MW00651555

Jessica Unbound: Gaia

Book Two of the *Jessica Unbound* series

S.G. Kubrak

Thanks for reading!
please leave a review
on Amazon.com

ISBN: 978-1-7375922-5-9

Also By S.G. Kubrak

The Jessica Unbound series
Jessica Unbound
Jessica Unbound: Gaia

The Dreams of a Freezing Ocean series
Dreams of a Freezing Ocean: Volume 1
Dreams of a Freezing Ocean: Volume 2 (forthcoming)

DEDICATION

This book is dedicated to two major influences in my life, one real and one imagined. To Lucille Ball, whose staunch determination to support the original *Star Trek* series gave it a rare second pilot, allowing it to become the cultural icon it is. My exposure to that series set me on the path of my love of science fiction.

And to the muse Calliope, ever present in my mind since I was a child. Her voice, and incessant prodding, has guided me along that path, helping me bring my dreams to life.

ACKNOWLEDGMENTS

I gratefully acknowledge the following people for their contributions and inspiration

Editor/Proofreaders
Monica Neumark

Nicole Neuman

Davene Le Grange

Cover Photo
Illustration of green spiral lines and patterns on a green background
This cover has been designed using assets from freepik dot com

Cover Design
Allie Shaw, DaxStudioz

Sensitivity Readers
Talia M.X. Shaw

Allie Shaw

Table of Contents

Part One:

Terra

Chapter 1: Dreams of Green

Closed doors, each a different color, stretched down a long hallway. Dark and forbidding, a thick miasma clouded the far end of the corridor, obscuring the end, if there was one. Standing there, gazing down the space resembling the maw of some great worm, she felt an overwhelming fear. Someone, or something, was pursuing her, at least she thought it was, yet when she turned to see behind her, nothing was there. Quietly at first, she heard the screech of an eagle, and she reflexively looked up, ducking her head in preparation for an attack from above. None came. Desperate to calm herself, she took a deep breath and held if for a few seconds, closing her eyes and willing her body to relax. The screech grew louder, each time sounding closer than the last. Her anxiety piqued until she could no longer stand still, it compelled to try each door to escape. One by one she tried them, one opening to a world familiar to her, yet she felt it was different somehow; another, alien and advanced, with stark-white buildings, seemingly molded out of plastic; and still another, a forest on the edge of a burning city; another opened to a bone-dry desert. Door after door with barely a change, and each felt as if it were the wrong choice and would lead to further danger. Frustrated and terrified, she turned and ran as fast as she could, plunging into the miasma, desperate for escape.

They can't get me if I hurry. They won't get me. The thought raced around her mind until she arrived at the end of the hall and stopped at a solid green door. With trepidation she reached forward and turned the electric-blue knob, opening it slowly. Pressure from the back side forced it open faster than she was able to counter and she was knocked to the floor. Bright green light poured through the open door, so bright that she had to turn her face away. Oppressive heat washed over her and she started sweating.

Squinting against the intense light, she could see a myriad of buildings stretching far into the distance. Each of them covered in glowing green lines, undulating and writhing, choking the buildings like a constrictor wrapping around its prey. The lines grew into gigantic tendrils of green foam, each of them growing larger and thicker as the buildings themselves shrank, collapsing in on themselves. After the buildings had collapsed, she heard voices. They spoke over each other, a cacophony with each voice clamoring to be heard. When the last building collapsed and the world grew still, the voices coalesced into one polyphonic voice.

We're here. All of us. It's because of you that we are this way. You turned your back on us. You let us go. Why did you do that? Why did you abandon us?

"No," she said to the voices, speaking into the milky-blue sky above her. "I didn't abandon you, I had to go home. I couldn't stay. It wasn't my planet. You know that."

We would never have left you. You left us to become monsters, to die there, and yet not die. How could you?

Jessica looked around for the source of the voice. Before the piles of rubble that were the buildings stretched a vast parking lot of abandoned cars, their rusting hulks arranged in rows. "Where are you? Please show yourself. I'm sorry. Let me help you."

You should know where we are. You put us here.

The voice sounded like her own, but different, mechanical, with a synthetic echo.

"I didn't put you anywhere. I don't know what you are talking about," she said.

Lies. Just like aways. You want to control us by lying to us. We know you aren't a god like you claimed to be. You don't have the answers, and everything you do is a failure.

Jessica shook her head, unable to see straight. Blinking quickly, she put her hand over her right eye, desperate to get it to stop turning toward her nose.

See? You can't even fix a turning eye. You fail. Like always.

"Please, I can save you. I promise, just tell me where you are."

"Right behind you. Turn around," the voice said, calm and soft.

Jessica spun, eyes widening.

"Dad?!"

Her father stood before her, dressed in a hospital gown, holding his IV tower.

"I'm so disappointed in you. You could have saved me, but you were too afraid. You're always so afraid."

"Dad, I was always there for you. What could I do? I did everything I could. I held on as tight as I could."

Her father turned his back to her as the ground beneath his feet opened up. He dropped into the abyss, the ground closing over him.

"No! Dad please! Come back!" She screamed.

She ran toward the spot and found herself outside of the doorway, back in the dark hall. Spinning around she looked for her father again, but could not find him.

From the spot where she saw him fall, a bright and blue light flashed, blinding her in its brilliance. She blinked rapidly, desperate to clear her vision as shadows played through the light, first large and then slowly decreasing in size until they were barely bigger than nickels. As they shrank, she heard clicking sounds, like those of metal on a hard floor. Solitary at first, the clicking multiplied until it became a wall of sound.

Looking at her feet she saw a wave of green foam spilling over the threshold. Frightened, she desperately pushed on the floor with her feet but they slid on the polished surface affording her no purchase.

Her hands similarly pressed and slid, getting her nowhere. The eagle screech came from directly ahead, inches from her face.

Get away! Get away now! her brain screamed and her throat constricted to the point that she felt her heart throbbing in it, each beat tighter than the last. Adrenaline coursed through her body.

GET AWAY!

The foam crawled up her legs immobilizing her body as it went, within seconds it was on her chest.

"Don't forget," she said as the foam covered her face.

Chapter 2: The Sleeper Awakens

Jessica Chao's eyes popped open, light-brown and flecked with green, they caught the bright sunlight streaming through the window. Her green and brown hair diffused the light reflected from her face, giving her entire visage an emerald glow.

"What the hell was that all about?" she whispered to herself, feeling the dream slipping away in her mind. Her body slowly relaxed in ripples of icy release.

Being chased in a dream was a common experience for her, sometimes on a nightly basis. Even after coming back from Terra --an alternate reality she visited six months ago-- with her newfound self-confidence, they still plagued her. Many nights she was jarred awake, screaming, and occasionally punching a wall to free herself. Her mother said stress. Millions of websites said everything from repressed memories, to gluten, to child abuse. Unsure of any of that, all she felt was that it was a horrible way to wake up.

Her eyes darted around the room as her brain came into focus, and she could smell the coffee coming from the kitchen. Yet she still lay there not wanting to get up.

"Babe?" called her best friend Katelyn Finnerty from the other side of her bedroom door. "It's eleven, are you going to sleep all day?"

Jessica bristled at the admonishment, after all Katelyn wasn't her mother, but she had known her since she was five, if anyone else could nag her…

There was a knock at the door, "Hello? Coffee? Babe?"

"Yeah, Kate, I'm up," Jessica answered, her voice hoarse and raspy.

The door swung open and Katelyn stepped in, an oversized coffee mug bounced lightly in her hands. She was still in her blue pajamas and bunny slippers, her long red hair tied loosely in a green ribbon.

Her blue eyes fixed on the coffee cup as she stepped slowly to the bed, attempting to not spill the overfull mug.

"I thought you were dead," she joked as she sat carefully on the mattress and handed Jessica the mug.

Jessica's stomach churned when the smell of the coffee overpowered her barely conscious nervous system. *'That's what the other one thought,"* she thought to herself, remembering the disturbing news of her counterpart in that other dimension who died from COVID-19. Terran Katelyn--the other-dimensional counterpart to this woman handing her coffee—thought that Terran Jessica was sleeping too, but she had passed in the night. Devastated from the experience, it took quite a bit of convincing for that Katelyn to accept that Jessica, this Jessica, was her double from another dimension and that she had not lost her mind from the grief.

Not that your best friend from another universe arriving with an android, an emulated AI, and a real live alien is an everyday occurrence. This Katelyn, Katelyn Prime as Jessica called her, didn't know any of that and Jessica wondered if she should tell her about it soon, if at all.

"Okay, your mom is coming over in a bit," Katelyn said as she got up from the bed. "More dumplings!"

Jessica rolled her eyes as the annoyance licked at her brain. Still groggy, the petty thought lingered in her mind; Katelyn circumvented her and spoke to her mother without asking. Maybe it was jealousy, or possession over her mother, or that she had one less person in her life since her father died and she held her extra close. It was ridiculous and she knew it; Katelyn was family and when her parents retired to Florida, she essentially lost them too. So close was the connection that Katelyn even called Jessica's mother "Mom."

Jessica shook her head and waved her hands. "Hey, I'm sorry. I had a really messed up dream. I guess I'm still trying to shake out of it."

Katelyn looked across the room at Jessica's mirror, and pulled her hair back tighter into the green ribbon. She addressed Jessica's reflection. "Sorry, babe. You've been having a lot of those in the last few months. Anything you want to talk about?"

"It's uhhh, the usual nonsense. Dad was in this one…" Jessica's voice trailed off.

"I didn't hear you at all this time. No zombies? You didn't kill yourself again, did you?"

Jessica shook her head. "No, actually, it was different, but not really better."

Katelyn turned from the mirror and looked at Jessica properly. "You know I'm always here for you. No matter what's going on. You can tell me anything, even if its really weird."

Jessica smiled and sat up in bed. Embarrassed, she changed the subject, "Did we run out of dumplings again? I don't remember eating all of them."

Katelyn nodded emphatically.

Jessica knew Katelyn had a serious fetish for homemade dumplings, and Jessica's mother, Ai Li, did her best to keep them stocked. It was unnecessary, but she was doing everything she could to make "a normal life for the girls." Jessica suspected it was really to keep herself busy after the loss of her father Kevin.

"You know, Mom is single if you want to marry her," Jessica joked after taking a sip of the coffee. Katelyn made it just the way she liked it.

"Right, that would make me your step-mom, nothing icky there." Katelyn stuck out her tongue, mocking her.

Jessica laughed and pulled herself out of the bed, she shook her head trying to get her muscles to relax after the intense dream.

"I gotta get a shower," she said, then pointed at her head. Katelyn nodded and tilted her head to the right.

"Headache again?" Katelyn asked, taking the coffee mug back and putting it on Jessica's dresser.

"What else is new?" Jessica said, stepping into the hallway and turning into the bathroom.

"Mom will be here in a bit," Katelyn reminded.

Jessica nodded and closed the door behind her.

Chapter 3: Dumplings

When she stepped out of the bathroom fifteen minutes later, Ai Li, Jessica's mother, was already sitting in the living room of the apartment. The smell of her famous dumplings permeated the space and Katelyn was already sitting on the large blue chair, bowl of dumplings and chopsticks in hand. A fresh pot of rice bubbled away in the cooker on the counter.

"Hi, Ma," Jessica said, kissing her seated mother on the head as she walked toward the kitchen.

"This is the thanks I get? You don't want to see me; you just want food." Ai Li pouted, over exaggerating her lips.

"Ma, you know I can't resist your cooking." Jessica grabbed a bowl and took some dumplings from the plastic bowl Ai Li put on the counter.

"There are some green beans in the fridge too, you can eat those later." Ai Li added. Jessica squinted as she reached into the drawer to pull out her pair of chopsticks.

"What is it?" her mother asked, then stood up to walk over to her. She reached up and put her small hand on Jessica's forehead. "I knew something was wrong as soon as I saw you. It's a headache. You haven't been sleeping well."

Jessica bristled at the accusation, yet knew her mother was right. She always was.

"Yeah, Ma, it's no big deal. I was hoping the shower would take it out. But…" Jessica explained. Katelyn quietly spooned some rice out of the pot then disappeared into her room. Jessica followed her with her eyes until she was gone.

"Ma, you know I don't like it when you treat me like a child," Jessica said, then rolled her eyes.

"You're not a child, you're my daughter. I know when you are sick. Your father would know too. Don't pretend we don't."

"Do you have to make a fuss in front of people?"

Ai Li brushed the green-dyed hair out of Jessica's eyes. "Katelyn isn't people. I know she's tired too. You both work too hard. You don't relax enough."

Jessica rolled her eyes then sat down on the couch. "Ma, you spent my whole life telling me to push myself and not be lazy. Now you tell me I work too much. Which one will make you happy?"

Ai Li narrowed her eyes, then came over and sat next to her. "Your father would say something about balance. I just want to make sure you are taking care of yourself when you aren't working. Maybe try to do it a little less. Get out more."

Jessica's eyes narrowed.

"That's why..." —Ai Li pointed to Katelyn's room— "she left. She thought it was lecture time didn't she?" she asked.

Jessica nodded slowly.

"Well, she would agree with me. She's serious about that new boy isn't she?"

"Ma, they stopped dating months ago. She's... single at the moment."

"You hesitated."

"Ma, that's her business not yours."

"I just want you. You *both* to be happy. Is that too much to ask?"

"No, it's not." Jessica conceded.

Ai Li's watch beeped, and she looked at it quickly.

"Ai ya! I have to get going. Tai Chi in half an hour." Ai Li bent gracefully and picked up her bag.

"That's all I have right now, I will make some more and bring them by tomorrow." She smiled.

"Ma, you don't need to keep us neck deep in dumplings, we aren't starving." Jessica said, rising to meet her.

"I know. Maybe I want to make them?"

"Well, it's a lot. More than we usually get."

Ai Li's eyes welled just enough for Jessica to know she was treading on thin ice.

"It's okay Ma, I just don't want them to go bad. They don't freeze well."

"That's because they are made with love, and love doesn't freeze." Ai Li said as she reached out for the door of the apartment.

Jessica scrunched her nose, "Did you read that in a book somewhere?"

"Maybe." Her mother smiled, then stepped out of the door. "Love you."

"Love you too, Ma."

Jessica turned and headed down the hall to Katelyn's room and leaned over and spoke through the door, "She's gone now, you coward."

"I'm no coward, I forgot I had to take a phone call." Katelyn said, barely able to suppress a laugh.

"Since when did that stop you?"

"Oh it's ringing again, sorry." Katelyn's cellphone buzzed, louder than it would if someone were actually calling.

"Riiight."

Jessica spent the next two hours waiting out her headache, she sat up at her desk reading as Katelyn stepped out of the apartment for groceries, leaving her alone. Resigned to the pain, Jessica took an aspirin and lay down on the bed, breathing slowly. Her eyes closed gently, and she thought about her friends back on Terra, she missed them more than she wanted to admit to herself.

Jessica sniffed the air with her eyes closed. Jasmine? Vanilla? An odd scent filled the room and her mind instantly flashed back to Terra. "Lavender? How am I smelling this? I have to be remembering it."

Jessica looked around the room, sure that she had left something out that smelled like the flower. "No, that's crazy. The only way would be if a portal..."

The hair on Jessica's arms stood on end, and the lavender was now hinted with ozone. "What the...?"

In front of her, in front of the door to her room, an electric blue sphere appeared. It grew rapidly and filled nearly the entire space of the doorway. Electricity arced from one side to the other as the sphere changed color from blue to purple. It crackled with alarming intensity. The smell of lavender was overpowering.

"It...can't be..." Jessica said, reaching out to it.

As her fingers touched the event horizon, a figure stepped through the portal, the figure was tall, bore an austere countenance, and wore thick glasses.

"It worked!" The new arrival said, a bemused smirk on her face.

Chapter 4: Teacher's Assistant

"Gabrielle? When did— how did…?" Jessica stammered, flabbergasted at the sight in front of her. When she left Terra, she was told the gate would be closed forever and there would be no way back for her. As much as she would have loved for the opposite to be true, she never expected to see anyone from that dimension ever again. Yet here she was, Gabrielle Duncan, the teacher's assistant to her quantum physics class, standing in her bedroom, dressed in her customary orange and purple. A swirling purple portal open behind her, with the smell of lavender permeating the air.

"Good to see you Jessica," Gabrielle responded to her rambling. "It's been a long time."

Jessica raised her eyebrow at the statement, noticing Gabrielle seemed quite a bit older than the last time she saw her. "How long has it been?" she asked.

"Five years, two months," the TA replied, checking her smartphone; she frowned as she analyzed the dark screen.

"They drain out when you go through the portal," Jessica explained.

Jessica craned her neck around Gabrielle and looked at the portal still held open behind her, its purple luminescence brilliantly outlining her form.

"Ah, that's right, you told me," Gabrielle said.

Jessica wondered how long it would be until the explanation would come. "So… what brings you to my neck of the woods, Terran?" she finally asked. Jessica felt a flush of excitement as she was finally able to use the demonym so often laid upon her until she chose her own of "Unbound".

"Terran?" Gabrielle looked confused, then distractedly put the smartphone into her pocket. "Oh, that is me, isn't it? I'm the one from Terra and you are from Earth. Yes, I am here. This is going to take some explanation."

Jessica sat back on her bed, feeling it sag and hearing the springs squeak. As if she were awaiting a lecture, she gave the TA all of her attention. Gabrielle cleared her throat and took a breath, she thumbed her smartphone through her purple slacks.

"It's okay, just start at the top and take it slowly," Jessica encouraged her, knowing she felt lost without her electronic devices.

Gabrielle paused for a moment, then started into her lecture. "Professor Sterling and I have been studying the android body that you left behind five years ago. What we could gather from the architecture and design has taken us in new directions, ones that we have never thought of before. We have spent the whole time working as quickly as we could fearing that your extradimensional friends from Bellerophon, the Takki, would come to collect the body and take it back to their Hegemony at some point. That has not happened yet, and we aren't sure why."

"They haven't sent anyone? No one has come through the gate at Hierapolis?" Jessica asked.

"They have the luxury of time, maybe they are waiting. After a while, Professor Sterling and I went to Hierapolis to study the gate there, we found that several circuits and sub-systems turned on in the android body when we brought it close enough. We studied those systems and found that the body transmits a frequency recognized by the gate, probably to let them know when someone needs to open it. We can't find any control structures on it that would allow it to open from our location. It must be a failsafe to keep traffic monitored."

Jessica remembered when they arrived on Terra from Bellerophon, the Hegemony world where the Terran Gate was located, that only the emulant AI, Peek, could speak to the gate. "You reverse engineered it," Jessica said jumping ahead in the conversation.

"You're getting better at those leaps," Gabrielle complimented. "Yes, we did. It took three years, but we found out enough to allow us to create our own gate and portal system. The data is stored in a fractal pattern in several locations within Dee's broken body. That vibration frequency was the key to unlocking the whole system. You leaving behind the android's body when you went back to Bellerophon allowed us to do all of this. Even without its head, the body is an amazing piece of engineering."

Jessica looked at the purple vortex behind Gabrielle. "Apparently," she remarked.

"Unfortunately, the only alternate dimension we could contact is yours."

Unfortunately?

"The Hegemony is closed; we can't contact them from our end. They must be blocking us until a time of their choosing. Without any other way back we tried yours, using…"

"My hoodie!" Jessica cut her off, reflexively reaching for a sweatshirt hood that was not on her neck. "I left my clothes in the hamper and wore her—the other Jessica's clothes."

"Yes, exactly. With that we were able to attune to the vibrations of this universe and find you. We can't open random portals; it would be too dangerous. Katelyn gave us the clothes to experiment with. They were disintegrating from the vibrational difference and have now completely disappeared."

Jessica felt a twinge of sadness, she loved her "Smurf outfit"; PSU sweatpants and an NYU hoodie, blue and white and purple and white. Her "serious comfy clothes."

When she first started traveling through the dimensions, the differences in the frequencies made her sick, as she was slowly disintegrating. Eventually she would have died an excruciating death were it not for a vibration patch that Gatekeeper Orvalus, the Takki in charge of monitoring the Terran Gate, provided her. She reached back to the spot on her neck where the patch had been placed, but was no longer there. "Did you make vibration patches too?" she asked.

Gabrielle pulled her smartphone out again and frowned at the dead screen. "Unfortunately, no. That technology is far out of our reach. We can open portals, but have no idea how to vibrate something at the subatomic level. I only have an hour before I have to step back through. I can already feel my lungs having a hard time assimilating the oxygen in this dimension."

"What's the problem Gabrielle, why are you really here? I know this isn't a social call."

Gabrielle put the phone back into her pocket and drew a deep breath.

"In an effort to get as many people working on the project as possible, we started pulling in more grad students. We swore them to secrecy, signed NDAs, threatened legal action to keep them in line, et cetera. Professor Sterling financed the whole thing to keep it away from the Regents at the school."

Professor Sterling? My Quantum Mechanics professor? When did he get that kind of money?

Gabrielle continued, "Three months ago, some code was stolen from our private repository at NYU. Very specifically in one branch: the vortex stabilizer of the portal. We weren't sure why this portion was stolen until we looked a bit deeper and realized that there was another breach ten months previous to that. It was top level research on our gate system and what we know of The Hegemony, including the hardware schematics of the android. We tried to trace where it originated but came up with nothing. Whoever they were they covered their tracks. Our best people think that even the government is incapable of that level of sophistication, and it is clearly beyond us. We keep trying different avenues to find them and we have asked several of the computer science post-docs to help. Hopefully they will turn up something soon.

"Regardless of how or explicitly who, we hoped that they really wouldn't know what they had, or how to use it. Until last week, when we detected a gate signature that wasn't ours, going to a dimension we don't know about. It was brief, barely a few seconds, but definitely not ours or The Hegemony. This means only one thing: someone else has a gate, and they stole the tech from us."

Chapter 5: Refusal

Jessica looked at the swirling portal and then back at Gabrielle and held her gaze for a moment, excitement at the prospect of returning to Terra overpowered her. Desperate to blurt out "When do we leave?" Jessica held herself back, she didn't want to abandon her mother again.

"Well, that's a pickle. What are you going to do about it?" she heard the sarcasm come out of her mouth and it upset her before it finished leaving her lips.

Gabrielle looked stunned. "Why come and get you, of course, you are the key to all of this."

"Can't NYU find the resources to fix the situation? Where did all of my... uh her, tuition money go? What about the Feds?"

"I - I..." Gabrielle stammered, and fingered her phone though her pants, drawing it out and looking at the blank screen. She took another a deep breath, raspy and labored. "We can't go to the Feds, you know that. Can you imagine what would happen with the board if an actual federal investigation was started over this? How much trouble would we get in with the University? We could all lose our jobs, or worse, this could be militarized and we have to give up control to more conservative elements. No, we can't do that. This is more than someone stealing files now, this is someone making connections to other dimensions based on our technology. You can talk to The Hegemony and get them to help. You have a connection to the culture of the Takki that we don't."

Jessica stood up from the bed, her face hot with anger. "But you have no problem making an inter-dimensional portal using The Hegemony's technology, while making up your own —ineffective— safety protocols and throwing caution to the wind? This is exactly why KT wanted me to study Terra, and let it know if you all could be trusted to talk to their culture at all. Are you trying to make amends? Or just afraid that someone is going to take away your little toy?"

Jessica still couldn't believe her ears, she had no idea why she was saying this and not packing a bag and jumping through the portal.

"Jess… please… you're the only person who knows… anything about them," Gabrielle implored.

"Jess-ICA. Only my mom calls me Jess," she reminded sternly. The smell of the dumplings still hung heavy in the house, reminding her of exactly who she was, and who counted on her. "Goddamn it, I am not your errand girl!" Jessica barked.

Gabrielle backpedaled toward the portal. Flustered, she dropped her phone as she tried to put it back in the pocket of her purple slacks.

There was a knock at the door. "Babe, you okay? Who are you talking to? Are you burning those candles again?"

Gabrielle pointed to the door, silently asking if this Katelyn knew anything about the whole saga. Jessica shook her head.

"Um, yeah, I was just watching something on TikTok. Got a little upset. I'm cool," she lied.

"Okay, don't go crazy talking to yourself. I don't want to have to get a new roommate."

"Right!" Jessica tried to put some sunshine in her voice to not arouse anymore suspicion.

The pair in the bedroom waited for the sound of Katelyn's footsteps to fade before restarting their conversation, quieter this time. Gabrielle grabbed the smartphone and took another breath, drawing hard, then settling herself.

"Look, I know you aren't the Terran Jessica, and you have no obligation to help us out here. We took risks and are prepared to deal with them. But you are the centerpiece of all of this. You set the wheels in motion by agreeing to come to Terra and not turning around the instant you knew it was a test. Whether you want the responsibility or not it's yours. Your counterpart took her responsibilities seriously. I can't believe you are that different."

Jessica blinked at the rebuke. "If she *was* so responsible, why is she dead? If she was responsible, she wouldn't have been so afraid to get the vaccine and she'd probably still be alive."

The retort dropped into the room like a lead weight and the tension became equally dense, they stared at each other for several long moments. The TA finally broke the silence after taking another labored breath.

"I have to go. Since we know this location does work, I will be back this time tomorrow. Hopefully you'll have calmed down enough to make the right decision."

Gabrielle stepped back into the portal and it instantly vanished, leaving only the smell of lavender and ozone behind. The sudden silence assaulted Jessica's ears and she sat down on the bed with a loud squeak, dropping her head into her hands.

Across the room in the closet, Terran Jessica's black restaurant uniform used to hang in mute testimony to a life that could no longer be lived; it disintegrated weeks after returning. Although her uniform in this dimension hung right next to the empty hanger. She stared at the closet door and slowly the heat left her mind, replaced with regret. Jessica remembered the promise she made to her counterpart while in the shower on Terra, the promise she made to live her life without fear.

"I'm sorry," she spoke to the other Jessica's uniform. "You know how Mom is, and I worry about her. I have to find a way to tell her. I don't want her to be alone; there has to be another way other than lying. I'll figure it out."

Jessica flopped back on the bed and pulled out her smartphone;

the one she took with her to Bellerophon and Terra. Scanning through the pictures, she smiled at her friends in that other dimension, stopping on a picture of Terran Jessica's father Ellwood.

"I can't let anything happen to them… all right, I'll go. You don't have to nag." She smiled, addressing the phantom uniform.

Chapter 6: Liberty State Park

The next day, Jessica spent the afternoon doing one of her favorite things, sitting on a bench in Liberty State Park with her mother. The two sat soundlessly watching the passersby. The water taxis were in constant motion, churning the cold water in their wake. The early April warmth upset Jessica, it reminded her so much of Bellerophon City now, with its climate control shield. "I wish we'd have gotten any snow this year, I really miss it."

"You know," her mother replied, "when I was a kid, this would all be covered with snow in the winter, and the Hudson would be frozen all the way across to the city."

Jessica had heard the story of the way winter used to be hundreds of times from both of her parents, but she never tired of hearing it.

"Of course, that is what your father told me anyway. The Potomac froze over a lot, even until recently, but then that stopped too. You could ice skate on it until the twenty-tens. It's a shame, seeing everything wrapped in white is amazing. You'd have loved it, Jess."

Jessica nodded at the "amazing" part. "Someday mom, you never know what the future has in store right?"

"Yeah, but I won't see it. Maybe your kids will."

Jessica's eyes narrowed, and her hands twitched.

"So, speaking of kids, anyone you have your eye on?" Ai Li asked.

Jessica sighed, then answered her mother measuring her words. "Not yet mom, it's been a hard semester, you know that."

Ai Li looked down at Jessica's feet, and then up at her. "You know, your father and I were already dating when I was your age. Already living together."

"I'm not alone, Ma, I have Katelyn."

And half a dozen friends in another dimension that I haven't told you about.

"If you're going to have kids, you don't want to wait too long, its why…"

"It's why I'm an 'only', I know."

Her mother repressed a sigh.

"It's ok Ma-Ma." Jessica said, using the same voice that she had ever since she was a child. "I promise, I have friends, I brush my teeth, and wear clean underwear as often as I can."

"I love you. I just want you to be happy," Ai Li said.

"I know Ma, I love you too. Can we stop being mushy?"

Contradicting her own statement, Jessica reached over and hugged her mother tightly. In the middle of the embrace, she checked her watch behind her mother's back: four pm. The sun was hanging low in the early March sky. It was nearing the time when Gabrielle arrived the day previous.

Jessica sat back. "As a matter of fact, Ma, I have to go see some friends in a hour or so."

"A man?" Ai Li smiled, and raised her eyebrows.

"Uhh, yeah there are men there, but I'm going to see Gabrielle Duncan. We need to take care of some stuff at the physics department."

"Oh," her mother responded.

"It's fine, Ma, we are doing some research and came up with some great stuff. She needs me to help out with Professor Sterling on a few things. A lot of future involved in it. Yes, there are… males there."

She found it hard to think about the aliens and AI as partners in a romantic sense despite the obvious attraction between Poke and Terran Katelyn; the way she unabashedly flirted with him, and his shy, yet eager, reciprocation. Her mom perked up at the explanation of having a plan. "Is Katelyn going with you?"

"No, she's staying here, someone has to keep an eye on you," she replied, with full sincerity.

Her mother nodded, then leaned back on the bench. The glistening sunlight reflected off the skyscrapers of lower Manhattan and the orange and pink light flooded the sky and bounced off the clouds and water. The breeze died and the river lapped gently against the wooden pillars of the concrete walkway.

"Did you make a new batch…?" Jessica asked.

Ai Li patted the side of her backpack.

Chapter 7: Returning

"Kate? You home?" Jessica yelled as she stepped into the apartment and pulled her key out of the lock. "Katelyn?" The empty flat stretched out before her, dark and quiet, the door to the balcony closed tight. None of the lights were on. Jessica took the dumplings out of her pack and put them in a cooler bag that she kept in the freezer, then put the cooler back in the backpack, she knew she would have to ration these and planned on only eating a few a day —however long they lasted before the vibrational differences disintegrated them.

Jessica walked into her bedroom and quickly changed into her black work uniform, thinking it better to return in the clothes she left in so as not to confuse her hosts, although the ones she arrived in had long since disintegrated. She packed extra underwear, toiletries, and socks. Although she really had no idea why; an exact copy of this bedroom awaited her, only five years older, and hopefully untouched. Or was it? Was Katelyn still living in an apartment in Jersey City or had she moved on with her life? She had to be nearly thirty years old now. "That ought to be enough?"

Jessica cleared her throat and sat back down on the bed, it squeaked beneath her. Nothing to do now but sit and wait. Jessica scanned around her room trying to remember the whole scene. She regretted not taking a longer look when she left Terra the last time; so determined and anxious to get home that she rushed through the preparations, but could forgive herself the fact she was in an extreme situation. Closing her eyes, she took a deep, slow breath. The smell of lavender and ozone suddenly filled the room.

"Ready to go?" she asked.

"You bet your fat 'A' I am," responded Katelyn Finnerty, the Terran version.

"Kate!" Jessica practically jumped from her bed and threw her arms around her best friend, her other best friend from another dimension.

Katelyn laughed, deep and resonate, shaking her entire body, her smile stretching wide. "How are you babe?" she asked after kissing Jessica's cheek.

"I'm doing great! I missed you!" Jessica paused for a moment. "Well, I mean I just saw you this morning, but that you doesn't know you. Like I know you. You know?"

Katelyn stepped back, crossing her eyes purposely. "Yeah, that's not confusing."

"I was expecting Gabrielle to come through. They sent you in case I refused again?"

"Well, duh." Katelyn remarked as she looked around Jessica's room. "But I know you are all ready to go." Katelyn gestured to the backpack on the bed.

"Mom's pack eh?"

"Yep, filled with your favorites."

"Oh yeah, she taught me, by the way."

Jessica stepped back in shock. "Mom taught you to make the dumplings? She hasn't taught *me* how yet!"

"She said she was gonna teach you when you got married, but then you had to die and all."

Jessica smirked, and forgave the impropriety of the comment.

"You look great by the way," Jessica commented, studying Katelyn's face in return. "No crow's feet yet."

"Girl, I just get sexier, don't hate." Katelyn joked, and then turned to the bedroom door.

"Don't go out there, we don't want her seeing you," Jessica admonished.

"She's not home, right? What boyfriend is it this week?"

"Did you just call my best friend a whore?"

"No. Don't judge us."

Without getting permission Katelyn opened wide the door.

"Darkness. See? Nothing more." Katelyn stepped out into the hallway and turned right, going into her counterpart's bedroom. Jessica followed her, and then continued on into the living room to look out of the window, desperately hoping that the other Katelyn wasn't coming home at that moment.

"Kate, if she sees you…" Jessica called from the door leading out to the balcony as she scanned the parking lot across the street.

"Yeah, I know. But it's not like I'm gonna destroy the universe. We aren't the same person. No paradox here," Katelyn called from the bedroom.

Jessica pulled her smartphone out and searched for Katelyn's last known location; midtown Manhattan, right at the PATH station to Jersey City at 33rd street. "She's on the train, she could be home any time."

Terran Katelyn came out of her counterpart's room, wearing the other's green ribbon in her ginger hair. "God, I lost this like three years ago."

"Put that back, it's still not yours, if you take it with you…"

"Yeah yeah, *Mom*. I'm just saying hello to an old friend. You had three days to play with her stuff. I want more than three minutes. I'm presuming from your cloak-and-dagger that you didn't tell anyone?"

"It's only been a few months. I've been thinking about how, and I really didn't expect you to, well ever, come back."

Katelyn took on a serious aspect, "I didn't think I'd see you ever again. Gabrielle told me that they haven't tried to contact you either."

"No," Jessica answered forlornly. "They closed Earth off remember? I don't know why they haven't tried you yet."

Katelyn shrugged her shoulders, "I dunno. Kinda rude though."

Jessica gestured to the purple portal. "So, when do we go?"

"Look, before we head out, I have to let you know that things have changed a bit at school. Once we got hacked, Professor Sterling had a bit of a crisis. I've never seen him like this before, like he feels guilty that the data got loose. Like personally so he's been obsessed with figuring it out. But then he will suddenly get all excited, happy to see the progress we made. Babbling on like the portal is the best thing ever, staying up all night to work on systems, or tinker with this or that. Double fisting coffee and scotch. It's like he's cycling between moods."

"Did he talk to Ellwood? It's not like he doesn't know what is going on."

"You know, I suggested that, but I think it's a pride thing. I can't get either one of them to budge really. Old dudes. What can you do?"

Jessica laughed, not to make fun of the situation, but to vent the frustration.

Everyone deals with life changes in their own ways.

The lock on the apartment door clicked open, and Katelyn, the one from Earth, stepped through the door. She walked into the kitchen and put her keys on the counter.

"Jessica? You here? Did you burn the candles again?"

Jessica's eyes widened as she looked through the portal, through the open bedroom door, down the hall and at her best friend rummaging through the fridge. She threw her finger up to her lips to silence Terran Katelyn, who she could tell was desperate to say something. Jessica then tore the green ribbon from her hair, grabbed the backpack from the bed, and, wrapping her arms around Terran Katelyn's waist, jumped into the portal. It closed with a whoosh the instant the both of them cleared the event horizon.

Chapter 8: Terra, incognita

The purple haze cleared and Jessica could see the room in front of her. She couldn't recognize it and presumed it would be the physics lab at NYU.

The smell of lavender overpowered her senses, it came from everywhere. She reflexively pinched her nose and tried to wave away the scent with her hands.

Katelyn explained, "Yeah, we still can't figure that out. Earth really smells like oranges, it's intense but you get used to it. The professor thinks it's how our nervous systems react to the vibrations of the other dimensions. What do we smell like?" Katelyn asked.

Jessica thought for a moment, then answered. "Katelyn... Prime noticed every time the portal opened. Thought I was burning candles. It's weird. Bellerophon smells of cinnamon, but it's mild, and more taste than smell. This..." Jessica pointed to the air and shivered, "I don't remember it being this bad. I mean, this is crazy bad."

Katelyn laughed and turned around, then headed toward a large steel door in the far wall, just below a dark frosted window.

"Wait..." Jessica called to her, "you get used to it? How long have you been coming to Earth?"

"About a year. We managed to open portals regularly, but always to Hierapolis. We couldn't direct them until a few months ago, and those were baby ones in your closet. You need new clothes; I stole the good ones."

Jessica sighed.

Katelyn smirked and stuck out her tongue, "Look behind you."

Jessica turned around; suspended in the middle of the room was their gate, eight feet on a side, built out of steel or aluminum, appearing as if someone framed a doorway then forgot to cover it up after the electrician was done. Bundled cables snaked up and down the frame, some of which were bungeed on with zip-ties. The cabling ran under the floor to the back of the room and disappeared into a concrete wall. The ceiling was low, only a few feet away from the top of the gate, the recessed lights cast multiple cones of harsh, white light.

"Are you serious? That is what brought us here?" Jessica remarked, as she studied the device.

"Yeah, it ain't pretty, but it works. When it first went online things came back really messed up. The first mice we put through… not good. We fixed the issues. No worries."

Jessica squinted, taking her friend at her word, then shook her head. "Where are we?"

A male voice spoke over a loud speaker on the other side of the room, "Not in Kansas anymore."

Without searching for the voice, Jessica responded to her father indigenous to this dimension, Ellwood Muller. "Hi Dad. I guess they let anyone in here huh?"

"Only the father of the first human dimension-hopper. No one special."

Jessica laughed and headed for the door, then stopped suddenly. "Uh, Dad, the vibration patches, Gabrielle said you couldn't make any." Reaching up to the back of her neck, she felt the spot where she wore one a few months ago.

Is that why it smells so bad? Because I'm not wearing a patch?

"We have a few, Poke left them behind." Katelyn answered then led her through the now opened doorway.

"He left them for you, didn't he?" Jessica asked.

"Maybe," Katelyn responded, her voice pitching up. "Professor Sterling wants us to only use them if we really need it. Which is why we limited gate use to only an hour. Gotta ration them, we have no idea how long they last or if you can trade them between people."

"Mine disappeared when I got back to Earth, I think KT dropped it when I was in that holding bubble."

"Bubble?" Gabrielle Duncan joined into the conversation, stepping out of the observation room, Ellwood right behind her.

"Yeah, a bubble," Jessica responded, walking up to Ellwood and throwing her arms around him. He wrapped back around her, eyes closed and lips trembling.

"Where did this bubble come from? How did you know? How did you get out?" Gabrielle asked.

Still holding her counterpart's father, Jessica did not respond and buried her face in his chest. After their embrace, Jessica turned to Gabrielle. "When we got back to The Hegemony's gate system and arrived at Bellerophon, KT kept me and Poke in a bubble and took Dee's head. It didn't want us to come through the gate without the administrator at the Library."

"I don't understand, why would it not want you to come back?" Gabrielle continued her questioning.

Jessica stood back from Ellwood and looked up at him. She traced her hand along his cheek, feeling his now completely grey beard, his equally grey eyes smiled down at her. With a smile and nod, he welcomed her back, not needing to vocalize.

"It didn't make any sense to me either, until I got out. KT is really protective of their network; it was making sure all the pieces were in place before we could come back. It is their AI and all. I can't blame it."

"Why?" Gabrielle's eyebrows furrowed.

"It was—"

"A test, wasn't it?" Professor Sterling interrupted Jessica as he stepped into the hallway with the others. His hair had become decidedly greyer since the last time Jessica saw him; his face more careworn. He leaned fully on his cane when he stopped walking, breathed a soft sigh, and squared his shoulders. He wore the same corduroy jacket his counterpart on Earth wore when she saw that version last; the same ink spot on the left elbow patch.

"Yes, Professor," she answered. "All of it was a test. It wanted to be sure Terra was worthy of risking The Hegemony to connect back to." She dragged out the "worthy" with an acerbic tone.

"Interesting," he said, thumbing the head of the Chinese dragon cane. "And what did it come up with?"

Jessica ignored that he was now testing her as well, "Obviously it reasoned that it was the right move, otherwise it would have dropped me from existence."

Everyone gathered looked shocked, Ellwood shook his head disapprovingly.

Professor Sterling jumped in, silencing the collective gasp, "Fascinating. I had no idea that the network can be controlled with such accuracy. How does that function? Did it share any of that information with you?"

"No, Professor. I don't think it would have been in its best interest."

The professor nodded quickly then remembered his social graces, "Welcome back to Terra, Jessica Chao, this is the… well, my. Gate Research Facility, Echo Mountain, New York."

Jessica smiled and nodded, "It's good to be here… Where is Echo Mountain?"

The professor smiled and then responded, "It is our home away from home as it were. Away from prying eyes so that we can work uninterrupted and be allowed to keep our secrecy. A natural setting, where we can do the most unnatural of things."

Jessica held her head back and raised her eyebrow, she stammered at a response to his sudden poetic spin.

"It's a farm in the country," Katelyn clarified.

"We're not in the lab on campus?" Jessica asked, looking at the walls and noting the construction.

"Right, so something can go wrong and we blow up the city?" Katelyn chortled and grabbed Jessica around the shoulders. "C'mon, I'll show you around!"

Chapter 9: What's in a Name?

Katelyn and Jessica stepped through a series of steel doors until they came up to an elevator with a single call button. When it arrived they took it to the top floor opening into what appeared to be a country pantry. Old walls with peeling paint, barren and dusty.

Katelyn pulled back a blue gingham curtain and stepped into the kitchen. It was small and simple: wooden furniture, a wooden and enamel sink under a window adorned with flowered curtains. When they cleared the gingham, a steel wall closed behind them, then another covered in brown wainscoting with shelving attached closed over that. The shelves were lined with canned foods of one variety or another, their labels old and yellowed.

"Are we in someone's house?"

Katelyn laughed. "No babe, we aren't. It's just a cover."

They walked through a simple living room, with an old sofa and antique cabinet radio. A fireplace crackled happily in the middle of the long wall and Jessica felt herself enjoying the simplicity of it all, and the implied quiet.

"No electricity?" She asked.

"Nope, well not that it is obvious anyway." Katelyn pointed to mounted animals adorning the walls. "We made it look like a hunting cabin, if you stumble in you could stay here for days without knowing we were thirty feet below you. But we, however, could see your every move."

Jessica shuddered at the idea of the taxidermy literally staring at her.

Through the front door, Jessica and Katelyn stepped out into the bright spring sunshine of the eastern Catskills. The cool breeze drifted across the warming ground, filling the air with the smell of soil and plants. Jessica was rarely exposed to real country air — it intoxicated her and she breathed deeply.

They stood on the porch of a small house that sat at the end of a slim gravel driveway stretching through the forest. At the edge of the house's clearing, two grad students threw a frisbee back and forth, another sat on a blanket and strummed a guitar.

"Where are we?" Jessica asked, waving hello to the students who noticed the pair.

"Umm, north of Jersey and west of Peekskill. 'Upstate' right?" Katelyn shrugged her shoulders.

Jessica looked around the compound. Other than the students and the house, there was no indication that an inter-dimensional gate lay beneath their feet.

"How'd this get here? There's nothing around."

"Yep, that's the point. Most of the material was brought in at night, and paid for with Professor Sterling's money."

"How much— how much does he have?" Jessica asked quietly.

"I haven't been able to figure that out. I'm presuming its old money; a tenured professor doesn't make that much. Anyway, the cars come and go from the only road at the base of the mountain, there is a tunnel from there into the complex. The power lines run in the same way. He owns the whole mountain, so the state let us get away with building permits. Personally, I think he has something on someone."

The pair sat down on the porch swing overlooking the driveway, Jessica swung her pack off her back and Katelyn took out her smartphone, it was unlike anything Jessica had seen before.

"What version is that?" she asked as Katelyn pulled up a three-dimensional model of the house, it floated above the surface of the phone, transparent, but bright enough to be seen against the April sun. It reminded her exactly of Orvalus's communicator on Bellerophon.

"We made it; it was easy to construct after we dug into the information in Dee's body. Those tech folks are pretty amazing."

Katelyn showed Jessica the plans for their facility and their relation to the rest of the New York State area.

Jessica said, "You guys think it is a good idea to be adding all this new tech to your culture? Are you ready for this? I mean, you didn't put in the hard work to get all of this, you're standing on the shoulders of giants."

Katelyn looked at her, "Babe, you can't just drop that on all of us and expect us not to use it? They are hundreds of years ahead of us. We'd be fools to not take advantage of it."

"But just because you can doesn't mean you should."

Katelyn paused for a moment and then smiled. "Yes, Dr. Malcom, I hear you. But we aren't cloning dinosaurs here."

"The chaos theory still holds. Besides, what if The Hegemony comes and takes it all away from you? They were worried you were a threat already, what if you prove it?"

"I thought you decided to live without fear? That sounds like fear in your voice," Katelyn retorted.

"Look, the data already got stollen. You let a genie out of a bottle. Who knows what else got out, or who has it?"

Katelyn looked out over the lawn and into the trees, she put the cellphone down and the model spun slowly. "We don't know who did it. That's why we need you. It also freaked us out. Think about it, we know that we aren't alone and that someone else in the universe has these and they could show up at any time. We need to be ready for that."

"Yeah, Gabrielle told me, I'm not getting into that fight with you too."

"It's more than that though. I miss you, Jessica. We all do. It might be selfish, but we also wanted you to come home. It's why I helped out on the project."

Jessica smiled at the admission from her friend from another dimension. It wasn't a surprise to her, but it was nice to hear. After spending so much time alone during the pandemic, and after her father died, she loved being missed. It was selfish, but she had to admit it felt good to belong.

"Jessica… Chao?" the three grad students she saw in the clearing stepped onto the porch and looked at the pair.

With a quick look of approval from Katelyn, Jessica addressed the trio, "Yep that's me, but I don't go by Chao anymore."

Katelyn cocked her head to the side.

"I needed to find a name for where I am now, not where I am from. It's 'Unbound.'"

"Cool!" remarked the student with the guitar.

"What is your Terra like?" the first one asked.

"Well, it's not Terra. We call it Earth."

The guitarist nodded, "The Germanic word. Cool."

The first hooked a thumb in the guitarist's direction. "Linguist," he said.

"Did you guys know that your planet smells of lavender?" Jessica asked back, her voice piqued with excitement.

The student continued, "You really smell like oranges, but it's not a bad smell. I thought it was my clothes at first, but then little girls, pumpkin heads, make chicken fly the coop."

"What?" Jessica asked, unsure of what she had just heard. Her ears started ringing, and quickly gained in intensity. Squinting hard, she put a hand on her temple and groaned.

"I—" the grad student's speech degraded to a series of grunts and barks, as if he was drunk and attempting to belch the entire alphabet.

Jessica looked over to Katelyn, whose face slowly melted in the sun, blue butterflies sprang from her ears. The lavender overpowered her and Jessica started retching. Standing up, she fell over, hitting the wooden floorboards of the porch. The floorboards curled to four gigantic wooden caterpillars, undulating toward her, their mouths opening and exposing rows and rows of green teeth dripping silver fluid. Heat poured out of their maws, searing the flesh on her face. She screamed, but no words would emerge from her mouth.

Help!

She heard her voice, disembodied from her.

Help! Me! Don't forget!

Jessica's world went black.

Chapter 10: Returning from Death

"Jessica!" Katelyn yelled. "Jessica! Wake up!"

"Dammit Katelyn, I'm up, will you stop yelling?" Jessica responded, although the words weren't coming out of her mouth, they bounced around inside her fogged mind. The world slowly came into focus like cotton being pulled off her face.

"Babe, you're mumbling. Come on, Jess, talk to me."

"Mom calls me Jess, you know that. Stop being stupid."

Gurgles and grunting came out of her throat this time, as she slowly regained control of her muscles.

The bright exam light Gabrielle used to look into her eyes blinded Jessica, who growled, imploring her to stop. Reflexively her right hand shot up from the cold exam table and swatted the penlight across the room. It clattered on the floor and skidded under a crash cart filled with medical supplies.

"I think she's awake," Gabrielle commented and then stood up from examining her.

"Easy, Jessica, you are among friends," the calm voice of Professor Sterling said from outside the circle of light around her.

"Goddamn light, are you trying to blind me?" Jessica tried to sit up, but her torso felt as if it were made of lead and wouldn't budge. Her head swam.

"Jessica gets mouthy when she's upset," Ellwood said from the back of the exam room, in apology for his daughter.

Gabrielle shoved her exam equipment back into her bag and gestured for one of the grad students to fish the light from under the cart. "Don't bite the hand that feeds you," she muttered, pulling her smartphone out of her purple jacket and texting someone.

"I'm sorry. What happened?" Jessica asked, blinking rapidly.

When she finished the sentence, she lifted her left arm and stroked the vibration patch now on her neck.

"Don't touch it. It could fall off. I've never put one of those on before," Gabrielle told her. Her phone rang, and with a nod to the professor she excused herself from the exam room.

Jessica pressed the patch hard onto the back of her neck and felt her stomach churn, then a pleasant warmth spread to the rest of her body making her feel calmer and more real. The smell of lavender receded from overpowering to a light hint of scent. "You gotta push them in a bit," she said, and then sat up on the exam table. "Thanks for taking care of me." Jessica smiled at the people gathered around her.

"That wasn't supposed to happen, was it?" Professor Sterling asked.

"I don't think so. When I ended up on Bellerophon it was like a few hours until I really started feeling the effects. I mean it started as soon as I arrived, but it took a bit to get critical. I've only been here half an hour."

Katelyn held up her fingers in a vee.

"Two? Wow, that did a number on me."

"Yeah, you were talking in tongues. What happened in there?" Katelyn pointed to Jessica's head.

Jessica thought about the vision she had had right before she passed out and decided it was better not to tell anyone. They had already been through enough and she didn't want them more worried. "I guess I just blacked out. I don't really remember what happened."

"Was that before or after you named yourself Unbound?"

"Unbound?" Ellwood asked, hoping off the cabinet he had been sitting on.

Embarrassed, Jessica blurted her explanation out.

"That's okay sweetie, I like it, gives you some mystery," Ellwood said. "Do we have to file that with city hall?" he joked, helping her off the exam table.

"In which dimension?"

"Now that you are stable, Unbound," Professor Sterling steered the conversation immediately upon the three grad students stepping into the room, "we can talk about what I need you to do."

Jessica replied, "I know what you want. You want me to help you find out who hacked into your... *our* system. Multiple people have explained that to me."

The professor smiled, took out his reading glasses from his sport-coat and put them on, and leaned his cane against the exam table. From his right pocket, he pulled out his smartphone. "What we found out in the two hours you were asleep will definitely cast some extra light onto the subject." Professor Sterling called up a file and an image floated above the display; a street-map slowly zoomed in on a warehouse in Newark, New Jersey.

Jessica fumed, looking closely at the display.

"Yes, our old friends apparently. Up to no good it seems, and not wanting to share," the professor explained.

"Wait, did they let you know it was them? They aren't very good hackers if they just gave themselves away like that," Jessica asked.

"They are indeed good, but ours aren't bad either." He pointed to one of the grad students -- the student who had spoken to her originally, and who now beamed from the recognition. "I'll let him explain."

The student cleared his throat and stepped up to the display on the wall of the infirmary. Tapping a few buttons brought up a dashboard of data, most of which Jessica had never seen before. "They covered their tracks well. Once you finished breaking your friend out, we managed to sneak a carrier interceptor onto one of their transmission lines. I'm surprised they didn't find it, actually. It was in the cable trunking. You needed a deliberate search to find it, and I guess they never did. This works by sensing the voltage change in the fiber optic line. It's almost negligible, but big enough that if you study the data for a long time, you can tell something is happening."

The student pointed at the screen in several places. "If you look here, here, and here, you can see spikes of data. This one here was right when we turned the system on, ostensibly when they were rebuilding their base. The second, here, was when we think they abandoned the location, which was only a month after you left. It was quiet for four years, until the day we saw them break into the system. They were looking for the stabilizer subroutine. This spike here."

"I'm not following you," Jessica said, her brow furrowing.

The student stepped back and started stammering, "It— I— they—."

"Slow down. Tell her what you told me," Professor Sterling counseled.

"Right," he began again. "The odds of that becoming active again on the same day we were hacked are small. It could mean that they were re-using the lines to transmit, then to break into our system. So, we have been watching it for a while, just in case. Then we saw that spike again, an hour ago."

Katelyn grunted, balling her first.

Jessica smiled at him playfully. "Well, they could be using it again, it could also be some interference or a power spike."

"You're right, so I tapped into the police surveillance camera for the warehouse complex and—"

"You hacked the police?" Jessica gasped. The professor smiled, as did Katelyn.

"I needed that information to solve a crime. That was the only stream I looked at... anyway." The student plucked another window on the display, and pulled up a video feed.

"It's really brief, the camera caught him right before he realized it. Look."

Jessica looked at the monitor, squinting at the blurry footage. Right in front of the warehouse, a male figure stepped out, then turned the corner and started to walk away from the camera. In a jerking motion, he pulled his hood up over his head and darted out of the frame. Just before the hood covered him, the camera got a clear shot of the right side of his shaven head; a large eagle tattoo covered the entire side. Its outstretched talons ready to strike for the kill.

"Son of a bitch," Jessica hissed.

Chapter 11: The Eastern Syndicate

Ellwood leaned toward the display and squinted at the image. "Who's the dude?" he asked.

Jessica sat back down on the bed and looked over to Ellwood.

"That guy was in the warehouse when we busted Dee out. I saw him in the back with all those other hackers. They just looked like kids dressed in black and wearing mylar pants. But that tattoo... I knew I spent too much time looking around."

The grad student continued, "What we managed to get from the police, other than this vid, is that a company called 'Transglobal Shipping' owned the building at the time, but—"

"Let me guess," Ellwood conjectured, "there is no 'Transglobal Shipping.'"

The student nodded emphatically after giving up on speaking.

"Why didn't Peek find all this out the last time?" Katelyn asked, referring to the emulated AI that was housed in Poke's temple, and who helped them infiltrate the warehouse.

Jessica shrugged. "I'm not sure, we were focused on getting Dee out, not their political structure. I'll bet ten bucks it knew and didn't tell us for whatever reason."

"That cheeky little codeblock, I'll bet it giggled about it the whole time." Katelyn chuckled.

"The kind of resources they need to do what they did... this wasn't a group of kids," Professor Sterling said. "They have arms, funding, and connections. Probably a syndicate of groups, a common cause, different goals. I wouldn't doubt it if they are local to the East Coast, with probably another branch on the West."

Jessica stared at the screen and tilted her head. "But, if it's that organized, why is this guy going back to a building he knew was compromised?"

How do you know so much about crime syndicates, Professor?

As if to emphasize the unheard point, Professor Sterling continued. "Evil organizations attract ambitious people who feel the rules don't apply to them. He probably has ulterior motives apart from their collective cause."

"We aren't evil. We have a gate that we paid for ourselves. How did we pull that off?" Jessica asked.

The professor smiled, "Not everything is as it seems Jessica. We also don't have a small army with us, nor are we in multiple locations."

Katelyn jumped in, "Awesome, a rogue hacker in a group of violent hackers. Bet he has some cool hacker name like 'Neo four million.'"

"Or Eagle," Jessica added. "Did you get anything else on these guys?" She asked the grad student.

"Not really. Their encryption is too good. The only info I got here is from the phone company and the police because they are easy to hack."

"So, you need my little 'AI in a brain-jar' buddy to come help and figure these people out?" Jessica asked rhetorically.

"Basically," the professor said, pre-empting the student. "We've done everything we can to find more about them, but we can't. They might have reverse engineered different parts than we have. We need an advantage they don't have."

Jessica smiled at the grad student, silently thanking him for his information.

"Thank you, that will be all," the professor dismissed the students and Jessica waited for the group to leave before she started speaking.

"Okay, I don't have my wings here. How do we get back and forth from Turkey with a pair of aliens?"

"We have the jet; we can get there no problem." Katelyn gave a thumbs up and headed to the door, characteristically ready to go at a moment's notice.

"Customs? Border security?" Jessica asked at Katelyn's back, who waved indicating that someone else would handle the problem. Ellwood chuckled to himself.

"Let's get there first, and we can figure that all out later," Professor Sterling said.

Jessica's gaze drifted back to the video display, in the loop of Eagle turning the corner.

I knew you were going to be trouble. Is your buddy with you? Where is your spy, Jason?

"Dad, are you coming with?" Jessica asked, tilting her head to the door. The professor pocketed his smartphone and headed out, leaving the two alone.

"No, not this round, I'll catch you when you get back. You know, I think it's time to tell your mother you are here. It's going to be another uncomfortable introduction, but it isn't fair to her. You're obviously not a one trick pony, never to return. It's time."

Jessica felt uneasy at the request. He was right, and her trepidation came from the desire to have only one mother in her life; in whom does she confide? Which one helped her with her first step? Who comforted her when she cried? Ai Li on Earth was obviously that person, but her counterpart was just as invested. Jessica accepted Ellwood as her father, why should she be hypocritical now?

"You're right, Dad," she sighed. "When we get back, I'll come down to you, okay? Wait, what have you been telling her anyway? How do you explain spending so much time here?"

Ellwood gestured to the door with his chin, meaning Katelyn.

Jessica nodded, "Thanks, Dad, that means a lot to me. Thank you for taking care of her."

Jessica stepped forward and hugged him, then she leaned back, breaking the embrace.

"Gotta go."

Chapter 12: The Jet

Jessica, Katelyn, Gabrielle, and Professor Sterling took the elevator to the bottom of the mountain into the garage. A black Model X awaited them.

"The same one as before?" Jessica asked, remembering the procedure to remove Dee's head from its broken body to make it easier to take it back to the Terran Gate. The space was cramped, but ample enough to perform the procedure in relative privacy.

"Yes," the professor said, leaning on his cane to summon the car with his smartphone. In a moment the crossover came to life and drove itself to the awaiting group; it silently slid up to them and opened its gull-winged doors.

"I put the seats back in, we have vans for that now."

The professor gestured to several black Ford Econoline vans. Darkened windows and nondescript New York State apportioned license plates gave them all an official, if not mysterious, look.

"Cool! What's in them?" she asked.

"This and that, mostly alcohol and shag carpeting," Katelyn quipped as she hopped into the middle row of seats in the Model X. Gabrielle followed her and got into the passenger seat, with the professor at the wheel. Jessica took her seat and the doors closed noiselessly. The Tesla drove itself out of the parking lot.

The bright sunlight flooded through the newly leafed trees as the Model X picked up speed along the country road.

"These are completely autonomous now?"

Gabrielle scoffed, and the professor nodded. "Level five. There hasn't been an accident on full autopilot in three years. There was a breakthrough two years ago when their competitor, Waymo's, AI became self-aware and upended the industry. The rest of the car makers are desperate to catch up. The iCar is close, but the fleet is much smaller."

Jessica went for the joke, "An Apple car? Does it have windows?"

Katelyn groaned.

After twenty minutes they arrived at a small airport. A single runway and two aviation hangars greeted them. They got out of the Model X, which parked itself in a protected space, and were greeted by their pilot.

"Good to see you again, Mike!" The professor greeted him, leaning on his cane to extend his hand.

"Professor Sterling, I got Gabrielle's call. I was just doing some maintenance, good timing." The pilot nodded hello to the group, then they boarded the plane, a Gulfstream G650.

Jessica looked around the interior then grabbed Katelyn's arm. "This feels like that scene in Pretty Woman," she whispered into her ear.

"Yeah, but you have been in a plane before," Katelyn reminded her as she took her seat, one of the single ones that ran along the starboard side.

"Not in a private jet. Like ever." Jessica's face was ashen.

"Babe, you flew across the ocean on a pair of wings. Twice. What are you worried about?" Katelyn shook her head as she buckled herself in.

Jessica's trembling hands clicked her seatbelt closed. She took a deep breath.

"Control," she said flatly. "I hate giving up control."

"We drove here in an autonomous car."

"I know, I didn't say it made sense. Besides, the wings felt like I was doing something and not just along for the ride."

Katelyn stuck her hand across the aisle and Jessica took it, squeezing until her knuckles turned white. The pilot, already in his seat, spoke over the speakers.

"Good afternoon, Professor Sterling and company, it's good to have you onboard again. Our flight should take us nine hours and twenty minutes. As requested, we are equipped with four reclining seats, the state room can sleep three, and other amenities are available to you. Professor Sterling wanted to make sure that everyone is comfortable. Once we're airborne, feel free to take a stretch, have any refreshments you like, and just relax. Whatever you need, you only have to ask."

With that, the attendant appeared from out of the back of the plane and waved hello.

Jessica leaned over, lowering her voice. "When did you find out he had this kind of money? He isn't rich in my dimension."

"Right after you left. He couldn't do this without us, and I guess he wasn't keen on hiding and lying about it the whole time. He took us all out to dinner at The Plaza and laid it on us. I still don't know where he lives though, he sleeps at the mountain when he's off, and that is never. He took a sabbatical to study the gate."

Jessica looked forward to the professor and the TA, he had a drink in his hand and was talking to her in hushed tones. Gabrielle pulled a valise out of the table in front of her. Jessica was focusing so intently on the pair that she didn't realize the jet had already taken off. Amazed with the ease of ascent, Jessica looked around, focusing on the professor's cane. "You know, he doesn't have a cane in my dimension either. Why didn't I notice this until now?"

"He's always had it, and he's been using it more often lately. Relax, babe, you need the sleep. You eye is really turning." Katelyn pointed to Jessica's right eye, which tended to turn toward her nose when she was tired, or had a headache.

Jessica leaned back in the chair, reclining it just enough to feel comfortable. Despite her apprehensions, and the thrill of being on a private jet. She fell asleep almost instantly.

Chapter 13: The Time Difference

Jessica's eyes opened as sunlight flickered over her face. White clouds danced, braced by a startlingly blue sky. The dull roar of the Gulfstream's engines filled her ears. She heard muttering from the front of the cabin.

"She's awake," Gabrielle reported, without looking back to check on her. Katelyn, who was standing in the aisle, smiled and grabbed the manilla envelope she was handed.

"You're gonna love this." She said as she took her seat across from Jessica, who sat up into her chair, stretching and yawning.

"Love what?" She asked.

"Your secret identity."

"Come again?"

Katelyn produced a blue US passport and tossed it onto her lap. Jessica opened it slowly. "Wha? 'Barbara Jones?'" she asked, looking forward at the professor. He nodded when he heard her say the name.

"You don't have a passport, so we made one for you," Katelyn answered.

"What? How?" Jessica asked, staring at the photo on the forged passport. "That doesn't even look like me." She pointed to the photo, a woman, a few years older, with similar hair and features, but bore no practical resemblance.

"They won't notice, nobody looks at faces anymore," Katelyn explained. "When we take your biometrics, they will match up perfectly. You could look like a horse and they wouldn't care. Besides, everyone knows an American when they see one."

Gabrielle came back with a smartphone connected to a card reader. She held out the screen which displayed an image of a thumbprint. Jessica obliged and pressed her thumb down, moving it around to make sure it had good coverage of the whole print.

"Good," Gabrielle said as she pulled back the phone. She took the phony passport from Jessica and ran it through the scanner. After a minute of swiping and typing, she handed it back. "Don't lose that. We can't get you a new one and the embassy will have no idea who you are, 'Mrs. Jones'. As a matter of fact, you died during the pandemic. It will be difficult explaining how you're still alive and in Turkey. We will be landing in a little bit, why don't you go freshen up." Gabrielle nodded her head to the rear of the plane where a full bathroom, including shower, awaited "Mrs. Jones."

Jessica got up and took a shower in the stall which was surprisingly accommodating given the size. The water was warm and soothing and she tried to linger; this was her first shower on a plane after all -- but she knew people were waiting for her. She changed back into the same clothes, which started to smell like oranges to her, and stepped out into the cabin.

"How long before my clothes disintegrate?" she asked into the air.

"A few weeks. They start to degrade as soon as they leave the field generated by the patch, but the process isn't fast. It affects people so quickly because of our metabolisms," The professor explained, handing Jessica a bowl of oatmeal and fruit as he did.

"Still tastes of lavender," she said, taking a spoonful, her nose curled as she chewed. "But I think it's getting better. Thanks for remembering I'm vegan."

Professor Sterling smiled.

Captain Mike made an announcement, "Folks, we will be arriving in Denizli Airport in an hour. The weather is nice and sunny, with some scattered high clouds. I've been informed that your car is waiting for you."

Jessica glanced out the window at the countryside below. It was exactly as she remembered it. In her mind it was only a few months ago. In this reality, five years had passed.

"Hey," she asked Katelyn as she took out her cellphone. It had no service and her calendar app displayed July 20th, 1969. "What year is it anyway?"

"2027."

Jessica shook her head, "Professor, why are our times so different? The gate to Bellerophon was a few days, not years."

"Time dilation and relative velocities Jessica. You know the equations, do the math," he said. Jessica rolled her eyes, sat down on the seat, and pulled out a piece of paper and a pencil that was tucked neatly on the credenza in front of her. Working backward from her present time to the date she remembered from Earth, she listed her assumptions and equations, writing then erasing several times. Katelyn came over and stood next to her, offering encouragement. After several minutes she blurted out a conclusion.

"The dimensions are moving relative to each other so the times are skewing away, every day here is a… month back home? Jesus, Mom!"

Jessica jumped up from the seat, "I can't be gone for months! She'll think I was killed or something! Turn back right now! I want to go home!" She ran up to the professor, her hands shaking, "Please, Professor, I can't! That will kill her!"

The professor turned to Gabrielle, who got up from her seat and went to the back of the plane. He motioned for Jessica to sit down.

"Jessica, we told you this information before you arrived, you knew of the time difference. We did inform you of that. You knew we were off by five years now."

"Yes sir, but I wasn't thinking of that because… because," fully panicking, she started crying, overwhelmed by the new knowledge and embarrassment that the anxiety had gripped her.

"I understand." He pulled a handkerchief out of his sport coat and handed it to her. "One of the great things about being an adult is that you are free to make your own decisions. You should also be given all the information so that you can make an informed one."

Jessica's face went red with rage, "Had I known...," her lips trembled.

"There is always another way." Gabrielle added into the conversation coming back forward and handing Jessica a bottle of water. "We will work it out."

"And if we can't?" Jessica asked, her voice piquing, "What am I going to do about mom? I'm not going to abandon her, not after everything she has been through."

The professor continued in a calm tone, "Then we need to do this as quickly as possible. Once we get your associates, we only need their services for a little while."

"But why haven't you asked them yourself? You don't really need me to do this for you."

"They won't answer us. I doubt they will refuse you."

Jessica looked out the window at the Mediterranean drifting by, her insides squirming at the thought of the clocks in all the dimensions running at different times. In her mind was an image of her mom, sitting in her apartment, inconsolable in the arms of Katelyn as yet another family member disappeared forever.

Chapter 14: The Gate to Hell

Once the plane landed, the group moved through security quickly; Jessica's anxiety raged the entire time. Katelyn was correct, no one really cared what she looked like, just   that her biometrics matched up. She reminded herself as they stepped through security and into the street in front of the airport: *Anxiety is not there to make you feel good about yourself, it's there to keep you safe.* Her mind chafed at the counterintuitive nature of the thought, and she shook it off with a deep breath.

Their car was waiting for them outside, a black Mercedes limousine, and she hopped into the back seat with no delay. In half an hour they arrived at Hierapolis and the Ploutonion. Jessica felt relieved at seeing the ancient ruin in the middle of the city, like visiting an old friend after a time apart.

A pool lapped in the middle of what appeared to be a marble bathtub. Walls went up three feet on each side. Looking to the far end of the pool, a small doorway opened in the wall, barely the size of a person, leading to a cave behind. The water in front of the bottom of the cave churned and bubbled.

Her first moments in this dimension lay at the base of that sunken bathtub, one in which so many animals had died over the millennia; suffocated from the carbon dioxide seeping out from the ground at the bottom of that placid pond. It nearly killed her when she first arrived.

Early in the morning, few tourists were around, and they had free access to the pool. Their driver, a Turkish citizen, warned them of the dangers of the place, and sat in the air-conditioned driver's seat of the limo while they headed to the water.

Once at the pool, Gabrielle reached into the valise she was carrying and pulled out a clear plastic bag, and inside the bag. In it lay a circuit board with several chips and wires attached. When Gabrielle stood in the water, away from the small doorway that led to the cave beyond, the circuit board lit up with a gunmetal blue light.

"Orvalus? Can you hear me?" Jessica called out, barely able to contain her excitement. "Orvalus, are you there? It's Jessica." Keen to see a sign of recognition, Jessica stared at the door. Professor Sterling stood above the pool, leaning on his cane, his fedora tipped rakishly over his eyes to shield himself from the morning sun.

"Be careful, ladies. If any of you get lightheaded, please come out immediately," he cautioned. "I can't carry you out if you are overcome from the gasses."

Gabrielle nodded, Katelyn jumped into the pool and waved him off.

"Jes...ica... me? ... you... he..." A deep baritone voice emanated from the cave, quietly and broken at first, but then increasing in intensity and clarity.

"Orvalus!" Jessica beamed, "I can hear you!" With that she ran into the cave, heedless of the warning given by the professor. Gabrielle moved in right behind her. Katelyn looked in the cave and then back at the professor, then back and forth again. She stepped out of the pool and stood beside him, and he reached over and patted her hand.

"Orvalus, can you open the gate?" Jessica asked as she scanned the stone archway inside the cave. From the outside, the doorway was just a stone post and lintel, from the inside it was clear this was an entry point to somewhere other-worldly; designs on the walls looked nothing like Turkish, Greek, or Minoan culture, and she instantly recognized the characters of the Hegemony alphabet. She could not piece together how the evidence was hidden from the world for so long.

Orvalus spoke, "This is not a gate, it is merely a... predetermined space to open the portal. We would not allow a gate to be unguarded in another dimension."

"But… how can you be talking to me now?"

"Our gate keeps a connection to any spot that it is locked onto, so that we may… open it as soon as we desire. It is good to hear your voice again Jessica, it has been a while. Are you safe? The carbon dioxide levels are increasing."

Reflexively, Jessica started breathing shallowly, she looked back at Gabrielle who was still taking full breaths and gave Jessica a thumbs up. "We're okay. Look, we were wondering why you haven't come to visit Terra yet. It's been five years," she said.

Orvalus responded, "KT is not in a rush to send an emissary just yet. Obviously, the Terrans have constructed their own gate system using the pieces of Dee's body that were left behind. That… complicates matters."

"KT must have thought they would do that, no? It must have computed that before we even got back."

"Apparently. KT thinks in cycles much faster than the rest of us. I am not privy to its thoughts on the matter, but it must have a plan. Is that why you are paying us this visit?"

Without preamble, Jessica jumped right into the events of the last twenty-four hours and all the information that she received since then. Orvalus stayed quiet through the whole recount and when she finished, he spoke.

"That is exactly what Peek thought. It knew the Terrans would find a way, it also knew that their data would get stolen. This does not come as a surprise, but I must admit it is disappointing. We hoped that it would not be exploited."

Jessica nodded and hung her head sheepishly, "Does KT know that?"

"I presume so. You speaking to me now must also be noticed."

Jessica continued on with her questions, "So, do you think you can send the boys over to us? We really need their help. KT can't turn its back and lock the Terrans out now. The problem won't go away by ignoring it."

There was a pause in the conversation.

"Orvalus? Are you still receiving?"

Another pause, longer this time.

"Orvalus?"

"One moment, Unbound," came his curt reply.

Katelyn said from above the pool, "How's it going? There are people showing up. We can't stay."

"Orvalus, we must know. We don't have a lot of time, people are coming," Jessica explained.

"I can see that; it is nearing mid-morning for you. Dee is consulting Administrator Dux. This could… be some time. Perhaps you can come back after the crowds have left?"

Immediately Jessica felt crestfallen. All this way only to have to wait more.

"Sure, Orvalus, we'll be back after nightfall."

Jessica turned on her heel and headed out of the cave, ducking under the low lintel. Gabrielle followed quickly.

"We will talk then," Orvalus said after them.

Chapter 15: Poke and Peek

Jessica and company spent the day wandering around the ruins of the city of Hierapolis, which she did not get to do the last two times she had been here. The first time she was learning to fly. The second time she was under immense pressure to get Dee's head back through the gate and prove to KT that humanity, or Terra at least, was worthy of reconnection to The Hegemony gate system. The day passed, and just when she had taken all that she could of plaques full of explanations of the fall of the Roman Empire and the history of the city, night fell and the tourists went home. As the last tour-bus rolled off, the circuit board in Gabrielle's valise glowed blue. Jessica ran into the pool, splashing water as she went.

"Orvalus, can you hear me?" she called into the air after ducking into the cave. She was already becoming light-headed.

"Yes, Friend Jessica, we hear you," the voice of her blind alien friend Poke responded, speaking in Standard, which sounded like barks and grunts to the unknowing.

"Hey, big guy! How are you?"

"I'm doin' good. How you doin'?"

Jessica laughed at his improving use of Terran slang.

"Kate, it's Poke!" Jessica called out of the cave, prompting splashing and the arrival of her best friend. "Hey, babe, you coming to see me or what?"

Poke took a few seconds longer to respond than he should have. "Yes, my dear, I will be there soon."

Jessica grinned and translated for Katelyn, whose face flushed.

Orvalus spoke again. "KT has allowed us to send you these two. Provided that you do not lose any more technology and that you stop them from… proliferating any more. You are also charged with shutting down that unauthorized gate. If you all do not come back exactly the same as you left, with everyone undamaged this time, they will not be able to return, and KT will close the Terran Gate forever leaving you there. It will also stop all gate traffic again, as it was in The Trials. Is that understood?"

Wow, that's excessive. No pressure.

"We understand, Orvalus." She said, trying to remove as much emotion from her voice as possible.

"KT is serious. No… funny business. Administrator Dux cannot take more time away from her duties running the city to assist you this time, the number of visitors has increased dramatically. She has also agreed to abide by what KT requires," Orvalus pressed.

"Yes, I understand."

"Very well, Unbound. Stand by for opening, please exit the cave."

Katelyn and Jessica stepped out of the threshold into the pool. The portal instantly snapped open and gunmetal-blue light filled the space; the smell of cinnamon filled the air. Out stepped, Poke; he had pale grey skin and stood so tall that he nearly bent in half to step through the portal. He wore faded blue jeans, a black hoodie, grey beanie, and black sneakers. He sported a pair of black Wayfarers. On his right temple three amber LEDs, arranged in a crescent moon shape, were embedded in the skin. Strapped to his arm was what appeared to be a large smartphone fit snugly against his bicep. Its screen was completely dark.

Katelyn ran through the water and jumped at the tall alien. He caught her with one arm and pulled in as tightly as he could, barely staying upright. Not wasting a moment, Katelyn pushed up and kissed him squarely on the lips. She moaned as she knocked Poke's sunglasses off his face and dropped them into the water, revealing his shocking green eyes which, lacking sclera, appeared as solid orbs.

Jessica smiled and turned away to give them their privacy as her vision began to grey.

"Carbon monoxide and dioxide levels are increasing, you need to leave the cave," Orvalus warned.

Jessica stepped out right away, and stood next to the astonished Professor Sterling.

"Katelyn? Katelyn? KATE!" Jessica yelled at Katelyn, who was now being held up by Poke, both of their heads a full six feet above the surface of the pool.

"She can't hear us, can she?" the professor asked.

"She can, she just doesn't care, and he can't see us anyway. I hope he knows it's her," Jessica explained while suppressing a laugh.

After another moment, Katelyn pulled back and took a deep breath.

"Oh, I'm swooning," she said, putting the back of her hand to her head and laughing slowly.

"That's hypercapnia, you dummy, get out of the pool!" Jessica yelled.

Poke, still holding Katelyn, took two strides and pulled them both out of the water, and the portal disappeared behind them. He turned to the direction of the trio, not quite looking directly at them.

"Hello Professor, Ms. Duncan. It's good to be here again."

"OH MY GOD!" Katelyn yelled, as she pulled herself tighter into Poke's arms. "You learned English?"

Poke's skin darkened to almost black. He looked down at Katelyn who was clutching his torso.

"Yes, I did, I don't want to... flex though."

Katelyn laughed, and playfully slapped him on the face, he smiled in response.

"Peek, can you hear me?" she asked.

"Peek is offline, we need to charge the storage device quickly."

"You okay? How did you know where we were?" Katelyn asked.

"I'll be all right, I remembered where you were and... got lucky?"

Katelyn smiled again, "Oh you sure will!" She exclaimed, unabashedly.

"Ohhh kaaay, that's enough. We'll get you a room on the plane." Jessica stepped up and hugged the tall alien, giving him a kiss on the cheek.

"It's good to see you, my friend," she said, and gently stroked the darkened LEDs on his temple. "Both of you."

Chapter 16: The Emulant

In the dark of the evening, just outside the city of Hierapolis, the limousine sat, engine running. It bothered Jessica to be wasting so much carbon without actually moving to their destination, but the extra power was required by their smallest member whose internal battery was completely drained by going through the portal. Katelyn held Poke's hand and softly spoke to him, reassuring him that his symbiote would be fine.

Jessica asked, "How long has it been on Bellerophon? How long have we been gone?"

Poke looked away from Katelyn and tried to approximate Jessica's location in the car.

"Fourteen months, twenty days, and a few minutes, Friend Jessica. How long has time passed here?"

Katelyn answered for her, "Five years. Five years that I haven't seen you. I missed you."

"That's strange, time is compressed for us, relative to you." Poke said.

"We've been studying that," the professor said, "but without access to your system, we aren't sure."

"It was only a few months for me," Jessica said, shifting her weight in the car and pulling a bag of cashews from the credenza. "We should figure out the ratio." She sat back in her seat, and shook her head with a frown.

"That is a great idea, Mrs. Chao. I expect you to get on that," the professor instructed without missing a beat. "Never ask a solvable question around a teacher," he said, raising his glass to her.

High pitched laugher pealed from the storage unit as its screen flashed on, and a bright yellow emoji, laughing with tears, appeared.

Poke's temple LEDs flashed on, a solid amber, Peek's sign of extreme emotion.

"Hey!" Poke spoke aloud, and then looked off out of the windows, "Yep, we're here. Uh-huh. Right." Poke held up his hand to let the others know that they were having a conversation. Jessica nodded as if Poke were engaged on a phone call. Katelyn reached up to the LEDs and rubbed them gently.

"Tickles!" came from the phone with the embarrassed emoji.

No longer living in the limitless Hegemony computer network, Peek's voice sounded child-like and innocent, with no clear gender.

"Right, Peek needs a few more minutes, but then it is ready to go," Poke added, reminding everyone that "it" was Peek's preferred personal pronoun.

The professor smiled, leaned forward on his cane, and set his whiskey down. He analyzed the LEDs in Poke's temple, physically turning his head with his hand and breaking Poke's gaze at Katelyn. "Explain to me how this works. How are you in there?"

Poke cleared his throat as Peek flashed wildly. "He doesn't need to know all of that. We should make a video. Ha-ha. Why can't you do that? No, why would I want to do.... No... I don't think so..." Poke gestured with his hands of a talking mouth, endlessly flapping.

"Tell!" Demanded Peek, its voice squeaking out of the storage device. Jessica raised her hands, gesturing for them to stop fighting.

"Fine. Peek says thank you for asking. It needs me to do the talking, it is a lot to push down though the speaker. It thinks it's faster this way." Poke smiled, then continued, "Peek wanted to be the first person to upload himself into the computer network. He had been working on emulating people for his entire career. When he was still a Takki." Poke stopped speaking as Peek flashed quickly in his temple, then said his conversation aloud. "Yeah, I know, that's your pronoun.

That was what you were, not what you are now. What do you want me to… yeah… okay…" Poke continued to relay the story, "There were a few emulants that worked but not… Well? Good? When *he* died they uploaded *his* personality and memories. Then Peek changed to *it* and worked on some of the first *de novo* AI, one of which became Dee.

"Peek likes to collect data, anyway it can. So, it moved to other dimensions, other systems in The Hegemony, any place it could go just to get data so that it could refine its algorithms, but… You want me to tell them? Yeah. Ha, okay I'll skip that. Peek was asked to restrict itself a bit so it volunteered to be a symbiote for some of us that wanted it. When I was old enough, they implanted its receiver into my nervous system. I don't remember the surgery. One minute I was blind, the next I could see. It took me a while to get used to it, but now it's like my internal voice has a friend. It sounds weird, like someone living in my head, but it's fine. It can't read my thoughts or anything, just when I think about talking it hears me and vice versa.

"We figured that having an emulant still hooked up to a sentient biological would push us closer together, since the de novo were never alive, they can't feel the world, right? When we're home, it lives in the network but we are always connected. The LEDs run off my body with a thermocouple."

"Utterly fascinating," the professor gawked. "And it switched genders when it was emulated?"

"Switching implies a binary state. Peek prefers no gender since it has no body, but it was male, as it wanted me to tell you," Poke explained.

The professor nodded. "Thank you for explaining that to me."

"Ready!" Peek chimed from the storage. Poke immediately disconnected it from the power supply and strapped it onto his arm.

"Peek, do you know what we need you to do?" Jessica asked.

"Yep," the emulant replied.

The professor reached for Gabrielle's valise. "Great, let me get you your identity…"

"We fly!" chimed Peek from storage, and Poke shook his head, declining the offer to take the jet back.

Jessica sat upright at the thought of putting her wings back on and flying across the Atlantic under her own power again. "I'll take the plane back with them." She pointed to the professor and Gabrielle.

Poke pulled the cube containing the three pairs of wings from his pocket. Pulling one pair of wings off he held it out and Katelyn immediately snatched it up.

"Can I go?" she asked.

Poke handed the other pair to Jessica, and his temple flashed. "Peek says, 'Yep.'"

Chapter 17: The Long Way Home

In the soft purple glow of the morning light, Katelyn Finnerty floated above the ground. Gold wings extended from her back, majestically framing her against the eastern sky. She laughed with the unrepressed glee of a child learning to swim, or an eagle taking to wing for the first time.

"You're gonna be okay? It's a long trip," Jessica asked rhetorically. Once the wings came on, Katelyn was committed.

"Yeah Mom, of course I will." Katelyn thumbed over to Poke, who was double-checking his pockets.

"I watch. We got this," Peek answered.

Jessica laughed.

The professor reminded Katelyn, "Let us know when you get close, I want to make sure that the mountain is ready for you. We won't have long before you head back out again, we've already taken too long, and who knows what the Eastern Syndicate is up to."

"Yep." Katelyn nodded and then shot up into the air, Poke streaked up after her.

Goddamn, she even figures out alien technology faster than me.

Within moments, the two were mere specks in the rapidly brightening sky.

"Well, let's get ourselves back home," the professor said as he headed back into the waiting limousine.

Jessica hesitated for a moment, looking up at the sky. She fingered the green cube in her pocket. The folded-up wings felt warm against her hand and vibrated softly. She looked at the limo, then back up at the sky. "Coming." she said.

The entire trip back across the Atlantic, Jessica kept to herself in the back of the Gulfstream G650. Listless and forlorn, she looked out of the window at the distant horizon. The images of the dreams kept returning to her whenever she closed her eyes. She could almost feel the heat, the sensation of melting. Green waves, like a swarm of insects, flashed in her mind. She tried to figure out what they meant, and why she kept reminding herself to not forget. Forget what? How could she forget something that she didn't already know?

The last time she had recurring dreams like this was when her father, Kevin, the one from Earth, died. The dreams were always about him falling down into a dark expanse, begging for help as he did. The dream repeated: he fell and reached up to her, just missing her outstretched hand while she desperately clung onto some unseen support with the other. She silently thought to herself that if she actually did catch him, maybe he would still be alive. Maybe he was reaching out and she was the only one that could save him from the cancer. If she could only have reached him and pulled him in with both hands. But then she would have had to let go from the support The fear of falling *with* her father was stronger than her desire to save him. And she hated herself for it.

Regardless of the obvious need to be back on Terra, she couldn't think of a reason why she was having these dreams, or why they started on Earth and not when she reached Terra. It wasn't the vibration patch messing with her nervous system, nor was she vibrating at the wrong frequency and needed its assistance. As far as she knew, everything was fine with her and her life on Earth. It was Terra that was the problem, and in the end as long as she could get back home there was nothing to worry about.

Except the time difference issue. She knew she had to fix whatever problem the Eastern Syndicate had created and get back home as fast as possible, lest everyone back on Earth realizes she had been gone for more than a few days.

"How did I get back the last time? No lag?" she asked aloud.

"Last time?" The professor asked, sipping another whiskey and nibbling on a piece of bread.

"Yeah." Jessica jumped up from her seat and then dropped onto the seat behind him, but leaned forward around the chair to prevent the elder scientist from craning his neck too much.

"When I came back from Terra to Bellerophon, I was only gone a few hours, not the few days when I was here. Then, when I came back to Earth from Bellerophon, I was barely gone. Katelyn Prime didn't even realize that I was missing. I know that there is a difference in the rates of time between the dimensions. But it was like no time had passed. No time at all. How is that possible, unless..."

The professor leaned back in his seat and looked over his whiskey, a smile slowly growing on his face.

"Unless the time difference isn't just because that is the way the dimensions line up in space, the gates... at least the ones The Hegemony uses... can also go back in time! I forgot!"

Professor Sterling's cheeks flushed under his three-day beard.

"Finally," Gabrielle said.

Jessica turned her head over the seatback, "What do you mean by that?"

Gabrielle straightened in her chair, "Finally someone saw the obvious truth." She gestured over to the professor.

"So," Jessica looked back at the professor, "you don't want it to just hop dimensions, you want it to go back in time!"

Professor Sterling smiled.

"You couldn't find that in the data from Dee? How they control time?" she asked.

"No, the only data on time is about keeping the gate open and holding it relative to your location, there must be something else that controls when they send information back through the gate."

"Information? You mean matter is changed to a waveform when it goes through the gate?"

"Yes, all of the mass is converted to a waveform and beamed, essentially, to the other end of the gate or portal." the professor explained. "That's why you need the gate in the first place. You can't open a portal without the gate, and the gate must always be active for a portal to remain open. A gate can open a portal but not change time, when a gate opens another gate... that is when I think they initiate temporal displacement. At least that's how I understand it."

Jessica sat back in her chair, "Not quite. I was sent back to Earth from a gate to a portal. But we had the Silver Stone. Maybe that was the key."

"Silver Stone?" the professor asked, putting his whiskey down on the credenza. "They use something else?"

Jessica's eyes darted around the jet. She felt like she was admitting to a lie, but then remembered she could not have told them since it was the last thing to happen before she left Bellerophon. "It was this stone that Administrator Dux had. It's really old. They used it to control the portal back to Earth so they could open one up anywhere they wanted, and any time they wanted. I guess they keep a patch on it when they aren't using it. It looks like that." Jessica pointed to a single silver bead on Gabrielle's bracelet. Gabrielle looked down at it, and the professor drew a short breath.

"Fascinating," he said, then lifted his drink from the credenza and took another sip. "Fascinating."

Wanting to move the conversation forward and take some of the pressure off the TA, Jessica went back to the physical properties of the gate. "Running all of that hardware must use a lot of energy."

"Prodigious amounts," the professor replied.

"How are you powering all of this?"

Gabrielle reflexively raised an eyebrow, then quickly looked down at her cellphone. "I've got service again, we are getting close," she said.

The professor did not move. "Great, I want to get back and stretch out for a bit, this seat is murder on my back." The professor rocked back and forth, a faux grimace on his face.

"Fine. Keep your secrets, then," Jessica laughed.

The professor winked.

Chapter 18: The Waveform

The Gulfstream landed at the regional airport and the Model X awaited them at the terminal. The professor said farewell to the pilot and the team returned to the mountain. An hour passed, then two. The sun set on the warm spring afternoon, still with no contact from Peek and the others.

"Do you think they are okay?" Jessica asked the professor as they sat on the porch of the farmhouse eating an early dinner.

"You would know better than I would, I barely know the aliens." The professor had only spent a few minutes talking to them while he and Gabrielle performed an operation to separate Dee's head from its badly damaged body. That was five years ago. "You know Katelyn," he said.

"That's what I'm afraid of." Jessica pushed the plate away from her on the bench. "Just like her to not give a number to call."

Ellwood stepped onto the porch with his own bowl of stew. He had cooked the whole meal, and was characteristically the last to eat.

"You guys finished with this?" He gestured to his bowl by raising it up into the air.

"Yes, it was quite good, thank you for making it." The professor nodded.

"No prob, I know we need to go vegan when she is here. I wish we hadn't killed off her mother's dumplings so fast."

"Thanks, Dad."

The professor's smartphone crackled, "Professor? Are you free?" Gabrielle asked. "We just got another gate signature."

Professor Sterling took up his cane and stood with some effort. "Right, I'm on my way." He cast a glance to Jessica, implying that she should follow. Ellwood nodded and took her plate.

The pair hurried to the observation room, their gate was dark and harsh lights illuminated it from the top. Gabrielle and a grad student were at the screens, tapping away, wearing headgear to record their conversations for review later, as no one had time to take notes. Gabrielle pointed to the screen as soon as they arrived. "See here? Another one, the signature is very strong. I think they may have fully opened it. The waveform is approaching ours."

Dammit where are they?

"Can you isolate the carrier?" the professor asked.

"Yes, well generally, the extra power is unmistakable. I will try to triangulate it." Gabrielle leaned over to the keyboard of the grad student, not bothering to ask permission. She typed a few keys, then went up to the touchscreen and flipped through display windows. Jessica raised her eyebrows at the speed with which she did it; almost too fast.

The screen zoomed in on a section of north Jersey, next to Kearny on the Hackensack River. A visual representation of the waveform scrolled beneath on a separate screen, red on grey. It floated above a green wave that scrolled with no apparent pattern. Gabrielle typed more and flew between screens. "I don't think I can match them specifically, there is a lot of interference in the area."

The graduate student slid their chair back from the displays, giving the TA complete access.

"Interference from what?" the professor asked.

"Metallic objects, heavy metals, conductive fluids… looks like…"

"Eww! It's in a landfill," Jessica spat, scrunching her nose.

"Very effective, there is no way we could have localized it without knowing exactly what to look for," Gabrielle explained.

"But… they know we know what to look for." The professor scratched his chin. "We need to go, now, while they are still there," he said, grabbing his cane.

"Professor, we don't have the emulant, or half of our team."
Gabrielle stood up from the station and removed her microphone.
The grad student nodded emphatically.

"I know, but we can't let them get away from us when we know
where they are. We're just going to look."

Gabrielle grabbed a black backpack at her feet, then stood up,
tapped the grad student on the shoulder, and pointed to the map on
the screen.

Jessica followed Gabrielle out the door, who grabbed the professor
by the arm to help him get up to speed. "Geez, I haven't been to
Kearny in a long time. Like a street fair twenty years ago."

"I don't think you want to eat the zeppolis from his location," the
professor said.

Jessica shook her head and wrinkled her nose.

The trio took the elevator back down to the cars where Ellwood
waited for them, holding a bag with Jessica's things.

"Here, this is everything you have; the phone is charged up. I left
some food in there for you in case you get hungry. You never know."

Ellwood leaned forward and hugged her, longer than usual. "I
don't know when I am going to see you again so I will take the hugs
when I can." His voice lowered to a whisper, "I took a few vibration
patches and put them in your pack."

Jessica hugged him back, "I love you, Dad. Don't worry." She
kissed him on the cheek. "That one is for mom, let her know… well,
just give her the kiss."

Ellwood nodded as she jumped in the Model X. It left its spot
with the professor behind the wheel and Gabrielle in the passenger's
seat.

When they cleared the mountain and got on the open road Jessica
pulled out her cellphone and called Katelyn's number. It went directly

to voicemail.

"Where the hell are they? They should have been here hours ago," she growled.

There was no response from the front of the car, she presumed they were asking the same thing.

The Model X drove off into the night, heading south.

Chapter 19: The Landfill

The black Model X rolled to a stop a few hundred feet away from the gates of the landfill and Professor Sterling pulled the car under a dense thicket of trees within sight of the gates to the facility. Just beyond the gates, several dark trailers were scattered about a decaying black-top lot. Spools of power cabling littered the spaces between with no discernible pattern. The Professor pointed to the furthest side of the lot, at a nondescript grey building.

"See that?" He asked, "All those pipes coming from the hills are filled with methane, they process it there and then pump it into the liquid natural gas tank next to the building."

The skin and pipework of the tank sparkled in the orange, sodium-lamp light. Two pickup trucks were parked under the pipes, their cabins were dark and the beds empty.

"Do you think they see us yet?" Jessica asked, noticing the cameras tucked amid the razor wire on the fence.

"Probably. They're trying to figure out who we are. Gabrielle, if you would?" the professor asked.

In a flash the Model X went dead.

"I cut us off, even if they know we are here they can't get much out of us now. You can't see it, but the plates are covered too," the professor explained, then leaned back in his chair. "Now we wait for our people. Are you getting all of this?"

Gabrielle nodded and tapped the microphone and camera gear she had just strapped to her head.

Jessica looked out over the landfill behind the building; covered in trees and low shrubs, it was difficult to see the mountain of garbage that lay beneath the greenery. Occasionally a waft of sulfur dioxide would drift by, reminding them of what it was.

"A sanitary landfill, collecting tons of methane for profit or use. It's a great idea, no one would want to come check it out unless they were invited," the professor said.

"Or too curious." Jessica looked up and down the street as dumptrucks intermittently rolled by to the nearby industrial park. She checked her watch. "What if they don't get here in time?"

"Then I will go handle what I can," Gabrielle answered, putting her hand on her black backpack.

"What's in there?" Jessica asked.

Gabrielle turned to the professor, asking permission silently, he nodded quickly.

"It's an Electromagnetic Pulse bomb. Unless they shielded all their components, I can set this off and disable their gate. Hopefully most of their data is stored here too, but that isn't likely."

"You're gonna go nuclear on them? Literally? Isn't that a bit extreme?" Jessica asked.

"More than you know," the professor added.

Jessica felt her throat constrict as her heart started to race. Her hands grew cold. "There has to be a way to disable it without blowing the whole thing up. Do we really have to start down the path of industrial sabotage?"

Gabrielle reached into the bag. "This isn't nuclear, just a large battery. They stole this technology from us, and we have to rectify the problem. It's our responsibility."

Jessica sat back, thinking of how she was the reason why all of this was happening and she didn't want anyone else getting hurt to fix it. In the dark, she quietly slipped her pack on her back. A new dumptruck thundered in the distance, heading toward the Model X.

"Yep, it's my responsibility." Jessica said as she reached between the two seats and grabbed the bag with the EMP from Gabrielle's unsuspecting hands, tearing her bracelet along with it. In a flash she pulled the manual release on the gull-wing doors and rolled out as the truck passed. Getting to her feet, she ran between the truck and the Tesla, realizing how deceptively heavy the EMP was. Her knees wobbled while her feet found poor purchase on the broken road. She ignored the pain, and regret, and pushed as hard as she could, trying to stay to the back of the truck and out of sight of the driver.

Jessica panted hard as she ran next to the truck until it turned toward the industrial park, along the back side of the LNG tank, beneath the high-tension wires. Throwing herself onto the ground, she rolled into the green chain-link fence and   slammed into the grass. The EMP slipped from her hands and it bounced into the fence, sliding under it to the bare dirt beyond.

"Shit," she spat, looking at the sharp, filthy ends of the bottom of the fence. It lifted up enough for her to comfortably crawl under, but nothing held it up for her and it appeared to move on its own. Gabrielle's bracelet dangled in mid-air.

"Thanks," she whispered as she rolled under and wrapped herself around the bag, managing to keep her pack on her back. Turning back to the fence, she saw four footprints in the dust, so close together they were practically on top of one another.

"'Bout time you showed up," she whispered, desperately trying to contain her anger.

"Sorry," replied the invisible Katelyn.

Jessica scanned the area looking for a place to hide, and hoped that she had not already been spotted. She grabbed the floating bracelet and put it in her pocket.

Why didn't you put your wings on? You didn't think that through. Not enough time now. Jessica chided herself.

An LNG truck pulled up to the front gate of the landfill, beeping its horn.

"HEY! Youse guys in there? I got other pick-ups!" The driver yelled from his cab.

The door to the grey building opened, and two men in hard-hats and overalls stepped out. "Yeah, hang on." One called to the driver as the other walked toward the LNG tank, on the other side of which stood the semi-visible quartet.

"Shit," Jessica spat again.

The four footprints stepped back, with two disappearing completely. Jessica snorted and then focused on the man walking toward her; with her heart pounding hard, the world seemed to slow down. Lifting the EMP, she turned her hips to get a full swing, and in her mind, she counted down.

Three...

The other worker jumped onto the cab to check the orders from the driver.

Two...

The approaching worker pulled a hefty keychain from his pocket and searched for the proper one to unlock the pumps and hoses.

One...

Jessica raised the bag, and swung her hips, feeling her arms start to follow through.

"Hey! What the hell?" The truck driver yelled again, looking at the black Model X beeping from behind his rig.

The worker stepped back, looking up from his keys at the front gate, squinting against the overhead sodium light. Jessica pulled her arms in and swung around with the bag, falling back into the shadow of the LNG tank.

"Can you help me? I'm lost!" called Gabrielle from the Model X. The professor was nowhere to be seen.

"What's a woman like you doing driving around here at this hour, lady?" the worker called back, jumping off the delivery rig. The driver threw his hands up after scanning his watch.

"I'm sorry," Gabrielle responded. "I'm meeting my boyfriend… and my GPS doesn't work. I don't know what to do."

Jessica nearly burst out laughing, and bit her lip to contain her reaction.

The worker in front of her put his keys back in his pocket and headed toward the gate, ignoring his task for the moment.

"Idiots," Katelyn chortled at the damsel-in-distress ploy. "Babe, hurry, we can get in while they're distracted."

"Already ahead of you," responded Jessica as she threw her pack on the ground and pulled out her wings. She slapped the glowing green block onto her back and disappeared instantly.

Chapter 20: The Eastern Syndicate Gate

The four tore around the corner, jumping into the front door of the landfill office. The wood paneling of the grey building assaulted their eyes, and the smell of formaldehyde, chocolate, coffee, and cigarettes overpowered them. Invisible because of her wings, Jessica shook her head in revulsion. "Uck, this is nasty. What do you think we are looking for?" Jessica asked.

They scanned around the trailer. Old calendars from the early 1980s adorned the walls and everything was yellowed from years of fumes. A fridge, a small sink and cabinet, some tables and chairs, and a desk took up the floor space and an air conditioner labored in the far window. The short wall, opposite the kitchenette, was lined with display screens detailing the pressures of the methane collection heads and the LNG tank. One of the screens held six different camera feeds, one of which showed the approach to the landfill where the collection truck still sat; Gabrielle stood looking up at the two hard-hatted workers.

"Is this the wrong place? How can they be working out of this?" Katelyn asked, pushing calendars out of the way and moving furniture.

Poke explained as he looked around, "The building is larger on the outside than what we are looking at, there must be-"

"We hid our entrance." Katelyn interrupted, scanning the far wall.

Poke raised his hand and pointed at the chocolate-brown refrigerator. "There, there is much-- a lot of energy coming from that device, more than it needs to function." Peek's LEDs flashed wildly in Poke's temple.

Jessica and Katelyn immediately descended on it, and Jessica opened the main door. "Nothing in here but... penicillin." She squinted attempting to see beyond the moldy deli meat. She slammed the door and opened the freezer, which was so encrusted with ice that only a five-inch square hole was left. It held a solitary pint of vanilla ice cream, also encased in ice.

"Where is it?" Jessica asked.

From outside the building, one of the workers yelled, "Okay, great I'm glad we could help!" The delivery truck gunned its engine to start moving into the lot.

Jessica glanced at the monitor; the Model X had backed off with Gabrielle frowning from the driver's seat. The worker headed back to the LNG tank, and the other was headed to the office they were standing in. "POKE! Help!"

The two women winced, and immediately threw their hands to their ears, pressing until their knuckles turned white. Agony contorted their faces. All three wavered in visible light as their invisibility flickered.

Poke reached forward and grabbed the top of the fridge. With minimal effort he pulled it towards them, swinging the whole refrigerator open like a door on a hinge. A dark space yawned behind.

Jessica threw herself into the void followed by Katelyn. Poke followed and pulled the fridge back into place. They panted in the darkness.

"Where are we?" Jessica whispered.

"Behind the refrigerator, Friend Jessica," Poke answered.

"How did you open the door?"

"Peek found they were using an ultrasonic tone to activate the release but didn't know the exact frequency, so it used the whole sonic band."

"Sorry," Peek said from its storage device.

"How did we hear it? We aren't dogs!" Katelyn asked.

"The wings? Do they shift ultrasound?" Jessica asked.

Poke nodded. "They do, it helps when we are trying to hear sounds above our range. We take it for granted until it becomes unpleasant. There are stairs down here, two meters ahead of us." He pointed ahead. Jessica held out her cellphone and turned the light on, revealing the stair in the distance.

The four reached the bottom of the spiral and turned a corner, a long hallway stretched into the distance. The walls were lined with power cabling feeding from the wall behind them.

"Poke, do you see anything?" Jessica whispered as the group walked slowly down the corridor, lit only by Peek's LEDs and Jessica's phone. "This can't be the only power; I know it needs more than just burning methane."

"Yes, there is power beneath our feet. Battery packs maybe." Poke scanned the floor beneath them. "Dozens of packs, lined in parallel."

Jessica rubbed the strap for the EMP slung over her shoulder, pressing uncomfortably against her backpack. Her fingers trembled. "If I set this off…"

"Why do you carry that, Friend Jessica?" Poke asked.

"It is the professor's answer to the problem," she said.

"Want to see gate," Peek chimed in with Poke nodding in agreement.

They stopped at the end of the hallway in front of a large steel door. A camera peered down at them, and a single slot in the wall for a security card appeared to be the only way to access the room beyond. Poke turned his body to move the storage device strapped to his arm closer to the reader.

"They will know we are here once we open that," Katelyn said.

The lights flashed on in the hallway, and a cold male voice broke over a hidden loudspeaker, "We already do."

Peek broke into the card reader system and the door flew open.

Across the room a gate, nearly identical to the one at Echo Mountain, stood. Its systems were powered on and an orange field spanned the distance between the posts. The smell of chocolate was overpowering.

Next to the portal, the hacker with the eagle tattoo stood, revolver in hand, and pointed it at the invisible group. Without hesitating, Poke stepped forward and using the forcefield from the wings, shoved Eagle aside, smashing him into the wall. To the other side was Jason, the operative who disguised himself as a homeless man to spy on the group five years ago. He pressed a button on the console he was standing at.

Jessica and Katelyn dropped as a wave of ultrasound tore through the room and ripped through their shields, rendering them all visible. Peek flashed wildly and Poke, struggling against the sound, pushed his way toward Jason.

Jason shook, pulled his revolver from his hip, and pointed it at Poke. "I don't want to hurt you man, just stop."

Poke unfolded his wings and lifted from the ground. "How DARE you threaten me, puny mortal! Cease this senseless action and I will spare your soul," he barked.

Jason stepped back and grabbed the pistol with his other hand, desperate to steady his grip.

"I did not kill you the last time at your headquarters, but if you leave me no choice I will--" Poke shouted, and was cut off from a cry from Jessica.

"POKE! Behind you!" Jessica yelled, then jumped through the air as Eagle fired at the tall Takki. Katelyn pulled herself off the floor and rushed toward the assailant. Jason threw his hand in front of his face, dropping his revolver and catching Poke's wings as the alien sailed by with Jessica wrapped around his waist. With no control, the entangled group careened into the open gate. The instant Jessica made contact with the event horizon, they disappeared.

Part Two:

Gaia

Chapter 21: Pain

Jessica's body seared; she squeezed her eyes as tight as she could, bracing against the pain. Her ears rang, a persistent high-pitched whine. Her fingers and skin felt numb, as if she was wrapped in cotton. Her neck squeezed, a crushing feeling compressed her vertebrae and strangled her. The smell, the overpowering stench of chocolate, flooded her nostrils, and turned her stomach from the overload. Every joint screamed in protest as she drew her arms up to protect her torso. Her legs fought against her body, refusing to move.

Slowly her skin started to prickle and the numb sensation was replaced with heat, baking heat from all directions, like broiling in an oven. She tried to scream to let someone, anyone, know that she was still alive and needed help, but nothing came out of her mouth.

From complete darkness, red slowly filled her vision; dark spots floated and danced chaotically. Her ears rang a bit less, and she could hear hissing, popping, and snapping sounds, but she could not determine their source or nature.

With her lungs aching for air, she could feel her chest as it rose and fell, straining against the straps of her backpack and the EMP.

She searched her brain for the last thing she could remember clearly, but could come up with nothing. Only her name, and a vague idea of what she looked like. A residual in a dream more than a memory. Her self-image was ephemeral and fleeting, giving her no context.

A pain in her ribs, something hurt, stabbing and liquid. Moving to try to localize it brought more searing pain. Again, she attempted to call out, and nothing but agony issued from her. White-hot pain ran down her spine.

"Hey," a voice drifted up through the ringing, soft and masculine, or did she dream it? "Hey, you." Concentrating on her throat, Jessica forced out a grunt. Guttural and meaningless.

"Yeah, I thought you could hear me. Wake up," the voice demanded.

As she tried to pull herself out of her state, Jessica heard screaming, loud, and terrified, in an inhuman language that sounded more like barks and grunts. A deep, primal fear overtook her, and she sat upright.

Squinting against the light, Jessica could see building after building surrounding her. Low forms of only a few stories, each covered in vines; the facades revealed deep decay. The sun blazed down on her, streaming through a milky-blue sky.

The scream pealed out again.

She turned to her left. There, lying on the ground, the tall form of a monster was beside her. It had grey skin, no hair, and green eyes that lacked sclera. Terrifyingly, three pieces of glass protruded from its right temple. It screamed again, its body twitching.

"Get away from that, man!" the male voice commanded.

She turned to her right. A bearded man with long hair, about thirty years old, stared at her, his sky-blue eyes wide and darting. Jessica responded to him by pushing her feet away from the monster that lay beside her, and she forced her body across the broken ground; dirt, glass, and oil made it difficult to make any progress.

"What... what is that?" Jessica implored, as she pulled her feet in toward her.

"I dunno," the man responded. "It's scary as hell whatever it is."

Jessica stared at the monster writhing on the ground, her instincts screamed at her to get up and run as fast as she could away from it. She tried to oblige, but her scrambling got her nowhere.

"I'll keep you safe," the man said as he grabbed her shoulders and pulled her closer to him.

Jessica looked back and nodded, having no choice but to acquiesce.

She scanned her surroundings again and saw cars scattered around her, parked in neat rows. Vines and shrubs filled the gaps between the decaying automobiles, broken glass and clumps of oil scattered the sunlight, casting miniature rainbows around them. With the man's help, Jessica pushed herself back into the collapsed side-door of a van and tucked herself behind a rusted seat, the upholstery completely rotted away. The man pulled himself alongside her, hiding behind another similarly decayed seat. The heat was intense, hotter here in the van than outside in the daylight.

The monster sat up, yelling again, quieter this time, but more desperate. It looked around, reaching its hands out to paw at the ground and then up in the air in front of it, like someone searching for a light switch in the dark.

"I don't think it can see us," Jessica said, squinting against the sunlight and rainbows. The monster instantly stopped looking around and focused directly on her.

"I think it can hear though," the man said, his voice piquing.

It grunted, loud and garbled, then stopped to listen. Jessica froze.

It vocalized again, turning its head from side to side attempting to localize any sound. Jessica's heart pounded in her chest and her hands went cold and numb. Her whole body tensed.

The monster grunted again, pulled itself onto its feet, and shuffled toward them, its hands splayed out in front.

Terror tore through Jessica, and she climbed over the decayed seats, pulling herself into the driver's seat. She searched for a release to open the door but found none. Desperate, she punched the safety glass and broke out the front windshield.

"Hey man, you're bleeding! Stop!" the man yelled to her.

Jessica paid it no mind and tumbled out of the van, its frying-pan hot hood buckling under her as she rolled off it.

The monster called again, this time moving quickly toward the van. In moments it was at the door, frantically searching for them. The man launched himself to the rear of the decaying vehicle, kicking and screaming in desperation.

Jessica stood up, clutching the left side of her ribs. She pulled her hand back and examined it; bright pink blood covered her palm. Her vision greyed and lights danced in front of her.

The smell of lavender filled the air, replacing the overpowering reek of chocolate. Jessica turned to the orange sparks that filled the space between the cars she had just run from. Swirling orange light filled the area as two people materialized from the glow. The light quickly went out, leaving the pair on the ground, locked in each other's embrace. A woman with bright red hair, and a man, bald except for an enormous eagle tattooed on the right side of his head. Both of them with their hands wrapped around a pistol.

The monster turned toward the sound and the smell and screamed, guttural and terrifying.

Jessica held her hands in front of her, blood dripped from her fingers, with effort she stepped away from the new arrivals, then dropped in a heap in the dirt.

Chapter 22: Medmads

Disoriented and confused, Jessica opened her eyes and surveyed the room around her. The voice in her head told her that this was a routine that she was not a fan of.

"Where am I?" she croaked out.

A woman, dressed in green and white leaned over her and smiled.

"Ah, you're with us. Good. We didn't want to have to revive you, it's better that you wake up on your own," the soothing voice explained.

"Mom?" Jessica asked, seeing a face resembling that of her mother, or at least what she remembered her mother to look like. The woman laughed.

"No, my dear, but thank you for the compliment," her brown eyes smiled down at Jessica.

"Sorry," she apologized. Jessica scanned the room she was in; it was little more than a tent. Other people lay on exam tables, resting. Her recent memories kicked in, and she sat up with a start.

"The m—monster... where is it?"

"The alien? He's over in another tent, we aren't sure what to do with him."

"Alien?" Jessica asked, her voice quavering.

"Yes, my dear, that creature is not from this planet. But then again..." the woman sat back as if she were about to sit on a chair, Jessica heard the sound of hydraulics and then the woman was sitting next to her, leaning forward, "we don't know where any of you are from, you aren't Gaian for sure."

The name triggered a reaction in Jessica's mind, a memory that she had briefly referred to herself using the same descriptor. Yet she couldn't place it.

"So, where are you from, my darling?" the woman asked.

"I… I don't know." Jessica scanned her memory for anything that would tell her where she was from and why she was here. The other people in the room looked familiar, yet no more so than a neighbor she might pass on the street. "Do you know where they are from?" she pointed to the others.

"No, and they don't have the same signature that you do, you're from different places as well. We fixed them up, but their cells are using proteins differently. Lots of waste products, and not really gaining much nutrients from the IV we ran them."

Jessica stared at the woman on the bed next to her, more familiar than the others but her name escaped her. She turned back to the woman in green, and winced.

"We took care of the gunshot. The nanites fixed the injury, but you have the same protein synthesis problem, we can't fix that. You'll be sore for a while until they can heal you completely. Well, *if* they can."

Jessica lay back down on the bed, "Nanites?"

The woman sat back and flicked a display over her left eye, she scanned through the transparent screen, read something then looked back down. "Okay, let me start from the top: you are in the recovery tent for the Merry Medmads, District of Columbia, Tysons Division. You are on a planet where you don't belong. You were shot and we repaired the injury using microscopic machines called nanites. Your body is not properly synthesizing proteins or utilizing water, and you are, apparently, suffering from amnesia. There is nothing we can do about it. At this rate you will die in six days. You have a patch on the back of your neck that seems to be helping, but it is not enough. My name is Mercedes Gomez, Medmad first class."

"The patch isn't working? Why?" Jessica threw her legs over the side of the table and stood up, instantly arms extended from

the bedside and braced her. Mercedes likewise stood in a flash
and wrapped her forearm around Jessica. A metal brace ran down
Mercedes' arm and connected to a pack on her back.

"Planet? What planet is this?" Jessica asked.

Mercedes stood up, meeting Jessica at her height. "Gaia."

"Gaia? When… what year?" Jessica implored when she saw her
confused face. "Please, just tell me."

"It's 2078, 11th April."

Jessica sat back down on the exam table, confused. Rather than
asking for exposition on all of her whereabouts, she decided it was
better to focus on the here and now. Something told her it would be a
better way to live.

"So, my dear, do you remember who you are?" Mercedes asked,
then sat back on her bracing, which folded from holding her upright,
providing an instant chair. Jessica couldn't tell if she needed it to
stand, or if it was out of convenience.

"Jess… ica. Jessica…" she ran through her mental contacts, and
recalled her last name, *better to not use it I don't know who these people are.*

"Jessica Unbound," she said with finality.

Mercedes looked incredulous. "Well, my dear, you should stay
here in the tent, it's much too hot for you to go outside, especially if
you are dehydrated." Mercedes pointed to the pack of IV fluid taped
to Jessica's right wrist. "Hopefully that will do something for you, and
will probably need a refill in an hour or so. You'll still lose your water
to the atmosphere, try not to breathe with your mouth."

Jessica nodded and lay back down. "The others?" she asked.

"They are in the same state as you. Your alien friend… he has his
own nanites as well and they won't let us study them."

"He? He's a monster."

"No, my dear, you don't understand, and people fear what they
don't understand."

Chapter 23: Ahoy!

Several hours later, after falling asleep on the soft exam table, Jessica woke up. No jolts, no nightmares, just the sweet release of exhaustion and renewal. Until she tried to move. Then her body reacted violently, shaking and nauseated; she groaned from the table.

"Hey, hey it's okay, you're awake. They tell me you lost a lot of blood, relax."

Jessica looked up at the smiling face of a woman with red hair and green eyes.

"I did? Why do I keep waking up on my back with people staring at me?" Jessica joked, fighting back the nausea.

"I dunno babe, maybe you have a cool-ass lifestyle. Occupational hazard." She laughed despite all the unusual circumstances.

"I know you, don't I?" Jessica asked, slowly sitting up.

"Who would forget me?" the woman sat down on the table next to her.

Jessica peered around the tent, the lights were less bright, the air felt cooler. The other tables were empty, and a medic she didn't know sat in a corner, clicking away on a bamboo laptop.

"Where are those men?" Jessica asked, not seeing the other members of their party.

"You mean our friends with the gun? They are in the other tent. The Medmads took their weapons and checked them out."

"What does that mean? Medmad?"

The medic in the corner answered for Katelyn, "Medical Nomads. It's a portmanteau. We call ourselves 'Merry' because well, no one would want to hear 'Maniacal Medmad.'" She stood up, slipping her computer into a canvas bag that sat on the floor. Like Mercedes, she wasn't sitting on a chair, but leaning on the bracing exosuit they all wore. "Name's Meera. Medmad Third Class. I was just assigned to Tysons, this is my first deploy." She offered an elbow to the women, Jessica reflexively extended hers in the sign of greeting. Meera's jovial brown eyes danced back and forth between the pair, expectantly. After a moment she moved again.

"I almost forgot…" Meera pulled out a vial and held it up; cloudy fluid filled the container. "Here is your new IV. We recycled your urine and added a bit of nutrients back in from your stool. Hopefully your body will run a bit longer with it."

Meera gabbed Jessica's wrist and removed the existing IV, carefully placing it back into her pocket. A chirp sounded when it dropped in. Unlike the new vial, the liquid in that one was brown and thick. "We can't get the nanites to work in your body the way ours would." Meera snapped the new vial into place, and immediately Jessica felt the cold fluid radiate through her body.

"There are nanites in there?" Jessica asked, feeling violated at not having given her permission. The redhead raised her wrist, showing a similar IV.

"Well, I don't think you'd have wanted to die right?" Meera said, then took out her pen light and started examining Jessica's eyes and ears, she moved quickly and held open Jessica's mouth, peering in. "The nanites can tell me all I need to know, but I still like seeing for myself, you know?"

Jessica raised her eyebrows and smirked.

"By the way, Mercedes says we can fix your strabismus, is that something you'd want?" The Medmad held two fingers in front of Jessica's face and separated them quickly, she nodded when one did not track with the other.

"Um, that's ok, I kinda got used to it."

Meera nodded emphatically. "Okay, if you change your mind

though, I can program them and send them in to fix it. My uncle had the same, he loved it when I repaired it. He said it helped him see how smart I was. I know he was kidding; you can't see brains, I'm not the Glass Cat."

Her friend nudged Jessica, then asked, "Meera, how old are you?"

"Twenty-seven, I know, I look kinda old for my age. I spend a lot of time in the sun, which is why they said I would be perfect as a Medmad. We're always out helping local communities, and the Wayfarers. I love this life."

"No, your age fits you," Jessica complimented.

Meera bowed quickly then headed over to the edge of the tent and stepped through the canvas opening and into the night.

"I thought she was fourteen!" Jessica said.

"Me too. Hey, I'm Katelyn by the way." she extended a hand to Jessica.

"I know… somehow. I'm Jessica." She extended back an elbow.

"What's that about?" Katelyn gestured with her chin.

"It's how we say hello? Right?" Her forehead furrowed as she glanced at Katelyn sideways.

"Not where I come from."

Jessica opened her hand, and clasped Katelyn's. After a moment of trepidation she smiled, then leaned forward and hugged her.

A male voice called from the entrance to the tent, "Good, the two of you have met."

They turned around to see a man standing in the doorway; his greying hair drifted past his shoulders and framed his wrinkled face. Through the open tent flap, they saw trees and a pink, light-flooded sky behind him. Hot air drifted in.

"Ahoy, my name is Richard. It's nice to meet you." He bowed to the pair.

"Hello," they spoke in unison.

Richard looked around quickly, eyebrows lifted, a quizzical smile on his face. "Is something the matter?"

Jessica shook her head. "No, everything is fine. It's nice to meet you Richard, I'm Jessica, this is Katelyn."

"Nice to meet you. The Medmads told me about all of you. Interesting story. Explains the alien in the next tent."

Katelyn stepped forward. "I want to see him."

Richard let her pass and she strode with determination into the oppressive heat. He looked back at Jessica who shrugged her shoulders.

"Are you in charge here?" Jessica asked, slowly getting up and heading toward the flap.

"No. No one is in charge. We are Wayfarer Nomads; we don't have bosses."

"You're a medic too?" Jessica stopped mid-stride.

"No, I'm a nano-engineer. I program nanites to recycle buildings and man-made stuff."

Jessica stepped out of the tent into the heat. It hit her like stepping into a furnace. Richard tapped her on the shoulder and pointed to a building on the other side of the clearing they were standing in. The five-story office building glowed green in the gathering darkness. The top levels, devoid of glass and facade, slowly melted into the structure.

"My work," he said. "Well, their work, but I tell them where to go." Richard held up his left arm and wrapped around his wrist was a clear-screened display, it spooled data across its flexible surface.

Jessica stood, gobsmacked at the display before her. The building in front of them melted as tendrils of green foam snaked away from it and into the distance. She recoiled from the scene. "My dream, I saw these in my dream… worms, are they worms? They are going to eat us!"

"Que? Eat? No, they are eating the building, not us, we are perfectly safe."

Jessica stared at the tendrils, watching them writhe over the ground and pulse with added mass. The organic nature of the act chilled her.

"You're safe," Richard reiterated. "They can't harm living beings; they saved your life."

Jessica suddenly felt dirty and violated; these machines were crawling around inside her body at this very moment, doing God-knows-what. Her knees wobbled, and she reached out to Richard for stability.

"Breathe, you're fine." He smiled and gestured behind him.

In a moment Mercedes was standing on her other side. "Easy, my dear, you're safe. They have saved all of us at one point or another. Even the planet itself."

Jessica took a deep breath, and steadied herself. Just as she started to relax, Katelyn screamed from the other tent.

Chapter 24: Alien

"Jesus, that's really an alien? I didn't dream it?" Jessica asked Katelyn over her shoulder, panting from her short run in the heat. She stared at the tall, thin, grey-skinned, green-eyed monster sitting on an exam bed. It stared back with a concerned look on its face. The pieces of glass wedged in its temples glowed with an amber light.

"Ah, Friend Jessica, it's so good to see you feeling better! Please tell Katelyn that I am no monster!" it said.

Jessica looked from one of the pair to the other —Katelyn stood unmoving— then focused on the lights.

"Those lights. In your head. How... you speak English?"

"Apparently, I do, and those lights are my... what do you call yourself?" The alien glanced up to the roof of the tent, as if lost in thought. "Yes, my symbiotic emulant AI, its name is Peek."

"Hi!" Chirped a child-like voice from a small storage device on the desk, it was plugged into a battery pack beside it with a short cable that glowed yellow. The voice was charming and disarming, lightening the mood in the room.

"Hello," Jessica replied, then grinned.

The Medmads scanned the room, searching for the cause of alarm. Katelyn cleared her throat. "Why do you people freak out every time we say 'hello?'"

Richard stepped into the tent behind them and closed the flap, the space immediately started to cool.

"Because that isn't how we greet each other here."

"Then, how do you greet someone?" Katelyn asked

A smattering of chuckles filled the room, Richard grinned and suppressed a laugh.

"Ahoy!" He raised his hand, palm forward.

"Ahoy!" responded the Medmads in the tent, holding their palms forward.

Katelyn leaned over to Jessica and whispered in her ear. "They're pirates. You look for the parrot, I'll search for the rum!"

Jessica laughed, shaking her head and smirking.

The alien on the bed laughed louder than the rest, deep and resonant.

"My name is Poke." he said, standing up, putting his right hand on the center of his chest and bowing.

"Hel… ahoy!" Jessica responded; Katelyn laughed this time.

"I know you. I don't think you're a monster." Katelyn stepped up to Poke quickly. "Not hardly."

Poke turned a shade darker. Peek, in his temple, flashed brightly.

Eagle stepped up and addressed the group.

"Well, that's great that you all know each other, but I don't know you at all. Who are you and how did we get here? Why can't we remember anything?"

From behind him, the other man with a beard and missing front teeth shook his head in agreement.

"Beats me buddy," Katelyn answered.

"They found us fighting over a gun. What am I supposed to do with that information?" he asked.

"Listen, Eagle, it must have been something you did. I don't pull weapons on people." Katelyn shot back, throwing a hand on her hip. Poke smiled.

"What about that computer? Computers don't get amnesia," he demanded.

Peek started singing in a small voice:

Daisy, Daisy, give me your answer, do
I'm half-crazy all for the love of you

The bearded man looked at the small computer and cocked his head. "I know that song from somewhere."

"IBM, 1962, you idiot," Eagle shot at him. The other man stepped back, averting his eyes.

"That doesn't answer my question," Eagle said, stepping up to the table to look at the storage device. Poke stood quickly and blocked his path, staring down at the human.

Eagle stepped back and looked up, "Right, you're its protector. So, I'll ask again, who are you people and how did we get here?"

Katelyn stepped past Eagle and picked Peek up from the table. Disconnecting the power cable that had switched from yellow to green, she wrapped it in the band that Poke wore on his left arm, making sure it was secure. She gently rubbed the tall alien's shoulder as she did. "How do I know how to do this?"

"Cozy," Peek purred.

Jessica said, "I don't know why we are here or how we got here. But I don't think it's a good idea for us to be fighting and not trusting each other. We need to figure out how to get home."

"How do we know you didn't send us here on purpose? Or maybe you are the ones who have done something wrong and we are the ones who should be watching you? Maybe you broke out of prison or something?"

"You think so?" Jessica turned red from her neck to her forehead, she started shaking. "What makes you think you know so much more than we do? Who the hell do you think you are? You think you're just gonna force yourself into making the decisions?" Her fists balled.

"Woah, this is not productive. Stop it now." Mercedes strode into the tent and stood between the pair. "You. Outside. We have a tent for you and your friend." She gestured to Eagle and the bearded man.

"Fine," he said curtly, and walked out of the door.

"Can I stay here? The bearded man asked. "I don't really care who is in charge, I just want to figure it out."

Mercedes glanced at the women and then back at him. Jessica nodded.

Richard stepped over to Poke. "So seriously, how can it not remember? It's an AI, isn't it? I run plenty and none forget anything. It remembered your names."

"Not AI, emulant," Peek responded from Poke's arm.

"You were living? They uploaded you?"

"Yes. Old. Body died."

Richard looked at Peek's storage device, it was currently displaying the sad emoji. "I wonder if you are having a problem with your heuristics. You are attempting to solve a complicated problem and are stuck in a loop. Do you have any debugging information that I can see?"

"Encrypted. Don't know access code."

"You can't remember the encryption key to your own codebase? Autonomous call seeking. Definitely. You're in a loop somewhere. A lower-order heuristic attribute will help you to release the block. I'd run a diagnostic on you but your encryption--"

Katelyn shook her head, "Can we go outside or something and look around? Maybe that will jog its memory."

Richard turned back to her and smiled. "Yes, I just said that."

Chapter 25: Collapse

"What happened here? Why is everything abandoned?" Jessica gazed over the parking lot filled with decaying vehicles. The building, much smaller now, glowed green, illuminating the entire area. She wiped a bead of sweat from her forehead.

Richard cocked his head and studied her face for a moment. "You mean your world doesn't look like this?"

"Only in movies."

"The polar caps melted and flooded the coasts. Most of the major cities drowned and society… well it's different now from 'What Came Before' as we call it." He looked at his feet, then continued. "I grew up after all of that. We're trying to fix the planet, and bring it back to where it was before the First Industrial Revolution. The best way to do it is to rewind everything back, building by building, and replace it all with forest to pull the carbon out of the air."

Jessica looked down at the lime-green tendril that ran from the building through the parking lot and into the distance. It met a much larger green structure that looked like a glowing tree lying on its side. "These are nanites?"

"Well, kinda, its nano-foam conduit. The nanites are in it moving materials around on the atomic level. Everything they process runs to The Trunk. That's where we live when we aren't out outquisitioning everything that came before. We go around taking these old things apart and using the raw materials to improve the city." He pointed to the east, along the line of The Trunk. "Sometimes people don't want to go to the city to live, they like being out here in the wild, living on What Came Before. I can dig it. We Wayfarers are out here because we don't like to be penned in either. So, we give them help when they need it; new tech, removing toxins, helping improve crop yields, the works. 'Outquisition,' is the opposite of inquisition. We want to educate and help them help themselves instead of questioning and forcing things on people. We are strictly non-combative though; we only keep weapons for protection. If you want our help, you have to disarm, so we remove all weapons when we come across them, and that's mostly firearms. Unfortunately, we come across a lot."

"You deconstructed the gun when we showed up."

"Yep," Richard responded. "When you all arrived, we inactivated it and converted it back to the carbon and iron. The oxidizer in the bullets is a little more complex for us, and we close it off in a pod to be shipped to a safe location. Those nitrogen bonds get dicey." He gestured with his fingers, mimicking an explosion.

Poke and Katelyn came over, speaking to each other like old friends. The man with the long hair and beard was still in the tent.

"Why haven't you weather controlled this planet?" Poke asked, licking his lips between words.

"You don't sweat?" Richard asked.

"No, I'm Atlantian originally. The air there is very moist, so evaporative cooling measures don't work."

Richard studied him, "That's crazy, how do you remember that?"

Poke looked surprised, and Peek flashed a solid amber. "I... don't... I don't know. I just... know it." He held up his finger to indicate that Peek was speaking to him in his head. "Yeah. I remember that. No... Yeah... No. That's funny. Peek says it remembers being organic, and having been to Atlantis once on vacation. But apparently, we have never seen a Terran... or a Gaian before today. Which doesn't make sense."

"We've never met aliens before, so I'd say that makes us even." Richard smiled and patted Poke on the shoulder.

The office building sighed and collapsed into itself, and a cloud of dust filled the air. Richard's wrist communicator flashed and he read its screen. "I have to go, we lost connection to some of the pods. I have wandering nanites."

With that he bowed and walked closer to the building. There he met a short woman with a billowing orange and purple afro. She held up her hands to him, conversing in American Sign Language.

"Why can't the nanites pull the carbon out of the air if they can rearrange things atom by atom?" Jessica conjectured.

"Probably that would take too much energy with the molecules dispersed? I like the trees though," Poke said.

"Hey man, you guys seen, Eagle?" The long-haired man came from the tent; he scanned the area as he spoke.

"I thought he was with you?" Jessica asked him.

"Nah, I haven't seen him since he stormed out. Dunno what's up with him."

"Probably the same reason he had a gun," Katelyn snapped.

"Hey, that's got nothing to do with Jason." He said, holding his palms up and stepping backward.

"Who?" the pair of women asked.

"Jason... uh, that's me?" he responded, unsure of his answer.

Jessica shrugged her shoulders. "Okay, that's one less thing." She turned to the tents and caught Meera's attention, who promptly came over. "Did you see Eagle?" she asked.

"The guy with the tattoo? The last time I saw him was with you. Let me check." Meera pulled out a tablet and flipped though screens, her eyebrows knotted together. "I don't see him anywhere. Everyone can be identified by their nanites, it's a personal locator if their comm bands go offline." She pointed to a display on her wrist, similar to Richard's. "I think he might be out of range." Pressing a few contacts, she spoke into the comm band. "Amanda, do you see nanite cohort one six seven four three? I can't track it." Meera looked across to the woman with whom Richard was talking, she shook her head no. Then her voice, synthetic but feminine, came over the band.

"We lost the transmitter on the north side of the building; I can't track north of us. A few clicks just went completely dark."

Meera covered her band with her other hand and whispered to the group, "That's gonna really piss her off. Losing a transmitter is her anathema."

Jessica and Katelyn nodded.

Meera took a deep breath and licked her lips twice. She stammered and then spoke into her band. "Do you think… that…?"

"Shit," came the response.

"What? What is she talking about?" Jessica asked.

Richard came running up behind them, his face flushed.

"You're friend's pretty sneaky. He stole the transmitter when the building fell, and took off. We can't track him or the nano-foam pod he managed to steal." He held up a black backpack and opened the main compartment, revealing the EMP bomb. "And what, exactly, are you planning to blow up?"

"What?" Jessica spat and immediately turned to Jason. "What the hell are you guys up to?"

Chapter 26: Dissension

Jason met Jessica's stare. "Look man, I have no idea what that dude's damage is. He's all about having control and shit. I think the amnesia is freaking him out. I don't remember what we were doing before that and neither do you. I didn't steal a nano PCP or whatever the hell it is. I didn't bring no bomb, man." Jason returned Jessica's stare, eyes burning, and holding it until he dropped to his knees.

Jessica stepped back, "Don't bow to me. What are you doing?"

Jason rolled on his side and started vomiting. Dark brown coffee-ground chunks poured out of his mouth.

Before any of them could call for help, Meera was assisting him. Mercedes tore out of the tent, her exosuit carrying her the distance in one stride. Jessica reached up to her vibration patch. "Patches. They don't have patches. Poke and Katelyn don't either.

"Oh no," Katelyn mouthed.

Jessica yelled to Meera, "My pack! I was wearing a pack! Get my backpack!" and pointed to the tent, then she rushed to Katelyn.

Another Medmad ran up to Katelyn and checked her IV. "I'm okay, just getting dizzy." She sat on the ground, burying her face in her hands.

Jessica dropped to her knees as Meera ran out of the tent, black backpack in hand. She willed herself not to pass out and with iron determination she reached into her bag and pulled out four patches that Ellwood slipped in before they left New York. She pulled herself up enough to hold one patch against Katelyn's neck and then handed the other to Mercedes. "Push it on hard," she said, squinting.

Peek squawked from the storage device attached to Poke's arm, "Patches. Configure."

Mercedes pressed the patch onto Jason's hairy neck, and then moved over to Poke, she spoke directly to the storage device. "How?

How do I do that? How do I configure it?"

"Program. Rewrite. Account for vibration."

Mercedes stood up and snapped her fingers and, in a flash, Meera and other Medmads were at her side. "Get them back into the tent and keep them as stable as you can. Run them full IV's and try to circulate their nutrients. Open them wide. Richard!"

"Already on it! But we aren't done with this!" Richard yelled, gesturing to the other backpack he threw over his shoulder. He ran toward Amanda, who grabbed her tablet and a bag, then headed to the tents.

Jessica, being escorted by a rather burly Medmad, yelled over her shoulder, "Peek, you have to let them see the tech, don't hide it. We could all die, understand?"

Poke shuffled in their direction; Peek's LEDs flashed blue. Meera quickly followed.

Once on the exam tables, Jessica relaxed as much as she could. She gestured to Mercedes. "I thought you said we had time?" She asked coughing; a wet, sloshing sound emanated from her chest as she spoke.

"At the rate of protein synthesis, yes, I thought so. This is more than that."

Mercedes turned on her comm band and waved her hand over Jessica's torso.

"Your DNA is breaking down, my dear. Almost like radiation poisoning."

She swiftly ran her fingers over the display as Jessica shook her head.

"I've directed the nanites to focus on your DNA. Hopefully they can keep it repaired long enough until we get your patches working. But you're still vibrating wrong. The only thing we could do is literally rebuild and replace every cell in your body. We can do that, but we wouldn't want to do that out here, otherwise we would put you in unbearable pain. We need a fully functional hospital." After she finished her scan, she put her hand on Jessica's chest. "Stay with us, my dear. You seem like a fighter, keep fighting."

Jessica nodded and shook her head. Growing increasingly weaker she whispered, "How long?"

Richard craned his neck up from an empty exam table; Amanda was furiously typing on her tablet, her face glowing with the iridescent blue of thousands of lines of code.

"This is amazing. I've never seen polymorphic code like this except in viruses, this data is… it's just loco. I don't even know the type theory it's using. What do you think, Amanda?" His face contorted in both frustration and excitement.

Amanda, quickly signed with her left hand, and typed with her right. A data cable ran from her tablet to the vibration patch, glowing blue.

"That's right, I see what you mean. It's going to take us too long to do this," Richard said. Amanda got up and reached over to the next exam table and pulled at the storage device on Poke's arm. Groggy and in pain, Poke pulled back, twisting her wrist, she growled out a moan from deep in her chest.

"Poke! No!" Jessica ordered.

Amanda reached over and typed on her band; it spoke for everyone to hear. "I know it knows how to do this; we can't do it. It has its own vibration patch, doesn't it?"

"Poke?" Jessica implored.

He relented, and in one motion Amanda took the storage device containing Peek and dropped it on top of the vibration patch, then reached down and pulled a large vial out of her bag. It glowed with the lime-green light of nano-foam. Popping the cap with her thumb, she poured the foam over the patch and Peek. Poke's temple flashed green in random patterns, and he winced in pain.

"It's… okay?" Poke said, still unsure of the term. "They are talking. It's too fast for me to understand."

"Please rest," Mercedes reiterated, putting her hand on Jessica's forehead. "Let them work."

Chapter 27: Patches

Jessica rocked on the exam table, switching her weight between her glutes and flexing her legs. The pain and nausea were overpowering her, and she fought to keep herself conscious. Katelyn had already passed out and she lay on the table breathing softly. Jason was similarly unconscious.

"Yeah, you see that? That's cool!" Richard exclaimed as he scanned through more lines of code that changed as he watched. Peek was interfacing directly with the nanites and re-writing their code. Richard continued, "It draws energy from the wearer and literally vibrates their whole body up to or down from the frequency they need. It's using ATP and cholesterol as a battery. Amazing. Jessica, do you feel hungrier when you are wearing the patch?"

"I dunno, I thought it was because I was stressed out." She remembered back to desperately wanting to eat an apple when they returned to Bellerophon, but didn't because she thought the act would be insensitive for some reason she could not remember. Remembering anything without trying excited her and her head swam. "I did notice that after KT took it off, I wasn't hungry at all."

Richard looked up from the display screen, "KT?"

Jessica froze for the moment, unwilling to give too much more away to this alternate dimension and risk contaminating it like she did Terra. Although she had given Peek the command to let them see everything to facilitate the work on reprogramming the patches, but she decided to be honest to make the exchange easier, concealment was not her strong suit --as her anxiety over not telling all of her family about her portal hopping adventures showed-- and decided to drop it. "I don't know. It's important somehow."

Richard gestured over to Katelyn lying placidly on the bed. "No, that's a different Kay tee."

Why are there two Katelyns? How do I know both of them?

Jessica looked at Amanda who was scrolling through code with one hand and physically holding nano-foam in place with the other. Her orange and purple afro was tied back with a silver ribbon.

You were there too, weren't you?

"There are multiples of us. More than one Katelyn, more than one Amanda. I've seen her before." Jessica said.

Amanda pointed to herself, raising one eyebrow.

"Yes, you... or someone like you."

Jessica's ears rang with a sudden fullness, and she swallowed hard trying to collect her thoughts. "Multiples. Counterparts." She whispered, then finally passed out.

"Goddamn it, I'm getting really tired of this!" Jessica roared as she sat up on the table, her head as clear as a bell. She could feel the vibration patch pulsing softly on the back of her neck.

The heat from the early morning sun had already warmed the tent up to uncomfortable levels. Meera stood next to her almost immediately. "Ah, you're up. You do pass out a lot. I wonder why? We didn't find anything that would suggest that in your bio scan. Have you always been one to lose consciousness?"

Jessica shook her head and rubbed the back of her neck, her muscles ached. "Not until I stuck my face into a portal in my basement a few months ago. I think it messed with my already messed-up nervous system."

What portal? How did I know that?

"The patches worked great." Meera jumped in. "They aren't perfect, but they are doing their job and speeding up your rate to match ours. Hopefully the nanites will keep your nervous system stable so you don't keep losing consciousness. That must be terrifying.

Mercedes thinks you should be rested enough to head out with us tomorrow morning."

"Head out? Where are we going?" Jessica asked.

"We have to move on to Chantilly, they have a few issues going on with the settlement there. The Wayfarers are telling us that they are giving serious resistance to our help. We need to be there… just in case."

"How long was I out this time?" she asked, with a sigh.

"Long enough to avoid talking about this," Richard said from behind her, holding up the black backpack.

"I don't know what that is. I mean, I know what that is, I don't know why we have it."

Richard smirked and pulled the EMP bomb out of the bag, placing it on an exam table with a thud. "The battery is drained, but it's enough to neutralize a kilometer. It could definitely take out part of The Trunk for sure. You don't know why you are walking around with this? We put one on your patches on it so it doesn't disintegrate. No telling what would happen if the wrong wire shorted.""

"I don't. I may have known but I can't remember why. If you don't trust me, you can keep it for yourself and disarm it. I can't think of a good reason why I need that." Jessica reached into her pocket and pulled out Gabrielle's bracelet. "Or this," she said, focusing on the silver stone.

"You haven't given me a reason not to trust you, but I know we can't trust that Eagle guy. That's why we are going to go looking for him tomorrow when the Medmads break camp."

"How is he not dead?" Katelyn asked, moving over to the exam table and sizing up the bomb.

Meera shrugged her shoulders. "I dunno. Maybe he is, and we just haven't found the body yet."

Jessica squinted in thought.

Something about that guy. Computers.

Jessica concentrated on his face: cold lines, narrow eyes, unflinching stare, the eagle tattoo on the side of his head. He reminded her of one of those guys who hates authority and is always getting in trouble. A bad boy. Not in the sexy devil-may-care sense, but in the very real, "This dude probably shot up a school" kind of latent evil. She knew in her heart she didn't trust him. He breaks into things. Steals stuff. No regard for other people. She looked over at Jason, who was busy shoving a protein pack into his face, humming as he chewed.

He needs to have minions... control.

The memory flashed into her head like a thunderbolt. "He's a hacker. It's why he stole the nano-pod! Richard, is it hard to hack into the nanites?"

Richard took a break from showing Katelyn the bomb, he made no effort to hide his fascination at the device. "Not really, the code is open source and we don't use a lot of encryption. Wayfarers are entrusted with its security and that tech is way beyond any of the settlements we run into. If you wanted to do that, you'd have to be super smart and well-motivated. Or..."

"Or a hacker from another dimension with nothing to lose," Jessica said.

Chapter 28: Preparing

"Jason, you have to remember. What are you guys up to? Why are you here?" Jessica asked.

Jason stood up and came over to Jessica's bunk to answer her question. He attempted to smooth out his disheveled hair and beard. "I told you man; I don't know. I don't think my memory is good without the amnesia anyway. You guys showed up, we got into a fight. Boom, alternate dimension."

"A fight?" Jessica looked to Katelyn.

"Yeah, like the gun wasn't a big clue?" Katelyn responded, arching her eyebrow.

Jessica shook her head. "I guess I must have forgotten that, sorry. So, we are on opposite sides of something, but none of us know what that something is. If Eagle is a hacker, then you must be one too."

"Maybe, man, but I don't really know too much about computers and shit. It's not my thing. I think I just work with him."

"Why do you work with him? Any clue?"

"Nah, no idea. I just remember that those dudes, the ones that Eagle hangs out with, gave me a place to sleep and lots of food so I didn't have to beg for it, but... I dunno."

Katelyn walked up to him and scanned him up and down, "Begging for food. I remember now, you're a homeless guy. We gave you food."

"Really? I know you guys are nice to me. He's..." Jason pointed to the opening of the tent, "he's a jerk. I know that."

Katelyn scoffed. "Well, that's obvious."

Jessica looked over the tent at her friends; the Wayfarers and Medmads were busy preparing for the move, except for Richard, Amanda, and Meera. The rest of the group stared at her, as if awaiting orders. She wondered why she was put in charge. Surely, she wasn't the smartest, the most capable, or the strongest; she didn't even belong in this dimension. Making decisions came easy to her though, and she had to admit she liked it.

Okay they want you to do something. Don't stand there like an idiot.

"Meera, do you think we should be stable medically if we take off now? Before it gets too hot today?"

Meera nodded. "We should be okay, your nanites are working properly now that we have stabilized you. Unless something weird happens. It's already thirty centigrade though, we have to be careful. I'll bring extra water."

Jessica's eyebrows knotted and her lip curled. "That's like… eighty-seven or something. Already? It's April!"

"The average high for April is thirty-three, be glad it isn't August."

Jessica found herself regretting asking what the average high was.

"Forty-eight," Meera answered, not hesitating.

Jessica and Katelyn gasped in unison. "My god, how did it get that bad?" Jessica asked.

Meera shook her head and shrugged.

Of course, she doesn't know, or realize how absurd that question is given her location on the globe. She was born into an altered world, almost alien. Bastards took too long to fix the problem.

"Richard, can we take some foam with us? Do they need you here?" Jessica asked, trying to get off the subject.

Richard looked at Amanda who nodded and signed "Okay."

"I think they will make do without us for a bit," Richard responded. "We will bring the comm relays and a few pods. We should fit you all with some comm bands before we head out." He called over to another Wayfarer who was packing supplies, and they pulled out four bands from a wooden box, handing one to each of the aliens. The bands locked onto their arms with ease, and synced with the nanites they currently had in their bodies, all but Poke who had his own.

"You can't shut yours down?" Jessica asked him.

"They aren't processing like they are supposed to. They need the Network to function, but they are still on. I don't know what else to do, I've had them since I was a baby."

Peek chirped from the device, "I fix. We will talk."

Jessica smiled and looked at her comm band; complete science fiction to her, and it was there, on her arm. She scanned through the data and found the band Amanda had already set up for the group. She sent out a ping and could hear everyone's bands vibrate and ping back.

This. Is. Cool!

Richard tossed each of them hats and sunglasses. Bamboo, metal, and glass; everything was natural or recyclable. Jessica realized that she hadn't seen any plastic anywhere. She presumed it was probably the first thing they deconstructed.

"You know," Richard stopped in front of the door, pulling his wide brimmed bamboo safari cap over his greying hair. "We still haven't figured out exactly how you got here other than that flash of light."

Amanda signed to him quickly, he responded to her, signing, "Thank you."

"She said we still have the residual data; we should start with where you all showed up."

Jessica pulled her cap down and tightened her sunglasses. "Let's do it!"

Chapter 29: The Wastes of Reston

The team stepped out into the heat of the early morning; it assaulted them like a sauna no one wanted. Sweat trickled down Jessica's ribs and stuck uncomfortably to her hips. The sun shone in the milky-white sky; a brown haze colored the horizon. All around them, rotting buildings loomed; some actively being re-wound, others waiting their turn. Vines covered nearly everything, smothering out what little native vegetation there was. She took her steps carefully, trotting over broken concrete, asphalt, and glass.

"It looks like *WALL-E* here. What's that haze?" Jessica asked, pointing to the horizon.

Richard didn't look up from his feet. "Fires. There are a lot of forest fires, what's left of The West is still burning. They aren't as bad on this side of the Mississippi anymore. But when fire season starts in June, all of this goes up." He gestured with his hands at the vine-choked underbrush.

"Hard to believe this was a year of growth. The rainforest in Canada? Is that still there?" Jessica asked, again not wanting to know the answer.

"Canada? Canada..." Richard stopped to think. "Oh, 'Canada'. We don't call it that anymore."

Jessica tripped over a vine, but quickly regained her balance.

"Ontario is still there," Amanda's synthesized voice spoke over their comm bands, "and Quebec. Everything else is different."

Jessica stopped walking and looked at Katelyn, who shook her head. "So, what happened to America?" she asked.

Richard answered, "You're standing in it, well what's left of it. It stops at the Mississippi. After that point no one really knows. The other side is completely different than What Came Before, it's just

'The Great American Desert.' I'm sure we will eventually get over there and outquisition that. I'm also sure there are people who need our help."

"Come on, we have to keep moving." Meera added, as she strode by on her exosuit, her head eight feet in the air; the suit's long, stilt-like legs propelled her effortlessly.

Jessica looked up at her as she crossed the sun, casting a long shadow.

In a few minutes the undergrowth cleared out and they entered the ruined parking lot where they arrived. Jessica saw the van she and Jason hid in, and the spot where she collapsed. The oil rainbows were muted, barely discernible amidst the heat waves coming off the broken ground.

"Sorry I scared you," Poke apologized, bowing slightly as he put his hand to his chest.

"It's okay," Jessica said, then smiled back at him. "You were panicking." She felt a twinge in her ribs where she had been shot. "I know what that is like."

From atop her perch, Meera commented, "It smells like flowers here. Do you smell that?" She asked.

Richard nodded and Amanda signed "flower."

"Finally, something other than chocolate. It's overpowering," Jessica said.

"There are cacao farms nearby, you're smelling that," Richard explained.

"You don't smell chocolate from the plants; they have to be fermented," Jessica said. "I can smell the lavender too, and now it's mixed with chocolate."

Meera pressed a contact on her comm band and she slowly descended from her perch. She put both arms through straps behind her back and pulled the struts from the legs up and onto her arms.

Like slipping on a backpack, the leg struts became arm braces. Jessica smiled at the versatility.

"You're smelling chocolate?" Meera asked Jessica.

"Yeah, it's really strong, we've been smelling it since the landfill. It's everywhere here."

"What landfill?"

"The landfill where the gate was. Right before we got here." Jessica rattled off the fact as if she were describing the sun coming up in the morning.

I guess I remember that.

"Gate?" Richard asked, his voice piquing. Amanda took off her pack and started to set up her communications relay. Meera activated her comm band and waved it through the air.

"Umm, yeah, the gates open up to another gate, unless you don't have one, then it just pops open a portal." Jessica instantly regretted explaining it, but was so excited to remember something, it poured out.

Shut up, will you?

"Like that orange light they came through." Jason pointed to Katelyn.

Poke stepped up and scanned the area so that Peek could analyze it. His temple LED stayed a solid amber.

"So, you came here on purpose... will someone else come to get you? Do they smell like lavender too?" Richard asked. He pulled a fistful of nano-foam out of his hip pocket and poured them onto the ground; it immediately soaked into the oil.

"I don't know what that purpose was." Jessica said.

"Location marked. I've let the other Wayfarers know that this spot should be considered dangerous. The Medmads will add it on their patrols," Amanda's synthesized voice spoke over the comm bands.

Richard typed on his band, and spoke as he did, "The nanites will clear the perimeter and establish a supply depot. I am seeing a lot of matter here with the same vibration as you had, and it's degrading quickly." He flicked a screen on his band, "I'll have them ignore that."

"Peek, buddy can you give me anything here? Can you fill in the gaps?" Jessica asked.

"Trying. Memory damaged. Hard to repair in this space."

"¡Aye!," Richard exclaimed. "I'm sorry I got so excited I didn't think about adding hardware. I'm going to have them make you some more storage space and computing power using the parameters we established from your connection. Does four exaflops and exabytes work for you?"

Peek cooed from the storage device, and its LEDs rippled.

Richard laughed. "I will take that as a yes then. We have plenty of carbon and silicon here, and we can make coolant as well. They are already getting started." He pointed to a spot in the oil where a one by six-foot box slowly emerged from the ground. Jessica recoiled but tried not to show it.

What are they doing inside of me?

She asked a question to clear her mind, "I don't get it, you can make supercomputers from garbage, yet the whole planet is still this messed up. Why can't you fix everything at once? What's holding you back?"

Amanda grunted as she took a transmitter out of her hip pocket and put it up on the top of the minivan Jessica had crawled into. Meera opened a package of protein and ate it, smiling between bites.

"First of all, this isn't a supercomputer, kids play with this capacity back in The Trunk," Richard explained. "You should see the ones in the city, they are a sight to behold. Second, the nanites require a lot of power to do what they do. Right now, the ones running in our bodies are harvesting fat and cholesterol to keep their engines running, and they are also drawing on our body heat.

"Third, they can't just make things out of thin air, they need resources and stable molecules. We're trying to restore the world by helping it along, using more power means that we will be contributing to the system that got us this bad in the first place. The damage took three hundred years to make, we think we can have atmospheric carbon back to nineteen-ninety levels in twenty years. But it will take another two hundred or so for the planet to heal.

"You can also forgive some of the population who have been through hell in the last fifty years or so. They don't trust the technology, and they also don't see the old world as a good thing, because they would have to adapt. Again."

Richard stopped for a second, surveying the broken landscape around him. "I've never seen snow, and only a few of the old timers remember it. But from what I have heard, it sounds like a pain in the ass. The only reason why I want it back is because I know it's not here anymore because of humans."

Jessica put her hands up in apology, Richard laughed and nodded. "Wayfarer's life for me," he said.

Before Jessica knew it, a structure had materialized behind her, complete with water and food. Richard gestured from them to sit and eat.

"Let's get some hydration and then head back out. I think we can track your man now." He held up his comm band, it displayed a pulsing red dot. "The transmitter can see his molecular trail now that we know where it originated. That data is all over here."

"Then he *is* still alive," Katelyn said, after chugging a metal canister of water.

"Looks like it, and he has a whole pod of my nanites with him."

Chapter 30: Amanda

"How long do you think it's gonna take to get Peek set up?" Jessica asked, pointing to the apparently not-so-super supercomputer growing steadily out of the muck.

Richard checked his comm band. "Probably an hour, give or take, then, well, they will have to do whatever they do," he said, pointing to Poke.

"In that time, the debris from the other dimension will have dissipated completely, and we won't be able to track him." Meera said, then lifted herself back up on the stilts of her exosuit and surveyed the area.

Amanda directed Meera while checking her band, her synthesized voice spoke from it, "Three five zero. Two clicks. That's where it goes out of range."

Meera spun around, careful to not step on her companions below. "Three... five...," she mumbled aloud, trying to get her bearings.

Amanda pointed away from the sun, over the baking parking lot, and past the ruined office buildings.

"Right! Thanks! I'm such a newbie." Meera pointed to herself and laughed.

Amanda rolled her eyes. "We have to keep going, he already has a day's head start," she said through her band.

"I should stay and make sure this works properly," Richard said, gesturing to the computer.

Katelyn sat next to Poke and put her arm around him, his skin darkened, and he smiled sheepishly.

"Working fast," Peek chimed from the storage device on Poke's arm.

"Let's get going then." Jessica looked at Amanda and Meera, and her insides began to swim. At first, she thought it was the patch not working properly until she realized it was her anxiety screaming at her. She was worried about leaving the only connections to her world behind, and what would happen if she needed those people. Poke lay down on a cot the nanites had created, and Katelyn sat down at the foot. Richard was poking away on his comm band, interfacing with the more rudimentary parts of the computer.

"Ohh kayy," Jessica said. "You four stay safe."

Katelyn exaggerated a wink and shot a finger pistol at her.

Jessica shook her head, thought of some choice —but playful— words for her, and decided not to use them in mixed company.

Out of instinct, Jessica signed to Amanda, "You're in the lead," and she responded with "Yes" and moved outside of the perimeter.

"Wait, you know ASL?" Meera asked, looking down at Jessica.

She looked at her hands and then replied, "I guess so?" then hoisted her pack on her back. "As fast as you can Peek, we need to know what we don't know. I don't like this."

The emulant flashed solid blue in Poke's temple.

Within minutes the trio was out of the range of the camp, passing though more of the same rugged and abandoned terrain. All around them rubble piles jutted out of the undergrowth like Maya temples rising above the jungle. Cars and buildings were everywhere beyond, a veritable bowl of desolation, but in an orderly collapse. Not as if some unforeseen catastrophe had suddenly surprised the culture, but rather as if it were planned, prepared for, even welcomed. No wind blew, and the sun, close to its zenith, baked the landscape. Jessica never felt so overheated in her life, and she wished there was something in her equipment that could cool her off. She wondered if the nanites banging around in her bloodstream were doing something to help her along.

Amanda's comm band pulsed every few seconds, growing stronger on the heading of three-five-zero. Meera occasionally moved in front of the group, pointing to areas that were more easily traversed.

Intermittently she needed to be reminded of the heading, and fell back a few paces. The effort was hardly wasted as the exosuit did most of the walking for her; she cruised along above the other two, looking down at them with professional concern. "How you holding up?"

Amanda jumped over a fallen tree, burned to a carbon husk. "Okay," she signed and kept moving forward.

"I'm hot, but all right," said Jessica, hopping the same tree, not quite as nimbly.

"How do you know ASL?" Amanda signed.

"I don't know. I think someone in my family is deaf. I can read it better than I can sign."

Jessica asked, "You aren't deaf, you're aphasic right?"

Amanda pointed to a car buried under some vines, helped Jessica steer around, and then responded in ASL. "Yes, I was a baby when it happened. Got sick. Some kind of virus. Damaged my brain on the right." She finger-spelled part of the next sentence, Jessica could barely keep up. "When the Wayfarers outquisitioned my village, I was already ten years old, and they gave me a book on ASL. I learned it and taught my friends. I can speak, but it's hard. The words are a jumble. I am more expressive this way anyway, I think, so I didn't want the Medmads to fix it."

They dodged a pile of concrete and rebar, and Amanda continued, using a sign that Jessica was unfamiliar with.

"... was in that group, and already knew some ASL. Kinda. I took pity and taught him too. I use the comm band when I know there are non-signers around."

Jessica nodded, realizing Amanda had used Richard's name sign, which looked like "R-bug."

"I'm not really sure who my parents are; I grew up in a creche. He's the closest thing I have to a father."

Jessica felt a pang of recognition, but was unsure why. She laughed and thanked her, not wanting to press her and make her feel like a bug under a glass.

Amanda thanked her back; Jessica could tell she appreciated the effort.

After a few more minutes hopping rubble, Jessica called out, "Meera, where are we going? Do you see anything up ahead? I mean, anything... interesting?"

Meera stopped for a second and let the others catch up. "A whole lot of the same, except for that," she said, turning to the east; she pointed her long, thin arm toward the horizon. A large building, bigger than the rest in the area, loomed, the blazing April sun sat threateningly behind it. Vegetable fields filled the area around the building, taking up the space where cars would have parked in another time. She could see people in the fields, tilling the soil with hand-tools. There was no technology that she could make out, nor armed guards.

Jessica clambered atop a tall pile and squinted against the sun, sweat pouring from under her cap. "That's a... hospital?"

Amanda stepped up beside and checked her comm band. "They aren't on our network. I'm not getting any signal from them at all," she responded from her band.

Jessica sat down on the pile and quickly took a large gulp of water.

"The trail leads there?" Meera asked, leaning back on her exosuit that cradled her lower back and thighs.

"Yes," Amanda responded.

"We're gonna have to go in at some point. Might as well do it while the sun is still up," Jessica said, capping the water bottle and wiping the sweat from her forehead.

A flash caught her eye and she heard a loud ping come from Meera's exosuit; she spun, looking for the source. Another rock bounced away from them as she searched. Then another. Amanda flicked her right wrist; from it sprang a shaft of dark metal, a foot in length and crackling with electricity.

"Don't move!" A voice called from behind a large pile of debris. Masculine, but young, barely a teen "You can leave with that other guy. We couldn't help him, and we aren't helping you. Get lost!"

Amanda held up both hands in front of her, palms forward. The electrified baton hummed, illuminating her face in its blue light.

"Okay," she voiced with great difficulty. She twisted her wrist and the baton turned off and slid back onto her forearm.

A voice from the west responded, much older and gravely, "We told you we aren't going to help you. Just like we weren't going to help him."

Jessica's hands shook, she was desperate to diffuse the situation as fast as possible. She turned to the direction of the voice. "We don't want anything; we are just looking for him. If you tell us which way he went, we will be on our way."

No one moved for a moment. A hawk screeched in the distance, and June bugs began calling to each other. A whistle pierced the air, coming from the hospital. It quavered across the landscape in an unrecognizable pattern.

"Fine," the man said after turning his attention back to the women. "You're lucky she can see you. Okay, move forward slowly so we can keep up. You, Medmad, come down and walk like the rest of us humans," he commanded.

Meera cast her gaze cast down to Amanda, who blinked slowly. With a sigh she pressed her contact and the exosuit sunk back down to the ground.

"Told you Pa, they aren't the same," the younger male said, still hidden in the rubble.

A man stepped out of the bushes, tall, with grey hair, and a long and tangled grey beard. Piercing grey eyes looked out from a wrinkled face. Jessica froze in place.

"Dad?"

Chapter 31: The Hospital

"Dad?" The man asked, his nose curled and head turned at an angle, as if to defend himself.

That's not your father. You're in another dimension. He just looks like him.

Jessica's stomach did somersaults and her legs trembled. She tried to reverse herself and her suddenly bone-dry mouth sputtered out her words.

"I— I'm sorry, you don't look old enough to be someone's father." Jessica could not shake the feeling that this had happened before under different circumstances. Instinctively she relaxed, knowing how this person would react. Hopefully.

The man leaned against the walking stick that he carried with him, raising his left eyebrow. He smirked, pulling his bushy beard to the right. "You're a horrible liar."

The teen laughed.

"Okay, let's get going before we get heatstroke." The man turned and walked back into the underbrush, blending in almost instantly.

Jessica glanced to the right to see the other man, but he was already gone.

As they moved through the fields, they passed maize, a variety that Jessica had never seen before; purple cobs behind green husks with orange tassels. She reached out to touch one of them and the teen admonished her. "Don't do that. They are the only heirloom ones we have left, and we don't want you to contaminate them," his voice was stern.

"Why are they purple?"

He laughed, from the other side of the path than he was on moments ago. "It's Inca. Where do you think maize comes from?"

"Hey," Came his father's curt reply.

"Sorry," he said from yet another position in the field.

How's he doing that?

The group walked to the front of the building; the entrance was flanked on two sides by decayed buildings, their windows broken away and replaced with wooden beams. Several faces looked down at them as they arrived, curious and yet fearful. Children giggled behind them from another building, similarly constructed but much smaller. To their right a parking deck stood silent, its top level covered in soil and cultivated with various vegetables.

Jessica tried to take in the enormity of it; this was an actual post-apocalyptic society. Worse than post-covid. Not an event, or a speed-bump in the road of civilization, society had collapsed and these people were doing what most humans do: adapting and fighting to survive.

There were no gigantic thugs, no machine gun nests every three feet, no squalor or desolation. Everything was neat and clean, and a sense of order instead of chaos filled the area. Even though the faces looking down at her were cautious, they were also pleasant, even hopeful. She wondered if it was because there was a Wayfarer and Medmad with her, or was it something else? Had this culture endured the spasm of chaos she saw in so many movies, or did it evolve slowly?

"Jessica, can we play today? You said after the 'adult stuff' we could play in the maize. You promised! Cool hat! Is it new?"

Confused, Jessica looked down to see a small girl tugging at her jeans; bright brown eyes smiled up at her.

"Uhh, sweetie... I'm not— wait. I'm Jessica?"

"You're not? Heh you're funny!" The little girl pulled her arms in and giggled. Other children ran up behind her and started laughing as well. Jessica found herself surrounded by children of varying heights and ethnicities, all sun-darkened, they laughed, relaxed and familiar.

"Uhh..." Jessica vocalized again, turning to her group. Meera was scanning the area on her comm band, and Amanda shrugged her shoulders.

"Tony, your sister is weird," the first girl called out.

"That's not my sister," responded the teen, this time from the windows above.

"Now you're all being silly!" the little girl yelled, addressing the whole group. "When you are done, come play!" She ran off toward the fields, the gaggle of children hot on her heels.

"Yeah, I don't…" Jessica looked around; her face red with embarrassment.

"Come inside, you'll see," Tony's father said.

Jessica did as he asked and turned to the door following him into the building without hesitating.

Inside, it was cool and dark, a welcome respite from the overpowering heat outside. Most of the structure had been stripped of its interior walls, and the space was open. LED lights lit the space, and she could see power lines running to an empty elevator shaft in the center of the building. Groups of people congregated around various farming activities: sharpening tools, fixing equipment, inventorying vegetables. All of this stopped as soon as the group walked in and people fixated on the visitors.

From a snatched conversation Jessica overheard, "Why is she with them? This isn't what we decided." From another, "Did something change at the council meeting?"

They turned a corner and ascended a flight of stairs. The next floor still had its interior walls and a long hallway snaked away from them, doors branching off in regular intervals. The spaces were wide, big enough for gurneys and equipment to be moved around without issue. At the end of the hall, a frosted glass door had the word

"Administration" written on it.

As they walked up, Jessica heard Tony speaking in excited tones. Then another voice, female, and familiar.

Tony's father knocked on the door and waited for the reply.

"Come," called the female voice.

He opened the door and let the group walk in ahead of him. Jessica stepped in to see the woman standing behind a desk wearing canvas pants and a cotton shirt, both dyed black. Slightly shorter than she, the woman had the same dark brown hair, with light brown highlights, exactly like hers when she spent too much time in the sun. The woman's sun-tanned face smiled at her, showing apprehensive eyes.

"Ahoy, Jessica," she said, rising from her chair, and holding out her hand, palm forward. "It's nice to meet you. I'm… well, I'm you."

Chapter 32: The Gaian Version

Jessica Unbound stopped moving and stood transfixed. Her arms went numb, and her lips turned to ice. "I— you…wait… uhh…"

The other Jessica motioned with her fingers, and a wooden chair slid in behind her twin who felt as if gravity had increased four-fold in the last ten seconds. Dropping into the chair, she desperately pulled air into her lungs, feeling her world greying around her and the tendrils of reality that kept her centered in her universe slowly slipping away.

This can't be happening. I am not looking at myself. This is impossible. How can this be happening?

Strong hands gripped her shoulders and she was aware of a voice behind her, soft and female. Through her tunnel vision, she saw the Gaian version of herself move from behind the desk and sit in front of her; shadowy and ephemeral. Her vision only provided blacks and whites fraying at the periphery, like ivy growing over a door.

You can't be me. I'm here. You should be… dead?

In a flash her mind stitched together everything she had experienced in the last two days: the amnesia, the aliens, falling through the portal, sneaking the EMP bomb into the landfill to destroy the Eastern Syndicate gate, Eagle.

"THE GATE! I REMEMBER!" She shouted out, catching the other Jessica by surprise.

"Yep, your buddy, Eagle. He was here this morning. He kept babbling about needing to get back to the gate before you did, asking us to fix him without letting the Medmads know he was here. He knew he was from another dimension and didn't know how to get himself back. When I spoke to him, he acted like he knew me. And he didn't like that fact."

Jessica Unbound sat back in her chair.

Meera, hovered behind and put a finger on Unbound's neck, manually checking her pulse. "Wow, that's fast."

"She'll be okay, she's strong," the Gaian said, lifting a bowl to Unbound's face. "Here," she handed it to her sitting counterpart, "Mom's recipe, you should eat up."

Unbound looked down and into her hands a full bowl of dumplings had been placed with an old pair of chopsticks suspended into the corner. She picked up a dumpling and ate it; almost the same as her mother's vegetable dumpling recipe, but heavily laced with chocolate. She chewed slowly and swallowed cautiously. When the food hit her stomach, it helped to center her. "I'm sorry," she said slowly, "I have never met my double before. It's a little… overwhelming."

The Gaian smiled, "Don't apologize, the same thing happened to me the first time I met my double."

Unbound dropped her chopsticks into the bowl, looking up at her counterpart incredulously. "When has this happened to you before?"

"Never."

Both Jessicas smiled.

"Now, before you start asking me all those questions," the Gaian said, "You know, the things that you would ask to make sure you and I are the same person, I need to remind you that we aren't alone. So here are my answers: Two times. Only if I have eaten chicken. I miss them too."

Unbound sat upright in her seat and blushed hot-red. "We're not in the same time or place, how can we have the same experiences? It not even the same year."

"I really don't know. You're the one who came from a different dimension, not me."

Unbound nodded and polished off the last dumpling. "Mom?"

The Gaian shook her head and blinked slowly.

Unbound felt a chill in her stomach, but it was fleeting. Her logic took hold and reminded her that her mother was safe and sound, on Earth and waiting for her to return. "We came through a portal that Eagle made. It was an accident. We were trying to stop him in that other dimension, which isn't the dimension that I am from. We have these patches on our necks that keep us from disintegrating." Unbound leaned forward and turned her head, exposing the vibration patch.

"Impressive," the Gaian responded.

"Yeah!" Tony's voice echoed through the room, neither of the Jessicas bothered to search for him.

"He didn't have one of these did he?" Unbound asked, knowing the answer.

"Nope." The Gaian reached over her head and took another bowl of dumplings that were handed to her by her father. "He was glowing though, this green color, sickly like pus."

Meera looked over at Amanda who shook her head and raised her eyebrows.

"He's a hacker," Unbound explained. "He took some of the nanites they have. He reprogrammed them so they could keep him alive. What was he asking for?"

Gaian Jessica went back to her side of the desk and put her feet up. Her shoeless soles looked like brown pie crusts, calloused and scarred from years of surviving in her post-apocalyptic world.

"He was looking for any tech we could give him. Wanted to see if we had a hospital computer, and if we connected to other places around here. He said he wanted to see our... what's the word... network?"

Amanda signed quickly, "You don't have a network, we can't see you. The Wayfarers must have come by here. Why did you refuse them?"

The Gaian looked at her, narrowing her eyes.

"She's using ASL, don't you know it?" Unbound asked.

"AS...L? I've never heard of it."

"American Sign Language? How do you talk to your Deaf community?" Unbound asked.

The Gaian sat back. "We take care of our own, everyone is heard and no opinion is left out."

Amanda huffed. Meera stepped back and bumped into the Gaian's father, who quickly stabilized her with his hands.

So, we aren't exactly the same.

The obviousness of the statement relaxed Unbound more, seeing her counterpart as a separate person and not as a twin or an imposter. Pointing to Amanda she said, "She wants to know why you haven't let the Wayfarers in to help you out."

"Or the Medmads?" Meera asked.

The Gaian's eyes darkened, she drew a deep breath and stood up, pushing her chair back from her desk.

"Look out that window behind me. Do you see that blasted world out there? That is what science and technology did to us. It stomped all over the planet destroying everything it touched. I've been to the city; I've seen what it all looks like. Just another time-bomb going to go off and destroy the planet again. Those nanites that you all carry in your bodies are just waiting for their chance to get loose and turn the whole planet into grey goo. You keep finding faster and more exotic ways of destroying us all. Why do I want to be a part of that?"

Unbound raised her eyebrow, impressed by the other's determination and fire, something that she felt she still did not possess. She also knew that when she was that upset, it was useless to try to reason with her; it would only make her angrier. "I understand. We're not going to try to convert you here. Did you give him anything? Any information?"

The Gaian leaned against the wall next to her window, the sun cast a black shadow over half of her body.

"We did, actually. We have these drives that were left over from What Came Before. The kids use them as building blocks. It's the only tech thing that we have that is portable." She reached into her desk and pulled out a thumb drive, and tossed it to Unbound. "I dunno what is on there, and I don't care. You can have all of them."

Unbound stood up and pocketed the drive. "Thank you for giving this to us, hopefully it can help everyone. She put her hand up, palm forward. "Ahoy!" she said, and turned to leave the room.

Tony started laughing, and the Gaian smiled, holding back her own laughter. Her face softened. "You say that when you meet someone. Not when you leave."

"Oh, well, I knew that, I was just… testing you?"

"Dad, you're right, I am a bad liar." Gaian Jessica said to her father, and then pointed to the door of her office.

"Ladies, I have an appointment with some of the little ones to play in the fields. It helps them feel like part of the community. You are welcome to join us, or you can settle in for the evening. Either way, we will give you a place to rest, and provisions for the journey back, then you can leave at first light."

"We'll take the room, and I appreciate your hospitality," Unbound said.

"This is one of those 'do unto others' moments. Literally." The Gaian smiled and then excused herself. "Tony, take them to the guest quarters."

"You bet!" His voice echoed from down the hallway.

The trio turned to the Gaian's father. Unbound knew he wasn't the same man, but they were so similar that she decided to further trust him.

"That's just the word we use for it, don't worry. It's a couple of cots in the old MRI room. It's pretty big, but no windows, so you can't cause trouble. You'll be fine. I can stay with you if you'd like."

Reflexively, Unbound blurted out, "Yes!"

Chapter 33: The MRI

"I hate that damn thing. Feels like they are burying me alive." Jessica's father, Kevin, remarked as he stood outside the room, looking into the MRI. "It screams in your ears and you can't move. I found something that I hate worse than flying."

"I know Dad, but we have to see how the chemo has done. We have to do this."

"It's not we, don't say that. It's I. I have to go in there. Alone."

"I'm right outside. I'll be watching you the whole time." Jessica tried to calm him, while internally her stomach somersaulted and churned. Her hands shook and she hid them behind her back so he couldn't see, although she knew he knew.

He took a deep breath and turned to her, holding his hospital gown closed with his right hand.

"Thanks for being here, Button." He leaned forward and kissed her on the top of her head.

The green light above the door came on, letting them know that he could enter the room.

"Jessica, hello?"

Jessica shook out of her memory to see the face of her father's counterpart in this dimension staring at her, the same smiling eyes and soft tones; yet he was alive and well, and this MRI was cold and dark. It sat quiescent in the darkness, mute testimony to its years of service and to the dozens, perhaps hundreds, of lives it had saved by alerting its patients to the unseen problems deep inside them.

"It doesn't have to be like this," Meera commented as she looked into the gaping maw of the instrument. "Our nanites can do anything that this old thing can do. Faster, with less energy, and less fear."

"Garbage, all of it. I keep telling Jessica to tear this thing out, but she wants to keep it. She thinks that it might be useful one day," Jessica's father commented.

"We can help with that you know," Amanda interjected from her comm band. "If you let us come in and help, we can rebuild everything, and make this a place where we can heal the sick and really help your community." She ran her hands over the front of the MRI, sliding the cobwebs off its smooth surface. "Look what the Medmads did for Tony, you didn't mind them saving his life then?"

"His mother—" Gerard started, then looked oved at the youngster who was averting his face from the conversation. "We don't want outsiders… any *more* outsiders," he said as he pulled one of the cots from the side of the machine out into the open.

"Dad…" Jessica caught herself, "I'm sorry, what do you want me to call you?"

He sat down on the cot, groaning as he did and rubbing his knees. "I'm used to Dad, actually, but I don't want to freak you out. You can use my first name, Gerard."

Jessica let the information sink in. Gerard was her father's middle name in her dimension. The differences and similarities tore at her mind, and her soul; she felt guilty for having this connection to so many people that were not her real father, and yet were, as if she were betraying his memory by having this happen.

Tony broke the silence, "Dad, I'm gonna go have the kitchen send up some food for them. I think it's venison for dinner, my favorite."

Jessica jumped in, "Ummm, I'm…"

"Yeah, vegan I know," Tony's voice replied out from the hallway.

Gerard got back up and pulled another cot out from behind the ancient machine. He shook it gently and a dozen spiders fell off and ran for the darkness. "Sorry, we don't get many visitors, and when we do, they usually sleep out in the fields with the kids. They like it."

Amanda sat down on the first cot, took her comm badge off, and swung her legs up. It creaked softly under her weight.

Meera leaned back on her exosuit, pulled her bamboo laptop out of her bag, and started plunking away as soon as the screen lit up.

"How many kids are here?" Jessica asked, as she helped Gerard pull the last two cots out and set them up.

"You know, I really don't know. My Jessica takes care of things like that. Tony and I are the patrol, so we have better things to focus on."

"Did you see the collapse? Did it happen like it does in the movies?"

Gerard pulled the chair from the operator's room out and sat on it, his knees popped as he did. "Nah, that stuff sold books and movies, but it's not how it happened in real life. When I was a kid, storms kept getting stronger and it kept getting hotter. Every year. The last time it snowed I was twelve, so that was... 2026. A lot of people complained that scientists didn't do enough to protect us, or," he used air quotes and rolled his eyes, "*didn't warn* us of the impending doom we all faced.

"Floods happened, grids went offline, the poor neighborhoods swamped and never came back. Then The Metro, the bridges, and then Alexandria flooded for the last time. Gas got too expensive and the roads went to sssh...hell anyway. We were out here in Reston so it wasn't that bad. After the last pandemic the hospital was abandoned, so we moved in. You...*my* Jessica was born a few years after things settled down. When Tony came around, she became the mom to all of us. Kinda weird, but there we are."

Jessica did the math in her head. "Tony isn't really your kid, is he?"

Gerard smiled and shook his head. "Nope, we found him wandering in the fields by himself one night. Little guy. He was attacked by a bear we think. Took his arm, shattered his leg, and tore half his face. The worst part was the infection he got, he needed a pacemaker afterward. It really damaged his heart."

Meera winced and sat upright on the cot, she looked at him imploringly.

"I know, don't worry about it," Gerard said to her. "Medmads fixed him up as best as they could. The artificial arm and leg work great, the pacemaker is solar powered. I tell you that boy can throw a sling and hit a fly."

"That's why we never see him isn't it? He's embarrassed?" Jessica asked.

Gerard leaned forward on the chair looking Jessica in the eyes. "I think he likes it. Calls himself 'Little Bear' and is always stealthy. He wears a bearskin cloak a lot too to drive the point home." Gerard leaned back. "It keeps him outta trouble and he is the sweetest kid I know."

Jessica leaned back on the cot, feeling it creak beneath her as Gerard started telling another story about how he killed another bear with an old loose-leaf notebook. She could have sworn she'd heard that story before, but before she could press him on the veracity of the tale, she slipped slowly into a gentle and blissful sleep.

Chapter 34: Little Bear

Hours later Jessica's eyes opened and she drew a startled breath. The room was dark and cool, and the sounds of her new friends breathing softly filled the room. Standing out the most to her was the sound of Gerard snoring from the floor. She could barely make his form out in green light; he was sprawled on a blanket, lying on his back, exactly like her father back on Earth did.

Jessica looked around for the source of the light, and saw it coming from the opening of the MRI; not very bright, but luminous enough to cast its eerie glow. It emanated from a single LED that moved back and forth softly.

"Good morning," whispered Tony from the bed inside the machine.

Jessica held her breath for a moment, trying to remember everything about the night before and where she actually was. It disoriented her, and she squinted her eyes, trying to focus. "Tony? What time is it?"

The dark form moved in the tube, pulling itself out and sitting upright, he continued to whisper, "A few hours before dawn, so no one is up yet. Jessica wanted me to be here when you woke up because she knows you need coffee."

Instinctively, Jessica sniffed the air looking for her morning beverage but could find none, just the overwhelming scent of chocolate that permeated this dimension, and the smell of unwashed bodies.

"It's not here yet, I didn't think you'd be up. I hope I didn't wake you. Dad was snoring, he woke me up too." Tony got out of the tube and came closer to Jessica. She could see the bearskin cloak that he wore, and the green LED glowing from his right arm, just above the elbow. She hadn't noticed it before, but in the silence, she could hear the servos moving the joints of his prosthetic devices.

"Dad... Gerard told me about your... accident. Do you remember any of it?"

Tony sat next to her on the cot, his weight barely sinking the canvas. "I remember the bear and a lot of pain. Then mom picking me up and running to the Medmad's field hospital, a lot of loud talking, then I woke up like this."

"I have a feeling you want to come with us, don't you?" Jessica asked.

"Yep. Dad and Jessica... they are nice people and all, but this is pretty boring. I mean all we do is stay close to the hospital. We don't go anywhere, or do anything. Every time I see the Wayfarers in the distance, or when the Medmads come around, or when the Caravan shows up to trade, all I want to do is talk to them about the world outside. Jessica won't even talk about the city. I get it, but there has to be more to it than just this."

Tony breathed deeply. Jessica reached her hand out in the darkness and took his, grabbing the synthetic arm. He laughed and took the pair in his left hand, holding them firmly.

"I've almost died once already; I don't want to sit here and wait for the real one to happen. Mom was only forty-seven."

The news hit Jessica like a stomach punch. She did everything she could to not talk about her mother on this world; this wasn't the mother she knew, but the pain of losing a parent was acute for her, and she didn't want to revisit it for any reason. Tony continued.

"I know she wasn't my real mom; I don't know who she is and I don't remember her, but her life was so short obviously. When the caravans arrive, I keep thinking about sneaking into one of the carts and running off with them. Maybe they can take me somewhere exotic on the shore, like Springfield or Annandale. Heck, I'd settle to just get over to the Hazy Center."

Jessica raised her eyebrow. "The Hazy Center?"

"Yeah, it's an old museum filled with airplanes and space stuff. It's all What Came Before but I know there is still stuff there, that's where the caravans meet up to go to Pittsburg or down south."

Jessica pulled her comm band out and strapped it to her wrist, she turned on the screen and looked at Eagle's last known position. "Tony, is the Hazy Center, northwest of here?"

"Yep, it sure is!"

"I'll bet there was a caravan when Eagle showed up, wasn't there?"

"They just left before he arrived, you could still see them."

"I know where he is going!" Jessica stood up in the darkness, her head swam from the sudden rise.

"Who's going where?" Gerard's voice croaked out from the cot.

"Eagle. I'll bet anything he's been following the caravan. He's looking for tech he can hack. Probably to find a way to build his own gate."

"Can he do that? I'd bet that is some pretty high-tech stuff?" Gerard asked. Meera and Amanda stirred from their bunks.

Jessica got up and turned the light on in the room. "Folks, we need to catch ourselves a hacker. We should get back to the others and let them know what to expect," she said, energized and excited.

"Wait, before we all go off halfcocked..." Gerard looked down at Tony, who pulled himself into his bearskin outfit to hide himself from the light. Jessica could barely see the white plastic that covered the side of his face, his eye hidden behind a shaded eyepiece, like a lens removed from a pair of sunglasses. He growled slightly.

"Sorry, Tony," Jessica said.

Gerard finished his thought, "We're going to need to talk to Jessica first. She doesn't want us interacting with him. You know that."

"Da—Gerard," she stammered, "No matter what this guy does, your peaceful village is in danger here. I've seen this guy work before, he's a rogue and now he knows of a whole hospital full of old equipment that he can take advantage of if he can't find what he needs there."

"The vibration patches?" Gerard asked.

"He's figured it out. Somehow, he's…" Jessica spun to Meera then locked her eyes on Tony's synthetic arm. "Didn't Mercedes say something about replacing body parts?"

Amanda shot up from the cot, "He's replacing his molecules using the nanites," she signed quickly.

Meera's face contorted and her nose wrinkled.

"We need to see…me, right now!" Jessica exclaimed, grabbing her pack and heading for the door.

Chapter 35: Twins After All

"Jess, you're kidding me, right?"

Unbound bristled at being called the name only her mother was allowed to use, even if it was coming from her extra-dimensional twin.

"No, I'm not, Jess-ica, this guy is ruthless. He's a threat to us all and I could use the help. Besides, Tony wants to come. Eagle will come back here if he doesn't get what he needs, I know it. Stronger more than likely. Do you want to deal with him then, or now when we still have the advantage?"

"He's one man Jessica, how--?" the Gaian asked.

"One man with self-replicating nanites that are on their way to a building filled with old technology. Shit, the Space Shuttle is there!"

The Gaian's eyes narrowed and she cocked her head.

Another difference.

"I don't want outsiders coming in and disrupting our community like you already have. You have your supplies and you spent the night, but that's all I'm gonna give you. Now I'm not asking you to move on, I'm telling you that I want you to leave." The Gaian scowled as she spoke, her lips drawing white. She leaned over her desk at her twin — pain contorting her face— who immediately stood up to meet her gaze.

"Who the hell…"

"Ladies, this is not productive," Gerard interjected. The two continued to stare at each other, playing a game of chicken, neither wanting to give quarter.

The Gaian leaned in. "You haven't been through what I've been through, you haven't built this community with your bare hands. All you want to do is run, run here, run there, anything you can do to avoid planting your feet in and building something. You're a coward who doesn't want to take responsibility. You haven't watched Mom…"

The Gaian's lips drew pure white and she punched her right hand into her left.

Unbound glanced down only moving her eyes, and then quickly snapped them back at her mirror-image. "Dad died in my universe, spare me the sanctimony and stop talking about things you don't understand." Unbound leaned forward, her lips trembling.

"Jessica…" Gerard said softly.

"You spend your whole life holding back. All you do is worry," Unbound continued. "It doesn't make you a better person it just upsets everyone around you. You're desperate to keep everything under control because you're terrified of losing someone else in the family and you think you can prevent it. But you can't. People still die, and control can get taken away from you in a second. You can't make people do what you want them to, even if it's to protect them!" She railed at her mirror image with naked fury and spat with a quivering voice. Everyone in the room stepped back, looking utterly confused as to whom either of them was really addressing.

"Who THE FU…" The Gaian stood within inches of her face, and Gerard threw his hands between them, forcibly pushing them back.

"Okay, can we stop with the anger and…alternate-self-loathing? Jessica, you're literally fighting with yourself!" he barked.

The two Jessicas stared at each other, nostrils flaring and hands trembling, their faces twisted with rage… and recognition.

"Shut up…you big… idiot." The Gaian cracked first, her smirk tore across her face.

Unbound dropped her head and leaned on her arms, laughs mixing with sobs.

Meera looked back and forth between the pair, scanning both of them with her comm band.

The Gaian and Unbound sat back in their chairs, shoulders relaxed.

"We're running out of time, please Jessica," Unbound said.

"Are you going to hate me the rest of your life if I don't let you do this?" the Gaian asked her brother.

"I'd never hate you, but I'd never let you forget it."

The Gaian smiled in response.

"Dad, are you cool with it?" Unbound asked Gerard, she dropped calling him by his name. He was just like her father, the proof sat across from her, and he deserved the name.

"He's a big boy. He can make his own decisions."

"What do you need me to do first, Jessica?" Asked Tony's voice, already coming from the hallway.

"Please make sure you keep him safe, okay? He's my little bear," the Gaian asked.

Unbound walked around to the back of the desk, embracing her twin. "You, of all people, know I will."

Smiling and looking away from her, the Gaian addressed her father, "Dad, I need you to stay here with me, in case something goes wrong I can't deal with something happening to both of you."

Gerard nodded.

"So, what's the plan?" Amanda signed.

Unbound thought for a moment then spoke, "We need to go back and get the others, Meera can you stay here and help them out until we return? I'm sure they need medical services."

The Gaian's eyes narrowed and then she slowly relented. "I'm sure there is some preventative stuff you can do. No nanites okay?"

Meera put her right hand across her chest and bowed.

"Tony, you ready to go meet an alien?" Unbound asked.

"Yeah, let's go meet... wait, I thought you were the alien?" He asked, from the doorway, his voice piquing.

Unbound turned to the door and looked down at Tony, the white plastic side of his face reflecting the early morning sun, casting pink highlights.

"No sweetie, he's not from this planet, in any dimension. You wanted to see what's out there, and I'm gonna bring you right to it."

Chapter 36: All Together Now

Meera, her head eight feet above the rest of the team, scanned the area around the cornfields, looking for a sign that Eagle might have returned.

"Anything?" Gaian Jessica asked, shielding her eyes from the morning sun.

"Nope. I don't see anything on the scanners, but then he might have found a way to hide himself. I have no idea how much of the technology he understands. Actually..." She looked around again, as if she expected to see something different. She pressed a contact on her band and dropped the exosuit to ground level. "Actually, I don't think it even makes sense for me to keep scanning, if he shows I will be able to detect him without looking. And if he's changed too much about the nanites, I'd never see him coming."

"That doesn't make me feel too good," Amanda said from her band as she pulled her pack onto her back.

"Do you think you will be gone long?" the Gaian asked her twin, who smiled back at her.

"Missing me already?" Unbound asked.

The Gaian smiled and punched her in the arm. "I'll miss my brother. Not you."

Unbound looked back at her, not completely sure if she was kidding or serious.

"I'll have him back sooner, Mui Mui." Unbound smiled.

"Little Sister? I'm older than you!" the Gaian pointed to the wrinkles on her face.

"Oh yeah? When were you born?"

"2050," she replied curtly.

"Okay, try 1996. I'm like fifty-four years older."

Gerard laughed as he pulled the hood over Tony's face then rubbed his head playfully.

Gaian Jessica turned to the pair, "So, she's…"

"Jeh Jeh," Tony shot back excitedly. "Older sister."

"Can we get going?" Amanda spoke from her band, "I appreciate the family dynamics though."

Meera stood back up on the exosuit legs, "You'd better get going, you need to be back by sundown, right? I mean, you don't want to be walking around in the dark."

"Come on!" Tony called from the corn, already ahead of the women.

Within minutes they were in the field, passing under the eight-foot-tall stalks.

"Tony, don't go too far ahead, okay? I still want you to be able to hear me in case I need you," Jessica said.

"Yeah, no problem, Sis," he said, a few feet to her left. Her breath caught at the name; the first time she'd been called anything other than daughter. With no siblings of her own, she was never "auntie", "Jeh Jeh," or "sister." Her heart suddenly ached at the realization. The closest thing she had to a sister was Katelyn, and now, a brother, literally from another mother. She shook off the lump in her throat. Her comm band vibrated, and she held it up.

"Babe, you coming home or what?" Katelyn's voice crackled over the band, finally in range.

"Katelyn, that's not proper communication protocol," Richard's voice said in the background.

"Errr… Wayfarer One to Wayfarer Two, come in…" Katelyn's laughter crackled over the line, "…I can't, it sounds stupid."

They clambered on for an hour, hopping old cars, rubble, and burnt trees, with Tony leading the way. They stopped just after noon and hid in the shadow of a decaying building to cool off and eat. Eventually, their comm bands flashed, picking up the nanite cohorts of the rest of the group who stepped out from behind the rubble;

Richard in front, Jason, Poke, Peek, and Katelyn behind.

"New friend!" Peek trilled from the storage device strapped to Poke's arm, its LED pattern followed.

Tony, who was characteristically hidden in the bushes, spoke quietly to Jessica behind her. "Is that it? Is that the... alien?"

"Hai, Dai Dai, that's them," Jessica said, mixing English and Cantonese, then signed to Amanda pointing out where Tony was hidden and signing "Little Bear."

"There are two of them... one of them lives in the other one's head." She bristled at the inaccuracy of the statement, but felt taking the time to explain how the emulant functioned was more explanation than he needed at the moment. Tony stood in the dappled sunlight behind the bush, his mouth agape.

Poke turned in his direction, and knelt down as low as he could, leaning toward Tony.

"It is... all right little one, we are friends. We..." Poke cast his eyes to the sky looking for the words, and Peek flashed in his temple. "Right, we come in peace."

Tony laughed and stepped out into the sunlight, the bright rays shining through the plastic on his face revealed his tawny cheekbone behind, his shaded eyepiece glinted in the sunlight. Reaching up with his synthetic arm, he touched the LEDs embedded in Poke's temple.

Jessica winced at seeing through Tony's mask to the exposed bone below, and wondered why the Medmads didn't make the prosthetic completely opaque. Maybe they couldn't, or maybe he didn't want to. Regardless she tried not to stare at one of the few moments the teen stepped out of the shadows, literally and figuratively.

"You're aliens? What's it like on your planet? Do you like ours?" Tony stared up at the pair as Poke stood up to his full height.

"Our planet is nice, but yours is so interesting, Friend Little Bear. I have never seen a place so wild before, it must be a lot of fun."

Katelyn stepped up behind the trio, and put her arm around Poke's waist. "Hi. Name's Katelyn." She extended her hand to shake. Tony looked at the open palm and pulled his hood down over his face, recoiling from the exposure.

"It's nice to meet you," he said cautiously but pleasantly. "How did you know my name?" He turned to the Takki, more energetically.

"Friend Jessica signed it to Wayfarer Amanda, Peek told me." Poke pointed to his temple.

Tony stepped forward again to Poke, and a stream of questions issued forth. Katelyn bowed slightly, excusing herself, and spoke to Jessica softly. "What happened to him?"

"Attacked by a bear. Mom..." she caught herself then started again, "My mom in this dimension saved him. He's my... well the other Jessica's Dai Dai."

Katelyn looked back at the chattering teen, and smiled. "Well, then he is mine too," she said, and threw her arm around Jessica's shoulder.

"He's good with kids, who'd a thunk it, eh?" Jessica pointed to the Poke, emphasizing her Jersey City accent.

Katelyn smiled and nodded emphatically.

"I guess you guys remember everything now?" Jessica asked.

"Yep, Peek uploaded into that computer Richard made and decompressed itself."

Jessica interrupted. "What happened to our wings? The invisibility? Our memories?"

"Their gate wasn't tested that well, so it didn't know how to handle, well anything really. It couldn't compensate and ripped the wings out and dropped them. Bad code. We're lucky we came through at all, and didn't end up like some lump of flesh before we died in agony. At least, that's what Peek thinks.

Jessica scrunched her eyes and turned her head, she wretched but quickly regained her composure. Katelyn continued, "When Peek came back online it told us everything that happened, including the fact that it knew everything about Eagle and his buddies." She explained with a singsong voice and rolled her eyes, "But it slipped its mind to tell us that they were some multinational crime syndicate with delusions of grandeur."

Jessica chortled.

Katelyn pointed to Jason, who quickly cast his eyes to the ground, "Eagle is bad news. He tried to kill both of us, and this dude was on his side and knew who we were the whole time, he was in the van on Halloween too when that truck hit that kid and Dee saved him. He wasn't just the homeless guy in the park we gave food to, he was a spy. He's one of them."

Jason sighed and kicked at the ground. Katelyn pointed her fingers to her eyes, and then at Jason, she mouthed, "I'm watching you."

"I think we can trust him," Jessica said, loudly enough for him to hear; she meant it.

She motioned to Richard, "What do you know about the Hazy Center?"

"That place is bad juju."

Jessica raised an eyebrow.

"That was one of the first places we went to outquisition when Tysons Division was founded. We know there is a ton of tech there, and we wanted to make sure that it wasn't, you know, abused or anything. It's literally a storehouse of What Came Before. When we got out there, there was a survivalist group... what where they, Mandy?"

Richard turned to Amanda who signed with him for a few moments.

"Yeah right, The Chargers. The high school mascot. Weird, right? But those weren't kids, we got our asses...Well, they didn't want us there, lots of weapons and all, and we couldn't just send the nanites in, if they want to be left alone it's their right. Eventually they will run out of bullets, and maybe they will be more agreeable." Richard stopped speaking and his hand slowly covered his mouth. Entiendo! He's going there with my nanites. Isn't he?"

Jessica nodded. "How far away is it?" she asked, scanning the western horizon.

"About ten clicks, give or take," Richard answered, and looked southwest.

Jessica turned back to the team behind her as they hushed, waiting for her to lead. It scared her again, knowing that she could be putting them in real danger. She didn't have the luxury of Professor Sterling to guide her, for Orvalus to walk up and fearlessly take control, or even her father to offer some sage advice; the universe put her in charge here, and this was her call. She took a deep breath and steadied herself, feeling the tightness in her chest, and her hands grew cold. Tony disappeared into the undergrowth - getting ready to move - and it snapped her into action.

"Okay folks, we know that every moment he gets stronger, and we need to see just how strong he is before we engage him. I want us to get close enough to observe him - or them if the Chargers are still there - by nightfall. So, let's get a quick meal in here and then get moving." She looked up at the sun and held her hand below it counting her fingers between it and the horizon, a trick her father taught her for telling the time without a watch. "We've got about four hours of daylight left, so we should get close enough. The day is still twenty-four hours here, right?"

Richard nodded, then checked his comm band, verifying the time. His eyebrows raised at Jessica's accurate assessment.

"Great, let's eat!" she said, slapping her hands together.

Chapter 37: The Hazy Center

"Oh man, I was not expecting this," Jessica whispered to herself as she looked through her binoculars. Meera who had run over from the hospital as soon as Jessica and the others came in range, crouched down in her exosuit next to her. Richard was on the opposite side of Jessica, also looking through binoculars. Jason, a few feet down, squinted at the center and twisted his beard. They were in a drainage ditch that ran alongside a broken road, and leaned against the road side where three rotten school buses provided further cover. The road stretched down "Air and Space Museum Parkway" culminating in a guarded gate which once took admission tickets from school children on field trips; it was now covered in barbed wire and anything but welcoming. The gate kiosk was manned by a person covered head-to-toe in body armor, who scanned the surroundings with their own binoculars.

"Told you, bad juju." Richard nodded his head, trying to take in the sight in front of him.

"Why is he wearing body armor? What are they expecting?" Jessica asked, as she slid back down the side of the ditch to the grassy bottom.

"No sé," Richard responded, likewise sliding himself down and pulling Meera behind the cover.

"Maybe they want to seem tougher than they are? Paramilitary wannabes?" Jessica said as she looked back over the road to the others gathered on the other side, hidden under the trees. "It's probably just a show of force. If they're so tough, why haven't they spilled out and tried to take over the rest of the area?" Jessica asked, trying to make sense of what she was seeing.

Across the massive parking lot - which had been curiously kept free of debris and plant life - stood the remains of the Steven F. Udvar-Hazy Center. Its aluminum and steel structure perched atop a hill, with a singular, raised main entrance. Behind the building, and tangential to the nearby Dulles Airport, lay an enormous field full of corn, soybeans, bush beans, and other plants that Jessica could not recognize. Farther back, a fenced-off pasture held two dozen chickens, and farther behind that, another with several cows. No one was outside tending the crops or animals. The top of the building had mounted two .50 caliber Brownings that swiveled back and forth, scanning the area. All the windows were covered in steel plates. The sun hung low in the afternoon April sky and glinted off the solar panels covering the top of the building. A hot breeze blew off the blacktop.

"They have to have a lot of people, right? I mean, that is a lot of work to do. I don't see robots or anyone in an exosuit. Where is everyone?" Meera asked, as she held her comm band over the berm above her. She read the scene on her laptop that at her feet.

"Amanda, are you picking up a network, or any external communication?" Richard asked into his comm band.

Across the road he could see the antenna from Amanda's comm tower, it snaked along the side of a broken light pole. Deploying it was a risk, but they had to take it to get information.

"No," her synthetic voice responded. "I'm not picking up anything being broadcast, but there is a lot of EM coming out of that place, it's practically glowing."

"Uh, is that the caravan?" Katelyn's panicked voice broke over the transmission, prompting her group to slide back farther under the cover of the trees. On the other side, Jessica and her group climbed into one of the buses, being careful not to rock the vehicle on its decayed shocks.

From the east, a group of people on horseback approached. Three in the front carried shotguns held at the ready, while another three behind them held bows at their sides. Behind them, a converted school bus pulled by a team of four horses rolling at walking speed, still another pair on horseback, also armed with bows, walked behind the bus, the pair had scabbarded swords strapped to their backs.

Hiding behind a decayed seat, Jessica asked, "Why are they out in the open like that? Aren't they worried they will get attacked?"

"You do see the weapons, right?" Richard asked.

"Yeah but…"

"No one attacks the caravan; it would end trade for all the communities. The weapons are to remind you that they aren't worth breaking that rule," Richard explained.

"The Wayfarers let them keep their guns too… it's an unwritten rule…" Meera added to the conversation, then her voice trailed off.

"Exactly, you know that, but…" Jessica held her head up over the seat and looked around, "but if I don't know that, he doesn't either."

Katelyn's voice crackled over their bands, "Do we let them walk in, or do we tell them something's up? We can't just let them fall into a trap."

"Kate, if we stop them right here, we blow our cover, and then they will definitely know something is up. Even if Eagle isn't there yet the Chargers will get nervous." Jessica looked over the seat again as the caravan passed their location. The guard in the kiosk stood up, opened the door, and held out his hand bidding them to stop. The Brownings trained on them. "I don't want to make them any more nervous than they already are," Jessica added.

"Do you guys see them? The caravan just showed up," Tony said over the comm band.

Quickly Jessica's glance darted around the area.

"Tony? Where are you?" She asked, anxiety rising in her voice.

"I'm in front of the building, there is a fountain here. I'm behind it."

Jessica scanned the front of the Hazy Center with her binoculars, she traced parking lot to a silver arch of metal sticking up from a flat, black depression. With the barest hint of brown from his cloak visible, Tony was perfectly positioned to look directly into the front of the building.

"Little Bear, you have to tell me you are doing these things. I promised your sister."

"You *are* my sister," Tony responded, then laughed.

Jessica rolled her eyes and shook her head. Richard snorted.

"Okay, just…" Jessica was about to tell Tony to stay out of sight, but then she realized it was the equivalent of reminding a bird to use its wings when it flew. "Just be careful and let me know if you see anything change, yeah?"

"Hai, dai jie."

And I'm the 'big sister' too, now.

The guard at the kiosk let the caravan pass, and they rolled slowly down the shattered blacktop toward the building; the turrets tracked them as they moved. Jessica couldn't tell if anything was different about this interchange, but decided to trust her gut.

"How long does the caravan hang out someplace? Like, do they stay the night or move on?" Jessica glanced at the sun as it sank lower in the sky; maybe an hour left before it hit the horizon.

Richard explained, "They are self-contained, so they can do whatever they want. But we are pretty far from the next inhabited settlement in that direction, I can't see them traveling far at night. We outquisitioned the airport when we couldn't get The Chargers to communicate, there's… really nothing out here."

"So, the caravan is an indie?" Katelyn asked over the comm band.

"Sí, they didn't want to group with anyone so they could stay neutral. They don't refuse our help though, or anyone else's. It works for them."

"Another unwritten rule, eh?" Jessica commented.

Richard nodded.

"I see the caravan coming," Tony said over the band.

"Can you point your comm band at them so we can get a visual?" Amanda's synthetic voice asked.

"Sure, hang on."

Their bands displayed Tony's feed of the building. He zoomed in, showing the caravan arrive at the front gates of the Hazy Center. The leaders got off of their horses, their white clothing rippled in the hot breeze. The main doors opened and a figure stepped out, dressed completely in fatigues and body armor, with no skin or eyes visible behind all the protection.

"Lincoln," Richard said, recognizing the figure. Amanda sighed over the line.

"Why does that not sound good?" Katelyn asked quickly.

"He's a tough hombre," Richard explained, "killed the last Wayfarer before we could get away. But he was also the one that negotiated the peace which let us get our dead people and the wounded out."

"Lemme guess, Washington is the one we need to worry about?" Jessica asked.

"No, he's dead. At least that's what we heard from the caravan. The new jefe is some vato named Roosevelt."

Okay now this is a movie.

"Hey guys, can you see this?" Tony zoomed in closer to Lincoln, focusing on the space between his helmet and neck. A part of his skin was showing; and in the shadow of the building a faint green glow filled the space.

"Dammit," Jessica hissed.

Chapter 38: No One is An Island

"Well, there goes our plan of getting here before Eagle did," Jessica said with a sigh.

Meera looked at the feed on her laptop. "I don't get it, that's not how the nanites work. Those ones are for industrial use only, they aren't programmed for biology. I mean, when they encounter biology, they shut down as part of The Three Laws. You know; they can't harm anyone, they have to do what you tell them, and they have to protect themselves. In that exact order, one law building on the other. You can't 'infect' someone with them. It doesn't work that way."

"I'm gonna argue that everything is on the table now." Jessica reached out and grabbed Richard's arm. "I'm sorry. Has no one ever tried to hack them before?"

Richard took a breath then answered, "I told you, no one has the tech to do that other than us."

"Well, now they do." Jessica said with an air of acceptance. "What can they have a person do? I mean what's their full potential?"

Meera jumped in, "For one thing, they can keep you alive, any damage can be repaired fairly quickly." Meera pointed to Jessica's ribs. "They can provide energy from the stored fat in your body, pull the cholesterol out of your blood, give you more oxygen when you need it, fix your DNA, deaden nerve impulses, increase ATP cycling, augment glucose intake, switch you into ketosis...."

Jessica rolled her eyes at the litany of enhancements that Meera continued to rattle off. *Super soldiers. They can make you invincible.* After a moment Meera finally stopped and then blinked at Jessica.

"Is there any way to slow them down? Make it so the nanites can't work as fast?" Jessica asked.

"Physics is physics, not magic. They can overheat, push too many byproducts, run out of fuel, break under the strain, kill you… get hacked *obviously*," Meera explained.

"They are still machines. Unshielded machines," Richard pushed the black bag at his feet. Jessica stared at it.

"It's okay, they're not my kids or anything," Richard responded to her unvocalized question. "I hate the fact that they are being used this way, and I'd rather see them shut down than… perverted like this."

"Does that work?" Jessica pointed to the EMP.

"Si, it's in good shape considering it came through a portal. I charged it up while you were at the hospital. I don't know the yield, I think it's a few dozen meters, I'm not sure. We'd probably have to get really close to use it, like uncomfortably close."

Jessica looked across the road at the group still huddled under the trees, and then over to the Hazy Center to see Tony sitting under the dry water fountain. "We have to keep him away from the blast."

"It's more than that, all of our nanites will be destroyed, which will kick your patches off-line. If it doesn't wipe them out too," Richard explained.

"Not shielded." Peek spoke over the band.

"Why not?" Katelyn asked.

"No need. Hegemony safe."

"Must be nice to live in a utopia," Katelyn spat.

"Babe, that's not helping," Jessica admonished, using her bestie's preferred form of address.

The comm band fell silent as Jessica sat against the decayed chair. She looked out over the Center and the fields beyond. The sky was slowly darkening, filling with orange and purple hues to the east. In the west, the sun hung low, barely above the mountains on the horizon. Its red sphere hovered like a demon about to devour the world.

We're here because of me. This is all my responsibility.

She took a deep breath and cleared her throat. "Okay, I'll take the bomb in."

"What? You're crazy. We can't even get in there. How are you going to do it?" Katelyn snapped.

"This is my responsibility. I grabbed the EMP on Terra to blow up the gate so the Syndicate couldn't use it. That hasn't changed, I still have to fix the problem I caused. Alone."

"And you see how well *that* worked," Katelyn said.

Jessica recoiled at the retort and stared across the road imagining Katelyn's blue eyes piercing across the space, even in the rapidly darkening early-evening light.

"Goddamn it, Kate, I'm tired of dragging everyone I love into danger. You didn't ask for this," Jessica barked.

"I didn't ask for my best friend to die of COVID, but she did. I didn't make you go through the portal the first time, but I gave them the clothes to find your dimension. I was the one who came to get you. I wanted you back, and I accepted the consequences of that decision. I did ask for that. Now stop being so goddamned selfish. I'm not letting you die..." Katelyn's voice caught, and she stammered for a moment, interspersed with static over the comm band. "I'm not letting you die... alone...*again* you idiot."

Jessica sat for a moment, looking across the road at her friend, now completely hidden in the gathering dark. "Bitch," she said, then wiped the tears from her eyes.

"Oooh baby, I love when you talk dirty to me."

"Sooo... what's the plan?" Tony's voice piped in over the comm band.

Jessica scanned the area. Lincoln waved the caravan off, and without hiding their affront, they moved along the road in front of the building toward a ruin that lay beyond the center.

"Okay we do this as a team. Tony, can you catch up with them after they get a bit farther away? We're gonna need to talk to them."

"Already ahead of them."

"Kate, bring your team over here, and stay low. We need to figure this out."

Chapter 39: The Deal

"Eagle got to the Chargers before we did. He must have been moving overland faster than us. Jason, what else do you know about this guy? Don't hold anything back, anything you can tell us could help us get an advantage," Jessica spoke into the darkness.

"Yeah, not much. He's a jerk," Jason said. "Kept going on about how people are hiding things from him. Like, he thinks everything is a conspiracy, man. Like everything. Everyone is lying to him and shit. It's annoying. He didn't even trust the other Syndicate people. He had recordings of everything that went on. He even has film of you guys with the wings in the office."

Jessica thought back to when she, Poke, and Peek broke Dee out of its confinement, storming their warehouse with the aid of Ellwood.

"Wait... film? Peek didn't you erase everything before we left?"

"All gone," the emulant chimed from his storage device on Poke's arm. "Everything digital erased."

Digital.

"Yeah man, he had film, like you know old people have? Had his own room with the red light and all. I saw the movie, the three of you popping your wings open and floating out of the building. It was pretty cool."

"Let me guess, he told everyone about us," Katelyn interjected, her face illuminated from the soft glow of Peek's amber LEDs in Poke's skull.

"Yeah, they thought he made it up to convince everyone to give him more money for whatever. Which I didn't understand. That dude has less than I do, except for his films and his laptop."

"So how did you guys get to the gate then? If they thought he was weird?" Jessica asked.

"They think all of us are weird." Jason laughed, revealing his missing teeth. "We are. But I don't give a shit, they gave me food and I just hung out a lot. Sometimes there were girls…" Jason's voice trailed off.

Jessica sighed, then continued questioning. "I need you to focus Jason. How did you get in the gate room? How were you working on the portal?"

"He's good. I'll give him that. Doesn't eat or sleep much. Always plugging away on his laptop. Trying to figure out 'the pattern.' He wrote a lot of the software to build the gate and all. I just hung around cuz he didn't seem to mind. He knows you're working with the government; knows you're aliens. Wants your technology."

"We aren't with the government," Jessica explained.

Jason shrugged his shoulders. "Whatever, I don't care. He's right though, you're aliens."

Jessica swallowed hard and cleared her throat.

"Tony? You there?" she asked into her comm band.

"Yep, I'm talking to Razlo, he's the head of the caravan."

"What can he tell us?" she asked.

"Lincoln didn't want them to come trade even though they were the next on the schedule. This was their monthly meeting. Razlo has no idea what is going on there, except that Lincoln was acting really weird and didn't sound normal. Like he was sick or drunk or something. They were counting on that trade, they wanted to get some tech for that new settlement out in Chantilly. He thinks something is going on in the Center and wanted to get them away from the place as fast as they could. Sally was in the schoolbus but didn't feel comfortable coming out. She says 'hi' by the way."

At the mention of her name, Richard sat up straight and looked out of the glassless window, but the caravan was behind the Center now, far out of sight.

Jessica scanned around on the ground, thinking quickly. "Can they help out if we asked? He's a threat to all of us."

Tony hesitated before responding, "They aren't mercenaries, Sis. I don't think they would do that. They stay neutral on purpose."

"Is there anything they would trade for to help us out?"

"Hang on."

For a few minutes the team heard Tony conversing with the caravan's leader. Razlo's sing-song voice interplaying with Tony's light patterns.

"Hey, so he said they can give us four bows and two dozen arrows, but not the shotguns. He wants a comm band for it."

"Why does he need a band? We've already offered one." Amanda's synthetic voice spoke over her band.

"Says he wants to be the first to present it to Chantilly."

"What? We already have a team going there! No!" Meera retorted, practically yelling into her band. Richard reached out and held her shoulder.

"Dunno, it's what he wants. I can give him mine, and bring the bows back to you," Tony said.

"Little Bear, I don't think that is a good idea—" Jessica said.

"That's fine," Richard interrupted. "Give him yours but lock the channel on this one, so they can only talk to us."

"Sure… how do I do that?" Tony asked.

"You just…" Richard stood still for a moment, then moved. "I'll do it. Wait a minute." Richard popped open Meera's laptop and started pounding keys. "There, you can take it off and give it to him, but they won't be able to charge it or assign it to anyone else without having a Wayfarer present."

"Great!" Tony responded. The channel flooded with the sound of fabric rustling and clamps clicking. Tony's voice sounded distant as he spoke to Razlo, explaining how the device worked and its limitations, "The band stays on and broadcasts to everyone close by, right, until you press—" His band went silent.

"Shit, Tony!" Jessica yelled into the band, "Tony!"

"He'll be ok," Richard reassured.

"Babe, easy," Katelyn soothed.

Jessica yelled then dropped her voice at the end of the sentence, "He's our forward position. He has weapons. How do we coordinate with him?"

So says General Chao, huh? The absurdity of Jessica giving military-style orders flooded her head. She tried not to give into her self-doubt.

"Surprise!" said Tony from just beyond the drainage ditch. Jessica looked over the top to see Tony's green arm LED pulsing slowly.

"How? That's a *quarter mile...?*" Jessica asked, her mouth gaping.

"Your buddy is fast, I didn't think he'd get back to you that quick," a female voice crackled over the band, the same channel Tony left it on. Her southern drawl was smooth and unhurried. "Hey Rich, how you doin' darlin'? It's been a long time."

Richard cleared his throat. "I'm fine. It has been a long time. I—I missed you."

Amanda rolled her eyes.

"You say the cutest thangs. Meet me at the maintenance shed at the end of the road, I can get us in."

Chapter 40: Through the Tunnel

Meera turned to Richard and held up her comm band to illuminate his face. She raised an eyebrow.

"We met when she was coming through town. When I was stationed in Annandale, a long time ago," he spoke quickly and quietly.

"That's right darlin' and you never forgot me," Sally laughed over the band. "Now get goin'. I'll be there in a sec."

Richard looked at Jessica, who shrugged her shoulders and smiled. "Let's get," she said, twirling her index finger in the air, signaling everyone to pack up their stuff. "But be quiet, and stay low."

The team spilled out of the bus and ran down the cross street meeting the others   at the beginning of Localizer Road. Or what was left of the road. Unlike the main road leading to the Hazy Center, this one was not kept up; buckled asphalt and plants slowed their progress in the darkness. Poke and Peek led the way.

"Since when can you see in the dark?" Jessica asked.

"I can't, Friend Jessica," Poke tapped on the amber LEDs rhythmically pulsing on his temple. "Peek's interface can see in starlight and the nano-wires run into my eyeballs. That gives it the data it needs."

"I'm there, Sally's inside the shed waiting for us," Tony said, after moving back across the field with startling speed.

"How does he do that?" Katelyn asked.

"I dunno, I think the artificial limbs do something more than keep him from falling over," Jessica said as they darted across the bottom of the parkway and into the woods to the east of the shed.

"If you didn't get tired, you'd move faster," Meera said.

"We're almost there. How do we get in, Sally?" Jessica asked into her band.

"There's a passageway they use to move things in and out. I know it's there, we had to use it to trade for some motors in the basement back a spell."

"And they aren't guarding it?"

"They weren't before," Sally laughed.

"That isn't very reassuring."

"Don't worry, it will be fine."

As Jessica and the team made it to the ruined fence surrounding the shed she could see Sally waving from the door of the ruined building, her short, brown hair held back with a beret. "C'mon, hurry," she whispered.

What choice do I have?

When they were close enough to meet, Sally looked at Jessica and nodded, her sparkling brown eyes reflecting the lights from Peek's LEDs. "Howjadoo?" She asked, then pointed to a large set of steel doors, behind which was a staircase leading down.

"Quiet," Peek said from the storage device.

Sally pointed next to the stairs, the four bows sat, each with a quiver of arrows.

"Ya'll do know how to use them, right?" Sally said with a raised eyebrow.

"Well, one year in gym class…" Jessica replied.

"Seventy-pound recurve bows. Yeah, no problem," Katelyn said as she picked up a bow and pulled back on the string. "You'll be fine babe; we did this before."

Jessica took the bow Katelyn held out to her. She swallowed hard as she scanned the weapon. Made of carbon fiber, the black string, sights and attached quiver confused and intimidated her.

"Yeah, this oughta do." Katelyn held her bow and looked through the sight, drawing the string back against her cheek and holding it for a moment. "Yeah." She said again slowly relaxing the string.

Amanda signed to Richard, Jessica responded to her, "Exactly! They are wearing body armor, what are arrows going to do against them? It would be like throwing pins against a steel plate." Jessica picked up "her" bow and looked at the steel-tipped arrows in the quiver. The head had metal wings and screws along the sides, like retractable claws.

"These are Expandable Blade Broadhead tips and we use them to hunt deer and bear for trade, also to keep their numbers down; they can do the job sweetie," Sally explained.

Jessica looked at the razor-sharp tip and studied the mechanism. Once the arrow hit someone, the blades popped open to slice flesh as it moved with the force from the bow. She imagined it sailing through the air and hitting a deer in the chest, ripping through its flesh and dropping to the ground in a cacophony of agonized screams as the animal drew its last breaths. She shook and put the bow back on the ground, stepping away from it.

"No, I won't use it," she said, shaking her head.

"What?" Sally asked, pulling her chin in and knotting her eyebrows.

"That, I'm not using that. Not gonna happen."

Meera stood behind her, with Katelyn standing on the other side, still holding her bow.

"How do you expect to stop them, sugah? Harsh language?" Sally mocked.

Richard stood next to Sally, slinging his bow over his shoulder.

"Friend Jessica does not eat meat, nor does she kill," Poke explained, as he stepped up between both groups, the "crossed arms" emoji showed on Peek's display.

"The Chargers aren't our enemy, only Eagle is. I'm not going to go killing them just to stop him. They had no option in this situation," Jessica said.

"You don't know that darlin', they could have joined him," Sally implored.

"Wait," Jessica's face flashed red. "Aren't you supposed to be impartial here? The caravan is neutral, isn't it?" She was embarrassed at her shaking hands and hid them behind her back.

"We are, but the caravan doesn't stand for people who break the rules either. They refused us, they insisted we move along, and they didn't offer us refuge for the evening. They broke all the rules of hospitality," Sally explained.

"So, we kill them for it?"

"The Greeks and Romans used to," Poke said.

"That doesn't help," Katelyn said, her eyes narrowing.

Jessica kicked the bow away, "These arrows are meant for one thing: killing. I'm not killing them. I don't care what you think or give a shit about the rules of hospitality."

Sally stood there for a moment, with Richard looking at her.

Sally relented, "Fine. We do it your way. I'll *try* not to kill them, but if they are coming on too strong or if there is nothing I can do, they get an arrow in the head. You got that?"

Jessica nodded solemnly, and then turned to Katelyn silently asking for support. "Only to defend myself, babe, I promise," she answered.

"Well, I'm not gonna kill them with this, at least not that quickly." Amanda signed then held up her electrified baton. "Now I wish we brought more."

"What do we do with the last bow?" Meera asked.

"Leave it here. I'll bring it back to the caravan when we are done," Sally said as she divvied the arrows among the three.

"You're sure about that?" Katelyn asked, her tone acerbic.

"Oh, we will, I have a good feelin'. Let's stop jawing and get in there."

Jessica stepped back and bowed, eyebrow arched, allowing Sally to move to the stairs.

"About time," Tony whispered, already deep into the dark passageway beyond.

Chapter 41: IMAX

Why do I keep ending up with my clones around? Jessica thought to herself. *Mom, Dad. A brother I never had in the other dimensions, but no copy of Katelyn here. Why? How is this possible? In all of infinity, I keep ending up where I already exist. Or existed. Except Bellerophon.*

As they got closer to the end of the tunnel, Jessica could hear talking.

"They are here, upstairs from the door, they don't know," Tony said over his comm band as quietly as he could.

Jessica looked up ahead to see Tony just inside the doorway, crouched and looking around the corner. He waved then ran for a set of double doors recessed in a wall. Jessica could barely follow him as he darted across the open space. She breathed a sigh of relief when he got to the other side and hid behind a fallen ceiling panel.

"When we come out, we're gonna be in the basement by the old IMAX theater," Sally explained. "That was where we were takin' the motors out before. Their air shafts are huge. Some parts you can stand up in. We can get around the whole dang place up there."

"Or be sitting ducks," Katelyn interjected.

"Is everybody where you come from so positive, sugah?" Sally asked.

"Keeps me alive. *Sugar*," Katelyn answered.

"Hey, stay focused," Jessica scolded. She couldn't control Katelyn any more than Katelyn could control Jessica; but she also knew if she didn't say something, her bestie could spiral into an uncontrollable fit. She looked back at Amanda who stared at Sally. Jessica presumed she didn't like the newcomer either. Or was it jealousy? Since Sally showed up, Richard had grown quiet and more reserved.

One by one they ran out of the tunnel and into the old theater. The rotten seats reeked of mold, and the walls were covered in moss and bromeliads. It was hot, almost like a sauna. Jessica looked down the length of the seats to the bottom of the theater; the pit in front of the former screen was filled hip deep in murky water reflecting the moonlight that drifted in from the ruined ceiling. She sneezed from the air.

Sally whipped her head around and glared, putting her finger to her nose. Jessica shrugged her shoulders and pointed at her nose. She was terribly allergic to mold. Even after years of allergy shots she had seen no improvement at all and in fact it may have gotten worse the older she got.

Are the gates making all of this worse? I've been feeling like crap since that first time, what did it do to me? Will the nanites make it better?

"Stop," Peek said from the speaker on its storage device.

"I can't help it, I'm allergic," she said, in barely a whisper.

"No, Friend Jessica. There is something in the water," Poke explained.

Fear tore up Jessica's spine, and her arms reflexively tensed.

"Gators. They snuck in a few years ago, and the Chargers keep them here," Sally explained nonchalantly.

"Alligators?" Jessica said, full-voiced.

"Shh! Yes, gators. Be quiet." Sally pointed to an open intake vent along the far wall, just above the pit.

"We're in Virginia! There aren't gators here!" Jessica said again aloud, as if she hadn't registered Sally's reprimand.

"Cállate!" Richard whispered behind her.

Sally slung her bow across her back and stepped onto an exposed board on the rotten wall, just below the intake, then waved for the others to follow. Tony extended a hand down, to help her up.

When Jessica's turn came, she lifted one quivering leg up onto the board, and held it for a moment, unable to control the shaking enough to move.

"Babe, you okay?" Katelyn asked behind her, taking her elbow into her hand.

"I—I can't…" Jessica's glance darted over to the pit as an alligator splashed and slunk into the water. "I—I…" Jessica stammered.

"You will be fine," Poke said from his position at the back of the line. "It doesn't want to hurt you. It's not coming this way."

Jessica fixed on the alien's face. His full-green eyes stared at her and his grey skin reflected the pale moonlight. He looked no less threatening to her than the reptiles in the water. Jessica's mind screamed in a primal rage, devoid of language. She could only vocalize a grunt. Her hands pulled back as she pressed her body against the mold-covered wall.

"What's happening?" Tony asked, as he reached forward to help his sister into the vent.

"She's having a panic attack," Katelyn explained quickly as she turned Jessica around to face her. "Babe, look at me. Breathe sweetie. Breathe. Stop fighting."

Jessica's breaths came shallow and quick, and her peripheral vision began to fog, her mind envisioned the alligators leaping out of the water and pulling her down into a death spiral. Her nerves went dead in her face and her skin felt like fire.

"Jessica, listen to me. Jess!" Katelyn pleaded.

"Can't— can't…" Jessica repeated.

Poke stepped up and lifted Jessica off the board, attempting to put her into a fireman's carry. She looked into his eyes; cold, lifeless, and without sclera. She started to scream.

"Jessica!" Katelyn yelled, as she tried helping Poke lift her into the vent.

"Go!" Richard yelled to the team in-front of him. Sally, Meera, Jason, and Amanda scrambled into the vent system.

"Jessica, please!" Katelyn spat.

Jessica could hear everyone and see clearly what was going on. It was as if she were watching a movie of it all rather then living the event.

Hey, calm down. Everything is okay. You're going to get us caught. You're overacting. Stop!

Jessica focused into herself as deeply as she could, and willed her lungs to slow down their panicked breathing. She looked at the dark pit and could see the alligators listlessly floating in the water. Poke's skin, now a deep grey, reflected the dappled moonlight at her, and Peek's amber LEDs flowed their content pattern. The feeling of crawling ants played all along her face, and as uncomfortable as it was, she knew the attack was over. She took another breath; still shaky but focusing.

"I'm okay. I'm sorry, they freaked me out. I've never seen them in the wild. I couldn't stop thinking they were going to eat me."

"Lucky for them," the voice of Lincoln boomed through the theater, "they might still get that chance."

Chapter 42: Trapped!

"I'm sorry, guys, I really didn't think I'd freak out on you like that." Jessica fumed as she apologized to the team. Yet again. Her anger at herself was visible, her hands shook despite being bound together with zip ties and held behind her back.

The four sat in the fuselage of the famed Enola Gay, the very plane that dropped the atomic bomb "Little Boy" on the Japanese city of Hiroshima on August 6th, 1945. She stared at the hatch in front of her and imagined the nuclear weapon sitting there, armed and ready to go, about to vaporize three-quarters of the city, and kill ninety to one hundred forty thousand people. Her stomach churned.

I don't want to be here. This is all my fault.

"You know, when they say there is nothing like getting up close and touching history, this is not what I envisioned," Katelyn said, looking around the inside of the plane. She tugged at her arms, similarly tied.

Jessica took a deep breath and tried to assess her situation. The three of them were prisoners, bound up, and sitting on the hull of the plane. Poke was chained instead of tied. None of them were gagged, and Peek was left on Poke's arm in the storage device. Their comm bands had been taken. The other half of the team managed to sneak into the vents and avoid being captured like they did.

I wish we had the wings; we could have come in from the top and I never would have freaked out.

"What's the plan?" Katelyn asked.

"I don't know, the others weren't caught. Maybe they can break us out," Jessica said.

"Do you think they are going to come up with a plan?" Katelyn asked, and Jessica immediately hesitated as she thought of Sally taking control of their group and getting them caught, or worse, killed.

There was a thump on the fuselage, and the voice of Lincoln yelled through the aluminum, "SHUT THE HELL UP!"

Katelyn rolled her eyes then yelled to her antagonizer. "We're talking about you, babe. She thinks you're hot!"

"Yeah whatever, I know her, she's a pain in the ass. Miss goody-good and her weakling farmers."

Katelyn looked at Jessica and raised her eyebrow. Jessica did the same. *He thinks I'm the other Jessica. Why didn't Eagle tell them the truth?*

"You gonna feed us or what? Why are we waiting in here? Doesn't your president or whoever want to interrogate us? What are you afraid of?" Katelyn returned the antagonization, not letting up on Lincoln.

"I *said*, SHUT UP!" he roared. Katelyn winked at Jessica.

"Sounds like you guys are all hat and no cattle. I'll bet Nixon doesn't even know who we are."

"Roosevelt, get it right."

"Come on, we need some food. Get Agnew or whoever to give us something to eat."

Jessica shook her head out of frustration, and yet couldn't help laughing at her friend's irrepressible irreverence, even in the face of death. She loved her for all the things that she was, all the things that Jessica wasn't.

"Fine. Jesus, you're annoying." The trio heard the sound of Lincoln walking away from the plane.

"What does that get us, my love?" Poke asked. Katelyn smiled broadly and kissed him. Peek's LEDs glowed a solid, bright, amber.

"It gets him away from us so we can plan. It also lets him talk to us." Katelyn pointed to the front of the plane, where Tony sat at the opening to the crew tunnel.

"Those guys are such dummies. They have no idea I'm in here," Tony beamed, and pulled his hood down tight over his head, hiding his prosthetic in the shadow.

Jessica was impressed. Regardless of whether she really knew him or not, his tenacity and joie de vivre were something to behold. She trusted him like she'd known him his whole life.

"Do they know we are in here? Did they get caught?" She asked, referring to the other group.

"Nope, they are hiding in a vent. No one is really looking for them though, I don't get it."

"Does Richard, you know, still have it?" Jessica asked, referring to the EMP.

Tony gazed around the inside of the plane, aware of its significance. "Yep. It's still charged."

"Can you get it to me so I can use it?" She asked, prompting Poke to glare at her.

"I dunno, Sis. It's kinda heavy for me to carry, I can't be stealthy. I mean, I can carry it and all, but, I'd get caught bringing it to you," Tony said, hanging his head down.

"It's okay, we still have it. We can get—" Jessica was cut off by a bang at the bomb bay. The doors opened slowly, and Lincoln's head cleared the opening. "Okay, Eagle wants to talk to you. You can get something to eat afterward."

Jessica looked toward the Charger; his helmet was off. He had boyish good looks, with flopping blonde hair and piercing eyes that glowed bright green.

"What if I don't want to go, big boy?" Katelyn jumped in.

"Not you sweetheart, he wants her." Lincoln pointed to Jessica.

"Her? The farm-girl? Why? She isn't dangerous, you know that. You don't know who I am at all. I'm the dangerous one. I dragged her into this. Take me," Katelyn badgered.

"Can't you stop talking?! I don't know why he wants her. Let's go!" He commanded, then grabbed Jessica by the ankle, jerking her across

the smooth doors in one swift motion. She gasped at the   strength
of the man obviously augmented by the hacked nanites in his body.
She looked back at the crew tunnel for Tony, but he was nowhere to
be seen.

"You don't need to be so rough. I'll go," she said, stabilizing
herself on the smooth aluminum. She jumped out of the plane and
tumbled down on the concrete floor. Lincoln offered no help in
getting her up.

"Thanks," she said, dripping with sarcasm. Lincoln shoved her,
"Get going."

Jessica walked in the direction she was pushed, toward the back of
the hangar heading for the wall. She gazed around the building taking
in as much information as possible. Most of the large planes appeared
to be occupied by people. They weren't Chargers with para-military
garb; some were women who weren't much different than she, other
men who looked like they spent a lot of time out in the sun, a few
dogs running between the planes, and children.

There is a whole village here. That's who worked the fields.

"Move!" Lincoln barked as he shoved her again, pushing her to a
solid blue wall.

"Dude! Where do you expect me to go?"

Lincoln pointed to a set of stairs that snaked down the wall that
were painted the same color. Jessica surmised they were designed
to blend into the wall so that visitors wouldn't notice them. As she
stepped up onto the first stair the metal runners creaked beneath her.
A few steps more and Lincoln followed her, causing the staircase to
sag even more. At any second their combined weight could bring
them crashing to the ground.

Jessica glanced up to the top of the stairs to see another person
looking down at her. He was covered in body armor, wore a bushy

brown mustache, and sported pince-nez glasses perched precariously on his nose, with no arms stretching to the ears, they appeared to float on his face. Behind the glasses glowed bright green eyes, exactly like her escort.

"Roosevelt, I presume?" Jessica asked as she took the last stair and met him on the landing. She looked up at his massive height, as he stared down at her.

"That's right little lady, the one and only," he said, then smiled. Despite his jovial appearance, Jessica felt as if he wasn't someone to be trifled with.

"You're taking me to your leader huh?" She asked, offended at his use of "little." Roosevelt's eyes briefly dimmed, then returned to full intensity green.

"Of course he is," Eagle said from a platform overlooking a spacecraft she had never seen before. Leaning against the rail, he stared at her, his piercing green eyes focused and motionless with mechanical precision. His namesake tattoo glowed green in an undulating pattern, mimicking the bird's wings flapping and its talons opening and closing. After a moment, Eagle stood up and stepped toward her, his legs flowed more than stepped, with inhuman dexterity. Despite the cold space in the interior of the shaded building, he radiated heat.

Instinctively Jessica lurched back pressing herself into the large form of Roosevelt, who promptly grabbed her around the throat.

"Don't try to run Jessica, that's not how to treat an old friend." Eagle walked up to her and stood so close that she could feel the heat emanating from his body. Waves of vibration rippled off him, she could feel them in her skin. His eyes locked onto hers.

"I'm so very, very glad to see you," he hissed.

Chapter 43: Twisting

"I'll bet you are," Jessica said, snarling. She didn't bother hiding her disdain. Her knuckles turned white as she struggled to hold Roosevelt's arm away from her throat enough to breathe.

"Ooh, feisty. Every time I hear of you being anxious or scared, I know you are faking it. Just like everyone else. You never tell the truth, just anything you can to twist reality to your own devices," Eagle shot back.

Jessica looked Eagle up and down; his jeans and hoodie were tattered, threadbare in ways that weren't from natural wear and tear. Obviously, he wasn't using the nanites to replace the molecules in his clothes. Underneath, all she could see was black. She wasn't sure if it was black skin, or some kind of armor. Narrowing her eyes, she could discern tiny flecks of green snaking along the surface. The only part she could see of him that looked like flesh was from his neck up; there it blended in with his tattoo. His bald head didn't reflect light at all, nothing like how natural skin, especially on the scalp, would.

"Twisting reality huh? What are you doing then?" she spat.

Eagle's laughter grew in intensity from a chuckle into a full guffaw. He relished in the mockery, then slowly returned to his normal speaking voice.

"I'm not twisting anything. I am doing what I need to do to survive. What anyone would do. I'm not hiding it or pretending to be something I'm not. I've been using the nanites provided by our... new friends, to rebuild myself to exist in this world. As a matter of fact, I can exist in any world now. I would be happy to share this technology with anyone, all they need do is ask. Further, I offer this without all the incredible pain I had to go through to achieve it." Eagle paused for a moment, his green eyes darting quickly to the floor then back up at Jessica.

"Unlike you," he continued, "I know the truth. I don't waste time playing your petty games of being nice to those who are too weak to seize the chance. You all want to 'fix' this world, 'fix' that world, when all you really want to do is keep everyone under your thumb and tell them what to do. You're going to try to subjugate the entire multiverse and take away all of their choice. All under the guise of 'helping.'"

Jessica looked at him incredulously. His body undulated under the tatters of clothing and it unnerved her to see him moving in such an unnatural fashion. She had no idea what he was talking about, and wondered if the nanites had made a mistake while replicating his molecules. Or maybe he was just crazy. "All you did when you got here was take. You didn't give a damn about anyone else but yourself. You stole. Then ran. Then you tried to steal again, and when Jessica didn't give you what you wanted, you came here and enslaved them."

Roosevelt laughed behind her, stroking his long mustache and adjusting his glasses. From what she knew of the former president, it was a fairly good approximation of his mannerisms. "We're not enslaved, young lady. He set us free. The nanites that we have are a hundred times more useful than the ones those insipid Medmads gave you. They don't just keep us alive, they make us invincible. Eagle unlocked the nanites true potential. The Wayfarers and Medmads wanted to control us from the start, it's why we never gave into their absurd 'outquisition.'" Roosevelt pulled tighter and Jessica gasped at the sudden increase in pressure, she couldn't pull back against his arms and started choking.

Eagle leaned close to her face and spoke in a whisper. "You could have this too. All of you. I can give it to you."

Jessica struggled to breathe, and focused all her energy to shake her head no.

"And why not?" Eagle snapped, stepping back against the rail, sliding as he did so.

Jessica gasped under the Charger's grip. Eagle nodded and Roosevelt relented just enough for her to catch her breath. "So, you can control us? I don't think so."

"I freed them; I don't have anyone under my control. They are free to make their own decisions. They can leave at any time, and go anywhere they want," Eagle explained.

"Bullshit," she croaked out.

"Young ladies shouldn't use men's words," Roosevelt said after a long chuckle.

Jessica tried stepping back to throw his weight off and attempt to toss him to the floor, but he was unmovable. She drove her heel into his toes, and it felt like kicking steel. Wiggling her arm free, she drove the side of her fist directly into where she believed his testicles to be. Aside from more laughter, nothing happened.

"You see," Eagle began, "they are invincible. Why would they want to leave me when I have given them so much?"

"You want followers. People to adore you and tell you how great you are," Jessica said.

"I already know I'm great. I will make them great again. I will rebuild this world, and I will start by creating a new gate back to Terra. Once our worlds are connected, I will bring the Eastern Syndicate here and we can begin."

"No one will follow you and you know it. You want the gate open so you can come back and conquer Terra. Because..." Jessica looked up at Roosevelt's face behind her. "They don't know you're an alien, do they?" As she said it, she looked into his eyes behind his glasses. They flashed blue before returning to green.

"They don't need to know that, and it would only confuse them.

Withholding information is not the same as lying. I've done nothing immoral," Eagle explained.

Jessica didn't waste a second attempting to contradict him. She knew he was incorrigible and angling for an advantage. If he knew everything --like he claimed-- he wouldn't be standing here playing petty dictator. "You're missing something. You don't know how to get back, or you'd have killed us already," she said, hoping the realization would get through and damage his ego.

"Oh, I know how to get back, and I know exactly where to go to make that happen."

As he spoke, Jessica looked across the hangar at the ventilation shaft hanging from the gangway on the far wall. Amanda leaned out, barely noticeable. She was signing, "Arrow. Careful." Jessica took a slow breath to calm her anxiety and focused back on Eagle, using her peripheral vision to look around the space until she saw Sally in the cargo hold of the spaceship that occupied the spot where the Discovery was in her dimension. This was the Dreamchaser Tenacity. Its name painted in bright blue lettering across the fuselage. Without moving her eyes, she saw Richard behind the front wheel of the vehicle, knocking an arrow. Delicately, she moved her eyes and looked around for Jason and Meera but couldn't find them.

Eagle's eyes glowed bright green and an evil smile played across his lips. Jessica's eyes widened as an epiphany dawned, "You know where to go…? It's the hospital, isn't it? You need something from there. Something to make the gate. You couldn't get it on your own, but now that you have an army of thugs, you can just take that too huh? You won't let that go; you're going to keep coming until we stop you. I can't let you do that. I won't let you hurt my family because of my mistake. I'll do whatever it takes." Jessica's world slowed down as she finished the sentence. Eagle turned his head as his eyes narrowed, his eyebrow arched. The eagle tattoo spread its talons and the beak opened wide.

In a flash, Jessica dropped and pulled out of Roosevelt's grasp before he could close back in on her throat. With all her might, she tore from her antagonists, desperate to get out of the way of the impending arrow fire. Roosevelt stepped quickly toward her as an arrow flew through the air and knocked his pince-nez glasses off his face. He stepped back in shock.

"Very good!" Eagle exclaimed as he caught another arrow without looking at it. "This will be more fun than I thought!"

Jessica's eyes darted to the ship again, Richard and Sally had moved away, out of sight.

"It's no use looking for your friends. I control this entire building. They won't get out of here alive," Eagle snarled.

Jessica walked backward as far and as fast as she could, hitting the railing behind her. She knew she was easily forty feet up in the air, and that a fall from this height could kill her.

"Maybe," she said as she put her hands on the railing, lifting herself onto the top. "Maybe not."

Jessica threw herself over the side.

Chapter 44: No Place for a Rumble

Roosevelt sprinted to the rail in a vain attempt to catch Jessica before she tumbled over. He reached forward into the empty space, hyperextending his arms to an unnatural length to no avail. Jessica smiled at him as Meera carried her in her arms, running for the spaceship, her exosuit feet clanging rhythmically against the concrete floor of the hangar. Eagle followed with his eyes, a cold detachment on his face.

The pair slid under the ship to see a panicked Richard furiously typing on his comm band. Sally ran up behind them, bow at the ready. "What are you doin' darlin'?! We have to go!"

"I'm trying to hack into his nanites, we haven't been this close before and you wouldn't let me do this before you started shooting," he explained hastily.

"Now is NOT a good time!" Jessica yelled as she saw Roosevelt running toward them across the hangar at top speed; he would be there in moments.

"HURRY!" Amanda shrieked in her choked voice from the air shaft; Jessica shot a glance to the vent and caught her disappearing into the shaft.

"Richard! Hurry!" Meera screamed.

"GO!" he yelled; eyes fixed on his band.

Meera tuned and ran toward the opening of the hangar, toward the *Enola Gay*. Jessica, bouncing in her arms, turned to see Sally running behind and Roosevelt ducking under the *Tenacity*. She prayed Richard would do whatever he was planning and get away before the Charger could hurt him, or worse.

"Richard. We can't let him—" Jessica pleaded with Meera, who was running at full speed, eight feet up in the air. Jessica felt like she was in a plane just after takeoff, but one that couldn't quite achieve flight.

"Gotta go, I have to get you out. Part of the plan," Meera spat between breaths.

"Plan?"

Jessica's comm band crackled into life, as Tony's image appeared on it, EMP bomb strapped to his back.

"Tony! NO! That will…"

"I know Sis, it's okay, this is the only way we can stop all of them. Get out as fast as you can." His screen went dark.

"No! No, there are other ways we can do this, it will kill him!" Jessica pleaded with Meera.

"Too hard, we can't do it," Meera replied, then ran, faster than Jessica thought possible.

As Jessica looked forward, she could see a crowd gathered around the Enola Gay. People who didn't appear much different than the farmers at the hospital. They looked on with curiosity as the ancient bomber rocked on its wheels.

Poke? It will… it will kill Peek!

The terrifying reality of the plan came crashing in on her. Using the EMP would be a Pyrrhic victory; it could stop Eagle and the Chargers in one shot, and kill most of her friends at the same time. All because of a bomb that she brought with her.

"We can't let them do this Meera; didn't you take an oath?" Jessica desperately tried to think of a compelling argument to stop what she figured was straight up lunacy.

"I did. I swore to protect the planet and not let people destroy it again," Meera explained as she leapt from the ground and landed on the tail section of the Stratofortress.

"What about 'Do No Harm?' The Hippocratic oath?" Jessica asked as she was deposited onto the back of the plane.

Meera dropped her suit back down to her feet, and extended the legs to her arms, quadrupling their strength.

"The what?" she asked, her eyes narrowed, and panting.

Jessica rolled her eyes. "What's the plan now?"

Meera opened her mouth to speak when the pair jumped and turned around. Poke came crashing backwards through the aluminum skin of the ancient plane. Lincoln's hand wrapped around his throat. Poke's hands were, conversely, wrapped around Lincoln's fingers, desperately trying to pry them off.

"Poke!" Jessica scampered over the hull and wrapped her arms around Lincoln's wrists trying to pry them loose. From below she should see Katelyn swinging at Lincoln's torso with everything she had, punching and kicking as hard as she could, solidly landing jabs to abs, and doing absolutely nothing. Peek's LEDs burned a brilliant red, and at the brightest intensity she had ever seen them.

Reaching around Poke and Jessica, Meera wrapped her right arm over Lincoln's left and under his right, grabbing the wrist. She pulled to her right with her exosuit-enhanced strength, the servos screaming like mad. All of their arms locked in struggle until Meera's left fist slammed into his Lincoln's chin, breaking his grasp on the alien. Poke dropped and fell back through the hole. Lincoln reeled from the punch and slammed into the hull, but quickly shook off the blow and turned to his attackers.

"Great, that worked… now what?" Jessica yelled as Meera stepped back next to her. The Medmad slid her finger along her comm band, the display blinked bright red. Jessica could see the servos on the joints spinning in preparation; the struts quivered with energy.

"We kick his ass," Meera said with burning determination.

Jessica spun her head to the right as the plane rocked to the left.

"Need some help there, my friend?" called Roosevelt up from the floor.

"No, but you can watch, and I will show you how it's done," Lincoln responded, grinding his green teeth together.

Before the sentence left his mouth, Lincoln lunged at Meera, who barely caught him with her assisted arms. She pressed back against his attack, and lost ground rapidly. Driving her feet into the hull, the struts pulled back from her arms and braced her legs as the suit buckled the aluminum and tore into the fuselage below. The sound of twisting metal was sickening, and mixed with Roosevelt's laughter, it took on a surreal tone.

"You just need to know how to handle women," Lincoln spat. His eyes flashed blue, then green; back and forth in a random pattern. His body locked up, and he fell to the hull like a statue dropped from the top of a five-story tower. He gurgled violently, green spit pouring from his mouth.

"Unlike you, asshole," Katelyn snarled as she clambered onto the hull holding Peek's storage device against Lincoln's leg, "we watch each other's back."

Roosevelt howled from the floor, then tore for the ladder and onto the Stratofortress. Katelyn dropped back into the hole, leaving Peek's storage device connected to Lincoln's leg.

"Incoming!" Jessica yelled down into the plane as she ran to the opening. When she looked down, she saw Roosevelt attempting to climb the ladder. Poke and Katelyn held onto the top and kicked furiously attempting to keep him pinned and off balance. Amanda and Jason ran up behind him and grabbed his legs. Roosevelt pushed back and forth, knocking two of them loose only to have the other two grab on and lean in the other direction. The Charger laughed. "Where is Eagle? He needs to see this! Bully on you four! This is great!"

Jessica shook her head in disbelief and Meera jumped past her and into the hull. Locking her feet into one of the aluminum ribs of the fuselage, Meera extended the legs of the exosuit and slammed her shoulder into Roosevelt's neck pinning him against the ladder and catching Jason's arm in the process. Jason howled in pain and Jessica clearly heard his arm snap under the pressure.

"Serves you right, you heathen!" Roosevelt roared as he slowly turned his face to Jessica, pushing Meera back with his chin. The servos on her suit railed against his strength. "This is all you can do? Children commanded by another child. It takes six of you to slow me down, what will you do when Eagle gets here?" With that he breathed deep and pushed Meera back with his neck, pressing her feet into the ribs of the fuselage and tearing the supports for the plane. She fell out onto the hard concrete into a motionless lump. Her exosuit fully extended; it spat sparks from every joint.

In another shove, Roosevelt pushed Katelyn and Poke off, slamming them back into the hold where they started out. He kicked the ladder off the body of the plane, leaving Amanda swiping at his legs with her electrified baton. Jason lay on the ground, rocking back and forth, cradling his shattered arm.

"Now, as I said before, we are invincible. There is no way you can defeat us." Roosevelt stood up inside the plane and looked around the twisted metal. "This is such a waste; you were always on the wrong side. As it was in the past, it will be my burden to civilize you lot and bring you under the new order. Eagle will show you the way. The way to true freedom, and once you experience that freedom, you will dance upon the flowers, smelling the lilies, and playing with butterflies. Why are you all getting swimmy? Like that alligator does when I feed him da rabbits. Tell me 'bout the rabbits...."

Roosevelt's eyes flashed between green and blue several times, then he fell over, hitting the deck plating hard.

With a gasp everyone looked down to see Lincoln holding onto Roosevelt's leg, green foam crawled down his arm. Lincoln smiled at the group in the plane. "Pardon my actions from before, I was not acting like myself. My esteemed colleague here will not bother you any longer. Let's see if we can't make amends for the trouble we have caused."

Chapter 45: Missing

Jessica threw her wrist up to her face and activated the common channel, "Richard, do you hear me? Are you there?" Her question was met with static. "Richard, are you receiving? Sally? Respond. Tony?"

Jessica and Katelyn got out of the plane, hang-dropping from the now ladder-less opening. Amanda was already at Meera's side, holding her head up and running her comm band over her body.

"How is she?" Jessica asked, after rushing over and checking Meera's pulse on her throat.

"I think she is okay," Amanda signed. "Knocked out, hopefully she will wake up soon."

"Can we move her?" Jessica asked, seeing the inhabitants from the planes walking toward them, cautiously.

"I don't know, *she's* the medic," Amanda signed.

Katelyn came up behind the pair, "We can't find them on the scan, Eagle and Tony are gone too."

"Did the EMP go off?" Jessica asked.

"That would have been a very big bang, babe," Katelyn said.

Jessica dropped her head and shook it, then took a deep breath. She turned back to the plane as Poke did his best to cover himself with what was left of his hoodie and cap. Lincoln and Roosevelt stayed inside.

"Peek," she said into her band, "What about those guys? How much are you controlling them?"

"Not controlling. Nanites reprogrammed," the emulant answered over Poke's channel.

"What do you mean? They aren't the same guys, how are they completely different?"

"Nanites enhance dopamine."

"You gave them happy pills?" Jessica asked, standing up and looking into the *Enola Gay.* She could see Lincoln and Roosevelt chatting in the ruined fuselage. As if they were old friends relaxing after a hard day of physical labor, not the psychotic brutes they had been only minutes ago. Roosevelt caught her eye and he put his hand on his chest and bowed, smiling.

"Old program. Kept them angry. Amplified fear."

"Amanda, I thought these guys were crazy, even before we got here?" Jessica asked her, as she looked around at the slowly gathering crowd. Amanda waved at them and then signed to Jessica with her right hand, finger spelling, "Maybe they were scared and confused." Then she shrugged.

The nanites are enhancing neurotransmitters too? They have been doing everything else, why not? Isn't it still control, even if it's enhancing the feel-good side of someone's personality?

Jessica waved to a tall man who slowly walked closer to her out of the crowd, he mouthed a hesitant "Ahoy."

Jessica waved back, hoping that he was not an enhanced Charger in disguise.

"Thank you for taking care of those two monsters." He nodded over to the plane.

"I don't understand. Monsters? Aren't you all Chargers? Isn't this your... settlement?"

The man looked over at the plane with the corner of his eye, and locked onto Roosevelt, who tilted his head down in supplication.

"No, this is not our settlement. They dragged us in from the other areas to work for them. They weren't horrible, but we couldn't leave. They wouldn't let us talk to the caravan either, so we were trapped here. It was only the three of them after a while, and to be honest, the hangar is a lot more secure than being out in the open. But then that stranger showed up, and everyone got really violent."

There was a bang from the B-52, as Poke hauled himself back up into the fuselage, Jessica could see the discomfort on his face, unaccustomed to being around that many people without an adequate disguise. Some of the people jumped and moved away.

Jessica looked back, "Three? I thought Washington was dead?"

The man shook his head, "Adams is still out guarding the gate."

"Damn, we have one Charger and Eagle still loose?" Katelyn asked.

Jessica addressed the man again, "We have to find Eagle and our friends so they won't bother you again. Will you all be okay if we take these guys off your hands?" Jessica pointed into the plane, where Lincoln and Roosevelt were resting against the hull.

Meera groaned from the ground, bringing Amanda back down to check on her.

The man responded, "I think that would be a good idea. It will be easier, but some folks will be afraid of not having protection."

Amanda was already typing on her band. Meera ran hers over her own body, and smiled, then frowned when she saw the twisted remains of her exosuit. Jason came over to her, clutching his arm.

"Would you have a problem with the Wayfarers paying you a visit?" Jessica asked the man.

"We could really use their help. Most of us don't like being isolated like this," he said.

Amanda quickly gave the thumbs up.

"Sis…, need you. Eagle has them," Tony's voice crackled over her comm band, so weak she almost didn't hear it. Amanda quickly checked hers and nodded.

"Are you all right?" Jessica asked.

"Hai, but Eagle… consumed them? I could see their bodies in his… when he ran out of the building."

Jessica's eyes narrowed and her nose rose in disgust. "Do you know which way they are going?"

"To the hospital. Straight home."

Chapter 46: Adams and the Guard Post

"Great," Jessica spat. "Tony, keep an eye on them, but stay out of sight. We will get to you as fast as we can."

"You bet, Sis." his transmission crackled over the band and then went dead.

Jessica looked back at the man she was speaking to, who was already nodding at her. He bowed and then turned to the crowd, putting his hands out to corral them back.

"Meera, can you do this?" Jessica asked, patting the Medmad on the shoulder.

Meera nodded emphatically. "I'm okay, nothing is broken. I wish the suit were still working but there is nothing I can do about it now. I'd have to stop and let the nanites repair it out here, but that would take a while."

"Jessica, let's go..." Katelyn said, rubbing her hand on Jessica's shoulder.

Jessica nodded. "Yeah, I think they are in good hands, let's get going."

The group, now with two added Chargers, slipped out of the building into the late afternoon air. Jessica breathed deep and looked around at her people. She wasn't sure how everyone was going to get back fast enough to prevent Eagle from doing whatever it was he was focused on, presuming the Chargers wouldn't tire. Trying to get her bearings, she looked around. "Okay, I'm lost, which way is home?"

Roosevelt laughed and started off to the east. "This way to the hospital," he said, waving the rest on and heading for the guard outpost.

"The guard...Adams!" Katelyn exclaimed.

"Yes, he's still there. Don't worry, he's a pussycat, and I gave him the orders to be there. He knows his place." Roosevelt headed out, with Lincoln on his heels.

Jason laughed and rubbed his arm, which Meera had already splinted. "They are named after presidents! I just got that, man."

Katelyn shook her head.

"What was this 'plan' anyway?" Jessica asked Meera who, unaccustomed to walking long distances without her exosuit, lagged behind.

Meera explained with increasing speed, "We were supposed to get you and everyone else out of the building as fast as possible. Tony was going to run the EMP up and take out Eagle. I know what you are going to say, but he insisted. We needed to make sure you didn't see it happening in case, you know, it was really devastating to him. Richard thought you'd been through enough, and seeing your little brother… well you know, so soon might have been too much for you. Do you think you could have handled that? I know if I saw a loved one shut down like that it would probably mess me up. It's why they kept me in Tysons, it's safe enough to be on the periphery, but wasn't supposed to see any action."

Jessica blinked as she absorbed the torrent of information, then nodded in appreciation of their concern.

"We hoped Lincoln wouldn't put up such a fight, Friend Jessica," Poke explained. "We thought he would come to Eagle's aid and then we could murder two birds with one rock."

"Stone, sweetie, 'kill two birds with one stone.'" Katelyn explained, taking Poke's arm and rubbing Peek's storage device. "Are you not remembering everything in there?" she asked the emulant.

"Doing best I can. Hard to squeeze back in bottle," Peek responded in its child-like voice.

"Ahoy! Mr. Adams!" Roosevelt said walking up to the guard post, he raised his right hand and waved.

"Mr. Roosevelt," Adams responded, as he stepped out of the post and straightened up. "I was expecting you to come a lot sooner than this after the caravan left. Who are these people?"

Jessica turned to the machine guns mounted on the front of the

Hazy Center, they were trained on everyone, just like they were when the caravan first arrived.

Roosevelt continued, "These are new friends of ours. They came from far away to help us with our endeavor to civilize the wastes and to make the world safe for our kind."

Adams's eyes darted from Roosevelt to Lincoln to Jessica and back. In his right hand, he held the remote for the .50 caliber guns, and his thumb jumped nervously on the fire button. "This doesn't make any sense, brother. Why is she here? We don't talk to any of the settlements, especially with those halcyon farmers and their socialist ways."

"Yes, brother," Roosevelt continued with Lincoln at his side. "We're negotiating a trade for food and medicine. Lincoln and I feel that our staff won't be able to keep up any longer without trade. There are just too many in our settlement."

"Not enough?" Adams asked, his eyes narrowing. "We just take them like we always do. We are stronger, Charger's take charge, right?"

Jessica stepped back casting her gaze at the guns trained on them. Adams's finger stroked the fire button on the remote trigger.

"No, this isn't right, something happened to you. This is crazy talk." Adams responded.

"Adams, listen to me carefully." Roosevelt started in, "This is the way we are going to do things from now on. We've been wrong to cut ourselves off and cloister away in that building. We have no right to steal people to do our work. You have two options here: you give me that trigger and go to the center and get ready for the Wayfarers to arrive, or you leave now and make your own way in the world. You're your own man, and I won't force you. But just to make this fair..."

At that, Lincoln grabbed the trigger out of Adams's hand so fast Jessica could barely comprehend what was happening before he already had it. Adams stood motionless, eyes darting from person to person.

"It's your decision, brother. Stay with us, or exile," Roosevelt said calmly.

"I had some ideas…" Adams said hesitantly. "Ideas about how we could increase the yield on the farm, but I was afraid."

"Afraid of what, brother?" Roosevelt asked, reflexively attempting to fix his pince-nez glasses, which were no longer on his face.

"I was afraid you'd disagree with me, and then you'd be angry. But I've been quiet about them for too long, and I want to see what we can do." Adams said, looking straight into Roosevelt's glowing-green eyes.

Roosevelt stood motionless for a moment, then put both of his hands on Adams's shoulders, green foam trickled from his fingertips and into Adam's shoulder, who slowly relaxed, his eyes flashing blue. A smile grew on Roosevelt's lips. "Bully on you, brother! I knew you would see reason!" He started laughing, a full guffaw. Lincoln pulled the transmitter off the remote trigger, disabling it, and crushed it under his boot.

Roosevelt bowed to Adams, "Head home and get started, when I return, we have a lot of work to do!"

Adams smiled and took his helmet off. Jessica realized he was barely an adult. He smiled back, waved, and headed toward the Hazy center.

Roosevelt continued laughing until he quieted and caught his breath, then turned to Jessica and smiled. "I assure you, madam, I am not mad. Nor am I under the influence of these machines. I am simply tired of wasting time."

Amanda checked her comm band then signed to Jessica, "Speaking of time, they are moving fast. We aren't keeping up."

Roosevelt looked at Lincoln, and then at the abandoned school buses.

"Yes, I think we can," Lincoln said with a nod to Roosevelt.

Roosevelt bowed and gestured to the rusting bus, "Gathered friends, your chariot awaits."

Chapter 47: The Hospital

"This has to be the most messed-up thing I have ever done," Katelyn said as she held onto the decayed seat beneath her. The dilapidated bus rumbled along what was left of the Dulles Toll Road heading east toward Reston.

Jessica sat in the driver's seat, arms akimbo attempting to hold the old vehicle straight. "God, I wish this thing had power steering! This is so hard, and I really don't want to lose more weight while driving." A half-smile flickered on her lips as she said it, enjoying the terrifying experience.

"Jesus, man, I used to live in a bus exactly like this. Didn't move much though," Jason said. "This smells a hell of a lot better." He stood up and stuck his head out of one of the high windows; his hair blew in the breeze like a collie sticking its face out of the family station-wagon.

Amanda stood in the back of the bus, overlooking the escape door that was bereft of any safety glass. She was looking around nervously at the road passing by as the bus thundered along. Catching Jessica's gaze in the rear-view mirror, she sighed, "I don't like this, too fast."

Jessica nodded. "It's okay, I've been driving for years. I don't trust a computer to do it. No offense Peek."

"Not a computer, none taken," the emulant called from its storage device strapped to Poke's arm.

Meera got up and joined Amanda at the back of the bus. "How are you guys doing?"

Outside the bus the two Chargers ran as they pushed the bus forward; sometimes forcing it over bumps, other times holding it back as it careened from one pothole to another, all the while singing "She'll be Coming 'Round the Mountain." Roosevelt smiled at Meera between shoves. She smiled again and ran to the front.

"How fast are we going?" she asked Jessica, excitedly.

Jessica dared not look down for very long, and could only make out part of the display on the speedometer. "Uhhh, I think fifteen? Eighteen miles per hour?" she yelled back over the rumbling of the rubber-less wheels biting into the asphalt surface.

"What is that in kilometers?" Meera asked back.

"I have NO idea!" Jessica responded, so lost in the experience that she completely forgot the GPS trackers they all had on their comm bands. "How far are we?" she yelled to the back of the bus.

"We are moving at thirteen miles, or twenty kilometers, an hour and should be there in half an hour," Poke yelled over the noise, relaying Peek's information. "Unless something happens. Please be careful, Friend Jessica."

Jessica nodded quickly as she steered around a broken section of a decaying overpass. Chunks of concrete and rebar jutted out over the hole like gigantic spikes, ready to impale them at their reckless speed. "Doing the best I can!" she yelled.

"Jessica, can you hear me?" Tony's voice crackled over the comm band. "Sis, you there?"

"Someone get that!" Jessica yelled to the back of the bus, "super busy!" The bus rocked to the left as it scraped an abandoned ice cream truck, tearing the rusty bumper clean off.

Katelyn jumped into the conversation over the band. "I hear you babe, what's shaking?"

"Ehh, hai, uh, Katelyn," Tony responded. "Eagle just got to the hospital, exactly like Jessica said he would. It was weird though, he walked right into the building."

"You mean he went in through the front door? Didn't Jessica or someone else try to stop him?"

"No, he walked *into* the building. Smashed right into the wall on the west side. He's like, I dunno, four meters tall."

"METERS?!" the collective voices rang out from the news.

"Yep, I can't see Sally or Richard. I don't know what he's done with them. As soon as he went in, the building went dark. I hope Dad is okay." Tony responded; his voice filled with anguish.

"Stay safe," Katelyn said, looking at Jessica for confirmation, who emphatically nodded "Yes."

"I'll try, but if he leaves…" Tony cut his sentence short.

"We're on our way. Stay safe until we get there. If anyone comes out, let us know and try to get their attention," Katelyn said, with a nod of approval from Jessica.

"Right, I will," Tony replied.

Jessica slammed the steering wheel with her hand. "Kate, I need you to do this, can you drive please?"

Without replying Katelyn stepped up to the driver's seat and slipped into the chair as Jessica slid out the other side. She grabbed the wheel and drove the bus, straighter than Jessica could.

"Oh, shit!" Katelyn exclaimed, then laughed. "YEAH BABY!"

Jessica went to the back, past Meera, and addressed Roosevelt. "How strong is he? What are we dealing with here?" She asked. Roosevelt looked up to her and smiled.

"He's fairly formidable, miss. He's not just enhanced like we are, his nanites…"

"I know, rebuilt him molecule by molecule. How can he be four meters tall?"

Roosevelt watched his feet as he ran over a particularly rough patch of broken highway, one that Jessica barely felt. Katelyn, as usual, was doing a spectacular job.

"I don't know what a meter is, we use American numbers like feet. Guessing by the way you all reacted though, he must be immense."

"How?" Jessica asked, kneeling down on the deck of the bus to get closer to Roosevelt's face.

"He has many more nanites, he reproduces them at will. He just needs base material," the Charger replied.

"Running into a wall is more like digestion than destruction?"

"An indelicate comparison to be sure, miss, but not inaccurate."

Jessica thought back to when her father told her of "grey goo." The fear that microscopic machines would convert all the molecules of the planet into one seething mass of raw atoms with no color or shape. A gelatinous blob, the height of the Empire State Building, coveting the world. It was science fiction to her as a child, a cautionary tale designed to both encourage treating AI with respect, and for always building in a failsafe. Something to ponder, but not a realistic fear. Then she remembered that she was walking on an alternate Earth with aliens from another dimension.

"This is gonna be hard," Jessica said aloud, thinking more than reacting.

"Uh, babe? This is gonna be harder than we think." Katelyn pointed out of the bus, through the broken windshield. The hospital loomed in the distance, completely dark and lifeless, with a two-story hole torn into the side. The entire opening glowing bright green.

Chapter 48: The Not So Magic School Bus

"Stop the bus! Stop pushing!" Jessica yelled to the Chargers. Katelyn slammed her feet on the brakes reflexively, not knowing if they would actually work or not. Roosevelt, glanced over to Lincoln and nodded. The pair stopped running and leaned back, pulling the bus toward themselves. Katelyn spun the wheel to break forward momentum and punched the emergency brake interlock button, which instantly shattered from the pressure. The rusting school bus ground to a halt, its body creaking loudly in protest. It stopped on the last overpass before the exit to the hospital, so conspicuously that it almost screamed, "Look at me!"

"We have to hide this thing, where can we hide it?" Jessica frantically looked around for a place for the forty-foot vehicle and came up with nothing. There was nowhere that was both large and high enough to conceal it. The only space out of view was the road deck below.

"Why?" Katelyn asked. "He probably already saw us."

"I don't know, maybe he didn't. We have to hide it." Jessica could feel her anxiety clawing at her consciousness, she couldn't overcome it and listen to reason. "Push it over, everyone, out!" Jessica yelled, standing up and waving to the passengers in the rusting "chariot."

Once everyone was out and safely hidden behind the last sections of the broken Jersey wall, the Chargers pushed the bus over the edge. It crashed with a slow-moving thunder, sure to alert everyone within a dozen miles. Jessica listened to the sound with her shoulders pulled up to her ears, her face twisted in pain.

"Shit. That was…"

"Probably not a good idea, Friend Jessica," Poke said, finishing her thought.

"Great," Jessica said, flapping her arms to her sides in frustration.

"We can't do anything about that now, babe. We need to get out of here, we're sitting ducks," Katelyn gestured over the wall toward the hospital, a dark edifice silhouetted against the gathering darkness of the sky. The parking deck was brightly lit, however, and Jessica could see people moving around in the structure.

"I think we're going to have an audience for this," Jessica said, dropping off the road deck and sliding behind a thick pine tree, so old it must have been there since before the road was laid.

"They're waiting for us. Our family that is," Tony said from beyond the tree-line. "I told everyone that we were coming to deal with 'our friends.'"

Jessica smiled and stepped forward to greet her "younger brother," but he stepped back into the shadow of the bushes.

"Don't. I don't want them to see where I am. They don't know I'm here."

Jessica turned her back to Tony and looked toward the group, crouching low. She spoke into her comm band to him, despite him being right behind her.

"Are they gonna help us?" She asked.

"Nope. Jessica, our sister, said no. She doesn't want anyone getting hurt fighting that guy," Tony answered.

Jessica's heart sank. The rebuke from her counterpart in this dimension was deflating to her, even though she was never promised help in the first place.

"What about Dad?" she asked, hoping for something to go her way.

"I'm right here. I saw the bus heading toward the hospital," Gerard said, stepping out from the trees behind Tony, he recoiled at the sight of the two Chargers standing with her, to which the both of them stood straight and waved.

"Good to see you, my friend," Roosevelt said, as he stepped forward, both arms outstretched in greeting.

"Good to see you too, sir. I'm glad you came to your senses!" Jessica's father smiled back tentatively, taking his hand.

"What?!" Jessica exclaimed, turning around to look at the two. "How do you know these guys?"

"I know these guys from a way back. Who do you think helped negotiate the peace treaty?" Gerard explained.

"I thought the Wayfarers did that? Or the Medmads?"

Amanda stepped up and signed, "We did, but we also needed someone from the hospital to speak to them. Sally's father was there as well. Part of what we have been trying to accomplish around here is making sure that everyone is involved in our future, and not just a few people making decisions for the rest of the world. That's what got us in this mess in the first place."

"Wait, but I thought the hospital wanted to keep to itself?" Jessica asked, tilting her head to the side, trying to mentally piece together the information.

"Oh, we do, but we also didn't want to be left out of the discussion." Gerard smiled and clapped Lincoln on the shoulder. "The best way to be left alone is to tell everyone and hope that they ignore you. This guy was the one that resisted the most, after Washington, but I am glad you came to your senses as well." Gerard smiled.

Jessica boiled at the exchange. "Why didn't you tell me this? Any of this? Tony? What the hell, did you know this too?" Jessica turned to the bushes, ignoring his request.

"Nope, I didn't know that, but that was before I showed up."

Amanda signed, "Reminding you that we have something important to do. He probably already sees us." Then she pointed to the hospital in the distance, where half the west side of the building was missing and dust drifted up from the hole.

"Right," Jessica said. "I'm surprised he hasn't already moved on us. Gentlemen, can you... I dunno, feel what he is doing in there? Can the nanites talk to each other or something?"

Lincoln shook his head then spoke. "No, it's not like we're in radio contact with each other, we never had that ability. They've just augmented our bodies, not given us telepathy."

Jessica nodded. "Tony, I think we are going to need you to get close…" Jessica stopped speaking as soon as she heard the underbrush rustling, she knew he was already gone.

"So, do we wait until dawn or something here?" Katelyn asked, leaning against the Jersey wall and Poke at the same time.

"Something tells me that is a good idea. But something else tells me that Eagle is thinking the same thing," Jessica said.

The light was rapidly fading, getting too dark to move effectively through the wreckage and brush that surrounded the hospital. "Hey guys, do you think you can follow Tony? Take up some positions to get as much information you can before the sun comes up? The nanites let you see the world better, right?"

"I can go to the hospital without any problem, Friend Jessica," Poke said, stepping forward to address the group. Peek's following pattern of LEDs let her know that the emulant agreed.

"Ours can let us see the ground beneath us, not amazingly well, but enough to accomplish our mission. We can be at the hospital in no time." Roosevelt said, cocking his head over to Lincoln, who nodded in response.

"Okay folks, here's the plan…" Jessica started.

Chapter 49: Grey Traces of Dawn

The faintest of lights tinged the eastern sky as the April sun returned from its nightly slumber. It was already warmer than any April morning Jessica had ever known and she tried not to think about what lay ahead for her this day. Anxious and aching, she had been thinking about it all night as she fruitlessly tried to sleep beneath an old oak tree next to the side of the road. Birds chirped in the distance, and a red-tailed hawk screeched as it made its effort to catch breakfast.

Amanda was already up and eating from her rations. Jason was sprawled out on the ground next to a wrecked car, his hat pulled over his face and his beard dropping to one side. Meera typed away on her bamboo laptop, cataloguing her adventure for the Medmads to study in the future. If they survived whatever they were going to do today. Katelyn leaned against Poke all night, and only now did she start to stir with the growing activity.

Gerard coughed from the other side of the tree, where he'd been lying, studying the hospital and waiting for Tony or the Chargers to give him updates. Tony did so twice, once when they were half-way to the building, and another time when they had taken up position. Jessica could tell that the anxiety was grating on him. His responses to her questions were short. Not particularly curt, but not his usual easy demeanor.

"Anything?" she asked, her voice still hoarse from sleep.

"Nada. I don't like this. We should get started," Gerard said. He stood up and looked over the camp, the nods of his head indicating that he was mentally counting the team members.

"Tony, are you receiving?" Jessica asked, whispering into her comm band. Seconds passed as she heard only static over the band. She asked again, louder than before. "Tony? Do you read me?"

"Yeah Sis, I hear you. Good morning!" Tony answered, his voice clear and strong.

"Hey bro, how are you? What's your position?" She asked, looking through the trees toward the hospital.

"I'm right in front of you, well you know, at the hospital, but right in front of you." Tony laughed at the end of the sentence.

"Has anything changed? Any movement?" she asked.

"Nope, I haven't seen anyone do anything. Which is weird, because our sister would have already been up and out in the fields checking the crops by now," Tony answered.

Jessica looked around; the situation was almost exactly the same as when they arrived at the Hazy Center: quiet. The proverbial "too quiet." Scanning the horizon, she looked for any sign of the caravan but could see nothing new. The blasted landscape stretched out in front of her. The edge of the forest, the hospital, the miles and miles of asphalt and broken buildings. Sweat dripped down her ribs.

"Lincoln? Roosevelt? Do you copy?" Jessica asked into the comm band.

"That's an affirmative, little lady, ready to take on the day!" Roosevelt's enthusiastic reply came over the band.

"Ready," was Lincoln's characteristically short reply.

Jessica turned to the group. Everyone was awake, shaking themselves out of their slumber. Coffee was produced from somewhere and the smell made her stomach growl.

"You know, the longer we wait here..." Gerard commented, securing his hat tightly on his head. He was in what they called "Go mode" in her family. A restless anticipation to do something, there was no way he was waiting to get started any longer.

"Right," Jessica said, pressing a contact on her comm band. The bands on the team buzzed and one by one and they all disappeared into the bush.

"The deck just lit up," Tony's voice came from the band. Jessica looked up at the parking deck on the other side of the hospital, every light blazed and she could see the farmers looking out of the levels. They did nothing but stare out at the hospital; they knew what was coming.

"Fine, let's get started," she said.

A boom came from the side of the hospital, where Eagle had pounded his way in before, and a new section of the wall fell away. It dropped quickly as if demolished, instead of smashed into. The base of the rubble pile glowed green.

"Got them! I'm in contact with the nanites," Amanda called over her band, then turned to Jessica and signed quickly, "he's encrypted them. Hard."

Peek's voice crackled over the band, "Working." Poke, standing next to Katelyn, nodded and held his large hand over the storage device strapped to his arm.

Roosevelt's voice crackled over the comm band, "My good man, what are you doing? Don't you understand what you represent? You don't have to destroy what's left of this world. We can rebuild it together! You are welcome here on Gai—" his voice cut off the line in mind-sentence.

Jessica squinted against the light coming over the trees as she tried to locate the Charger, then she dropped her eyes down to the comm band. "Where is he? Where did he go? Tony, do you see him?" her voice rose in panic.

"No, Sis, I don't see him. I don't see Lincoln either, do you—" Tony's comm went dead. Fearing the worst, Jessica looked down at her band and saw his blue dot jumping around in his area. Gerard bolted into the brush, heading toward the hospital.

"Dad! Dad!" she yelled, trying to get him to return.

"That isn't the plan, man!" Jason yelled toward the building.

"Lincoln is gone," Poke said after checking his band.

"Shit. SHIT!" Jessica yelled running toward the hospital completely ignoring everyone that simultaneously yelled to get her to stop.

I can't let anything happen to them, I can't...

Jessica's heart pounded in her throat as she ran, her feet felt like they were barely touching the ground as she tore through the brush.

I can't let...

Jessica could hear her frantic breathing as she jumped over a pile of asphalt and bricks then dove, headfirst, into the hospital. She slammed into a wall of the children's wing, still painted with blue sky and green trees. A world that no longer existed. Pulling herself off the ground she turned, feeling the heat pour over her. Bright green light filled her vision.

"Did you think I wouldn't know where you were? You're going to help me whether you want to or not," an unearthly voice spoke.

Jessica couldn't clear her vision, but knew that she was accelerating upward. The next moment bright sunlight pushed out the green, and she looked straight ahead to the forest in front of her, the cornfields to her left, the parking garage to her right. When she looked down, her heart skipped as she saw her feet dangling twenty feet in the air. Desperate to break free, she tried to pull her hands up but could not move them.

"If you approach, I drop her. You will be responsible for her death," the voice boomed across the area.

Jessica twisted in the air, seeing long black tendrils holding her above the ground. They pulled her toward the building, and a large black and green mass that undulated and writhed.

"E-Eagle?" she managed to choke out.

"I am so much more than that now. Your friends are a part of me now. Everyone is here. Even your sister."

Jessica peered at the writhing mass and saw her twin's overalls drop out of the mass and onto the roof of the building.

"You can't stop me now. This world is mine," Eagle said, using her twin's voice.

Chapter 50: The USB Drive

"Jessica?" Unbound squeaked out as the horror tore through her body.

"She's in here. We are all in here," Eagle said again, this time in Richard's voice.

"What have you done to them? Where are they?" Jessica spat, kicking her feet and trying to break free.

"I've given them freedom. They aren't bound by their bodies anymore. They will live forever, truly unbound, not that gross caricature you call yourself."

"Live as your slave?" Jessica asked.

"I'm sure they wouldn't want to leave, but they can. I can reform them anytime I want."

"You want. This is all about you still. Your control. Put me down!"

"When I so chose." The mass moved across the roof of the hospital and lowered Jessica into the center of the building. From floor to floor she dropped until she reached a room she had been in before; the basement with the MRI. The machine now glowed bright green, nano-foam writhed over it. The main well of the device crackled with a green light, and ozone filled the air.

"You made a gate?" Jessica gasped. "How did you do that?"

Eagle put her down and pressed her against the wall of the room, opposite the MRI. "It was simple," he responded, now in his familiar Terran form, tendrils snaking out of his body and down the hallway. He seemed more sinister this way than as a seething blob of nanites. More determined. More evil. "The nanites helped me remember what I had forgotten when I fell into the gate and ended up in this hell-hole. We were testing our system that you provided. I was experimenting with holding the gate open long enough to establish a connection that didn't close instantly. I couldn't figure out how to do that." Eagle walked over to the MRI and put his hand on top of the machine, his fingers dissolved and met the other nanites covering the device, then they separated again.

"But once I absorbed your friend, he filled in the gaps, your AI left traces of its code in us, and I realized that I lacked a mineral that is the key to the system. It knows nothing of security. You really should tell it to not trust strange AI" Eagle held up the USB drive that he had taken from the hospital the night he visited. Similar to the one Jessica held in her pocket. "I knew exactly where that mineral was. Right here." Eagle tapped the machine. "Did you know that MRIs use beryllium because it's not magnetic? And so do x-ray machines, and power transmitters. Practically every piece of machinery in this building uses it. And it's exactly the mineral our gate back on Terra is missing."

"You're all powerful now, why didn't you just make your own beryllium? Why did you come here?" Jessica asked, trying to buy some time to come up with a plan; even though her plans had gone completely wrong the whole time she was on Gaia.

Eagle laughed in her twin's voice. "You don't get it, the nanites can't make elements, only restructure existing ones. I had to come here. The rest was elementary. Those solarpunk fools have this building wired with batteries, there is more than enough power to turn my gate on. I just need to test it. Since you are the one that gave me this opportunity, I will allow you to be the only Earthling to travel to four different dimensions."

Jessica barely flinched at the revelation.

"Yes, I know you are from Earth. A whole other planet for me to exploit and conquer."

"I thought you only wanted the truth?" Jessica asked, eyeing the cot that she had slept on two nights ago.

"Well, I'll tell you," Eagle said, his body rising from the tentacles on the floor. He spoke again in the combined voices of everyone he had absorbed. "It's so much more fun being powerful than smart."

Jessica lunged for the cot, breaking out of Eagle's grasp during his monologue. She lifted it over her head and swung it down as hard as she could, it moved an inch then stopped.

"Pathetic," Eagle said, lifting Jessica and shoving her head first into the glowing chamber of the MRI. The green field crackled and the smell of cinnamon filled her nose.

Chapter 51: Old Friends

"Welcome back, Jessica it is… good to see you," a deep baritone voice spoke to her. It was not in a language she natively understood, somewhere in the back of her mind she translated it. Jessica saw a grey hand reach to her through hazy vision. Her ears rang and her stomach churned. Clenching her eyes shut, she reached out her hand and was pulled to her feet. The vibration patch on the back of her neck burned, as if a red-hot poker were pushed into her cervical vertebrae, and she reflexively reached up to it in an effort to stop the pain.

"Do not touch it, the pain will… subside momentarily," the baritone voice instructed. She did what she was told.

"Orvalus? How… how did I get here?" Jessica asked, still groggy, her voice was raspy and hoarse as she coughed out the last sentence.

"I do not know. I was alerted to the gate being activated from an unknown world, and then you… fell through the portal. Are you all right?"

Jessica looked around the room. She was in the library on Bellerophon, the exact place she had appeared six months ago after bouncing through several versions of this very room, each drastically different from the last. "I think so, the patch is having a hard time…" Jessica pointed to the patch on her neck and swooned, Orvalus caught her and held her upright.

"It would appear that the patch has been altered by foreign nanites and you are experiencing vertigo, Jessica. How did you come to be in the transit system? Where are the others? This is not what we expected, nor was it part of the agreement." Orvalus guided Jessica to an awaiting chair and table, which had fruit in a bowl. A large glass of water sat on the table next to it. Jessica hungrily picked up the food and started eating and drinking. The massive form of Orvalus sat across from her, another chair growing from the floor to meet him.

"I didn't come from Terra," Jessica explained, "I was on another planet... err version, it was called Gaia. Really warm place."

"You were directed to stop the spread of Hegemony technology beyond Terra. It has further...escaped you?" Orvalus asked. Jessica could hear the disappointment in his voice.

"Yeah...sorry?" she said, unable to think of anything else to say by way of explanation that didn't sound like an excuse instead of a reason. *Will Rogers once famously said, "Never miss a good chance to shut up."* Her father taught her when she was a child, and she decided this was a time to use it.

"KT will not approve of this obviously. How did you end up on this... Gaia?"

Jessica finished eating a fruit that looked like a banana but tasted like strawberry. It was her favorite from the last time she was in this dimension. Leaning back on the chair, the pain from the patch subsiding, Jessica told the story. When she was finished, Orvalus leaned back in his chair and started laughing. A full-belly laugh. His white and gold tunic, that of the uniform of the "Keeper of the Terran Gate" reflecting the warm light of the floor panels.

"You always get in trouble, do you not, Unbound?" Said a metallic voice from behind her. Jessica spun around to see the android, D417a, standing in the doorway to the library. Its tall metal form, gold-irised eyes, and cat-like whiskers greeted her. Jessica jumped out of her chair and flung herself at the android, wrapping her arms around it. It was the reason she had sacrificed so much the last time they were all on Terra together. It was also the reason why the Terrans and now the Eastern Syndicate had gate technology.

"Dee, I'm sorry," Jessica said looking up at its face, the whiskers flashed a cool blue and white. From experience she knew this meant the android was content. As much as she assumed that AI, the de novo AI --not an uploaded personality emulant like Peek-- would lack emotions, she knew Dee had them.

Dee stepped back from her, giving her space. "You do not need to apologize to me. I was there with you. I know what you have gone through for me, and how much you will go through for all your friends. I never understood why KT did not order us to retrieve my body. It would have known that the technology would easily have been copied. Your species has evolved rapidly, you proved that."

Jessica turned and stepped up to Orvalus, who stood to greet her. "I'm sorry, I forgot to say hello, you picked me off the floor as usual." Wrapping her arms around the massive Takki, she couldn't connect her fingers in the back and contented herself with holding as much as she could; she heard his heart beat through his chest. Orvalus put a massive hand on the back of her head and cradled her. "I missed you too."

Dee spoke from behind the pair, "Administrator Dux is on her way to greet you. I asked her to be present as soon as Orvalus informed me you returned through the gate. I do not know why KT has not appeared yet, although I am sure it has some inscrutable reason."

Jessica stiffened. The two people she least wanted to see, and they were both due to arrive any second. Briefly she wished she were still on Gaia dealing with the enhanced Eagle. Then the memory came rushing back. Jessica ran over to the control panel next to the gate and operated the controls, trying to bring up Gaia's location on the monitor. Nothing she did worked.

"I believe KT has... locked out the system. It does not want any access at the moment," Orvalus said.

"I have to go back. My brother and sister, Katelyn, they need me!" Jessica said, trying another finger combination that also had no effect.

"That will have to wait," Orvalus said as the door to the library slid open, and the lithe form of Administrator Dux stepped in.

Chapter 52: The Pair Arrives

"So, you have returned, Unbound." Administrator Dux bowed to Jessica. Her iridescent purple and orange clothes reflecting the blue light of the portal cast emerald flecks throughout the library. The tall Takki was in charge of all aspects of running Bellerophon City, and was connected to all its information by various electronic devices and communications equipment. Jessica was unnerved by Dux's constant connectivity and devotion to her job, yet she respected her all the same. Jessica bowed to her in response, unsure of how to do it properly, she used the same deference she would to any elder on her mother's side of the family.

"It has not been very long, however. I think this is a testament of your inability to refrain from getting yourself in trouble." Dux said, her mouth curled up into a smirk.

Freezing from the comment, Jessica couldn't decide if it was a dig or compliment. Realizing she was taking too long to respond; she shrugged her shoulders. "Eh, you know me."

"Indeed." Dux pulled out a display screen from her pants and flipped through it, then pressed her earpiece quickly. "KT will be here momentarily. It has a lot it would like to speak to you about."

A chill ran up Jessica's spine, and her lower legs tightened from the anxiety. This was something she had anticipated. She had done the exact thing she was told not to do. One thing she was sure of, however, if KT had wanted her dead or banished, it would already have happened.

Jessica drew a quick breath and jumped in, "Okay, ma'am, can you tell me what it's going to say? I hate to be impertinent, but we have been down this road before. I wait for KT to show up, you are here before it arrives. We wait for a grand entrance and meanwhile the anxiety is killing me. I just need to have things explained to me quickly without hiding anything."

Orvalus looked between the pair. His throat jumped as if he was going to speak, but every time he almost vocalized it, it caught. He merely grunted and breathed heavily.

Administrator Dux raised an eyebrow and stepped back, locking her eyes on Jessica's face. "I would normally not tolerate such an improper line of questioning, but I know that you continue to be held up to standards that you are not accustomed to. Also, the stress of traveling through the gate system might be too much for you to bear given the circumstances. But you must learn to cool your temper, Unbound. It will be your undoing."

"It's gotten me pretty far up to this point." Jessica retorted, then threw her hands on her hips.

"Yes, it has. And yet you continue to be at the clemency of others." KT interrupted from the large monitor, just above the control panel.

Satisfied to finally get the ball rolling, Jessica spun around and bowed, relaxing as she did so. "Hello, KT, it's nice to see you again," she said.

KT's image appeared on the monitor. It bore the amber, more angular face that it was prone to using when it was being overtly logical and pragmatic. Jessica was not a fan of this face, she always associated it with a decision she was not happy with; more robotic, more of an emotionless, de novo, AI than uploaded, emulated Takki she knew it to be. "I did not think I would be seeing you again so soon, Unbound. You continue to prove me wrong." As if to accentuate the point, KT's face switched to its green visage, its lines less austere, more biological. Then, just as quickly, it switched back to amber. "The Gaians have completed a new gate, based on the information the Terrans acquired from you. Because of your arrogance, you have allowed our technology to spread to yet another system. Have you no sense of self-control?"

Jessica's face flushed; her hands shook. "You don't seem to have very good control of your property. I didn't do anything other than show up. Dee came with me to Terra on your orders. It also defended that child based on your laws of behavior. With all due respect, I don't clean up after people. We assumed you would be back to Terra to claim the body and you didn't. That's not my fault." Jessica's stomach did somersaults and she lost feeling to her face, her chest pressed uncomfortably against her heart.

KT's visage switched from amber to green and back several times. It made no sound for several minutes as Jessica's retort hung in the library. Dux kept her eyes on the floor, not engaging either of them. Orvalus watched the pair, his eyes drifting between them.

"So, are you gonna threaten me again? Close off Earth, strand my family?" Jessica started in again the words spilling out, "You don't want me dead; you'd have done it. If you wanted to maroon me, you would have done it. Now that you know where Gaia is, which I don't know how you know, you could shut that down too. There's a certain rhythm to this, and it always ends with a threat to close off Earth, then I end up somewhere I didn't choose again. I know you aren't powerless; I know you can wipe me out from existence the next time I pop into a portal. So, what gives KT? Why all the cloak and dagger? Just spill it."

Chapter 53: Explanation

Jessica stared at the shifting form of KT dominating the main screen of the five library control room monitors.

"You already know why I need to do this, human. The space-time continuum in your part of the multiverse is unstable. The more traffic that comes in and out of that region the further it weakens. At some point the very fabric of reality could come apart and we would be responsible for it. I am trying to prevent that from happening. That is all. I hold no malice for you or your world. I am trying to save all of us."

Without asking, Jessica sat down. "I understand that you've told me a dozen times already. I want to know why every universe I enter has a version of me there. But not the same version, there is no exact copy, and sometimes they are even dead. Why do I keep ending up like this, and why do you and I keep going at it?"

KT again held still a moment; the amber face motionless on the main display. Orvalus leaned against the wall and rubbed his chin, awaiting the emulant's reply.

"The reason," KT began, "is because of the state your mind was in when you stepped into the portal. It set in motion the chaining of all the quantum realities that were possible for you to exist in. The multiverse was set into a deterministic cascade in which all the possible outcomes contained a similar proton spin mirroring your universe perfectly, even to the exact moment of the Big Bang."

Jessica squinted her eyes, trying to get the stream of information as quickly as KT described it. She understood deterministic systems and chaos theory, at least as much as Professor Sterling had taught her. Jessica held still for a moment, then responded, "There is no 'me' in this universe. There isn't even an Earth."

KT flashed amber and green quickly, then settled on amber.

"Correct, there is no 'you.' However, the atoms that make up who you are and the planet you come from do exist. They did not coalesce into the system that you were born into, but are incorporated into the planets orbiting..." KT paused, Jessica shifted in her seat. "HD162826, in the constellation Hercules."

"The... stellar sibling?" Jessica's eyes widened and her eyebrow raised. "Sol's sibling star? We were both from the same interstellar cloud. There aren't planets there, well at least not in my universe anyway."

"Your knowledge of astronomy is considerable, Unbound. You are a credit to your professor's teachings." KT said, prompting Jessica to blush.

"Not really, when things are slow at the restaurant, I scroll Wikipedia endlessly. I can't really get into the stuff the others are talking about, it's too superficial."

KT did not respond, and Jessica fought off the urge to go on a tangent to keep the conversation moving along, like she was speaking to someone of higher social status at a cocktail party. She'd rather deal with Eagle and the possible loss of her entire family than be in one of those situations. She focused back on the matter at hand, "Okay, so the masses have to be the same, I guess. Why am I finding all these universes where I exist in one form or another though? Except this one?"

"I...I do not know, human. Perhaps there is something else in the determinism that is too small to reconnoiter, or an emergent property that I am currently not aware of," KT said curtly. Orvalus grunted and stood rigid. Jessica scoffed in her chair.

"I thought you knew everything?" Jessica said.

KT flipped to green and then back to amber. "To be able to predict all the permutations of the multiverse would require that I have the computing power of the entire multiverse, add the fact that I would also need to calculate the differences in N number of probable outcomes and the number quickly approaches infinity. You are here because you are here. Every universe you enter contains you because your mind was focused on something when you entered. Perhaps you wanted a place where you didn't exist but wanted the reassurance you would find something familiar."

"I ... made the multiverse?" Jessica asked, gobsmacked.

"No, human, you did not *make* the multiverse. Your mind forced the connection to all possible universes where you could exist. This one happened to be one of them, as well as an infinity of others."

"So, I exist in an infinity of universes?" Jessica asked. She was testing the emulant this time.

"You know that for a fact, human. I know from your mind that the concept is no leap in logic for you. The many-worlds theorem predicts it to be so. The waveform does not collapse. I know you are testing me, but you must try harder than that," KT answered.

Did an emulate just burn me? Was that pride?

Jessica remembered what Peek had told her the last time she was on Bellerophon: KT was once a Takki, the same race as Poke and Orvalus, and uploaded herself when the dimensional gates began to degenerate and break down. She gave literally everything she was to protect reality. Enough of her personality must have been emulated as well, and it must break out occasionally.

Jessica paused for a moment, giving the emulant a chance to recover, if it needed it. "So, what are we going to do? You held me in a transit bubble, you know where I was coming from, and could probably figure the reason. What is your plan?" Jessica asked, knowing that she was at KT's mercy.

"I am going to block all access to Earth, your vibration, and that from Gaia. You will not be able to return from this gate, or from Gaia," it said.

"And how are you gonna do that? You can't control Gaia, you can't make them do anything," Jessica retorted.

"Can't I? I bounced you here. I now know the signature from their universe and from Terra. If I detect anything heading toward Earth, I will divert it here," KT said coolly.

That means you are always watching Earth, you will always have a connection, even if you say otherwise. Jessica kept that to herself and simply nodded in acquiescence.

Chapter 54: Ultimatum

"However, human, I also need you," KT said after a momentary pause. "With the Terrans and now the Gaian's possessing our technology, I need to better monitor and restrict what they are doing instead of being proscriptive. I also cannot risk further contamination of our culture by sending anyone from The Hegemony into other worlds. Poke and Peek have seen too much, and they cannot integrate back into our society without creating damage. As soon as I allow them back into the system, Peek would reconnect and upload everything it knows, and that information would be instantly accessible to the entire Hegemony. I cannot have that. We already have a problem with separatists."

Unable to help herself, Jessica's mouth swung open with a gasp. "Those are real?" she asked, recalling when he mentioned it briefly to her the last time she was on Bellerophon.

"Yes, Unbound, they are becoming a problem." Orvalus answered.

"Indeed," KT said, "a faction of The People has broken off from The Hegemony and are determined to find the Lost Colonists; disconnected colonies in other dimensions. Their locations were lost during The Trials," KT reminded Jessica.

"Wait, so they know about The Trials? You let them know about that? Wouldn't that shake their faith to know that you lost control of the gate system and marooned people in other universes?

KT switched to amber. "All of the people know our entire history. I do not hide anything from them. The Trials are part of our history."

"You just said that you don't want Peek reconnected because of the chaos that knowledge could cause? Isn't that hypocritical? Don't you want to find them? I don't get it?" Jessica asked.

"Because, human," KT's form switched to her green face, showing the slightest emotion, "those colonies have been cut off since before

The Trials, and would not understand our culture as it is now. The separatists want to find them, and reintegrate them as soon as possible."

Jessica bristled, "So what? What is wrong with the truth? If you can monitor Earth, Terra, and Gaia, how can you not find your own culture connected to your own system?"

"Further," KT continued, ignoring Jessica's question, "we do not know the level of their culture, or how they have progressed. They could pose a danger to us and our stability. We cannot allow that without understanding them first and allowing me to prepare The People."

Jessica cut to the chase. "So, you want the little Earth girl to do your recon for you and test them, don't you? It's why you'll cut off Earth, but not the other two dimensions. Now you have the resources of the Terran gate, but also the guise of not having to use the Hegemony system. They won't know it's from you if we gate over on our own. What am I? Your 'chosen one?'" Jessica's head shook as she spat out her realization.

KT waited a moment, her image vacillating between green and amber. Finally, KT answered, green face showing, "You are perceptive, human. However, you chose the universe, not me. This situation would still exist without you, and there is no prophecy predicting your arrival. You are merely the best candidate and a fortuitous coincidence."

Jessica thought a moment, then responded, "I'll do it under a few conditions: one last visit before you shut the gate to Earth down. I have to get my mom. I can't leave her there all alone. She'll die without me, if I don't come back, she will just … die. I need to be there within a week after I left the last time. And Katelyn, I need to bring her too, I love her too much to abandon her. I want to take them from Earth to Terra, and I'm presuming they would need to come through here. One last time, and I will never bring Earth up again, and I will never ask to return. Then I need you to send me back to Gaia, right when I left. My friends are there, and I need to stop Eagle. Otherwise, he will be a threat to you eventually and you might not be able to stop him. You get your errand girl; you get to close Earth off. I will give up my homeworld and everything I know and do what you want. Just give me my mom and Katelyn, and let me save my friends. I won't do anything knowing that I have abandoned them."

"Unacceptable, Unbound. I cannot allow that, the instability—"

"Yeah, I know about your goddamned *instability*," Jessica shot up from her seat, cutting the emulant off. "But none of that is my fault. I didn't experiment with gates like your scientists did. I didn't disrupt spacetime. I didn't turn my back on my own people. I do everything I can to make sure my loved ones are taken care of. I'm not going to go get the witch's broomstick for you simply because you are too afraid to do it yourself. If you don't give me what I want, you don't get what you want. We call that compromise where I come from. If no one is happy, but everything is satisfied, it a fair deal."

Jessica stopped talking and stared at KT's green visage. The silence hung in the library like a lead weight.

Administrator Dux, who had been quietly standing in the doorway to the library to this point shifted her feet and cleared her throat. As far as Jessica knew, no one had ever spoken to KT so. The emulant's image switched to amber. "This is acceptable... Unbound."

Chapter 55: Homeward Bound

"Also, I need him to come with me," Jessica said, pointing to Orvalus. Grinning to herself at the realization of making yet another demand, what her mom called "pushing her trip." She leaned into it, "If I go back and tell everyone what is going on without proof, they won't believe me. I won't be able to get them to come."

"Are you in the habit of lying to your family? Why would they have cause to not believe you?" KT asked.

Jessica's face burned. KT had deliberately misled her when she first arrived on Bellerophon, convincing her that she was going home when she was, in fact, being sent to Terra as a spy. Jessica swallowed her emotions and calmed herself. It would not do at this point to call her benefactor a hypocrite again. She cleared her throat then spoke, "KT, I can tell you for a fact if my mom sees this guy with me, she will believe me instantly. You should know how much he would stand out on my world."

KT said, "Of course I do, that is why we have been using disguises since we first found your world after The Singularity. Gatekeeper Orvalus, do you agree to assist Jessica, and retrieve her mother and friend, and then return promptly?"

Orvalus bowed, "I do, KT. I will make sure they are all safe and I will return as quickly as possible."

Administrator Dux walked over to one of the alcoves in the Library, it slid open noiselessly. She reached in and pulled out a pair of blue jeans, black boots, a black hoodie and beanie. "We created these the last time you were gone, Unbound, in case Orvalus needed to come through the gate to extract you." Dux walked over to Orvalus who took the clothes with a bow. He instantly stripped out of his jumper.

Jessica flipped around as quickly as possible. "Geez what is it with you people? Don't you have any kind of modesty?" Jessica looked straight ahead, only to be confronted by the large monitor as well as the smaller ones. All of which displayed Orvalus, now completely naked, putting his boots on first.

"Can't you ..." Jessica clenched her eyes shut.

"It is ... okay, Jessica." Orvalus said, "we do not have a sense of embarrassment that your world does. We only wear clothes to show designation and to keep ourselves warm when needed."

Jessica shook her head quickly. "Yeah yeah, you're all evolved and whatnot. But you're doing it wrong, dude. Pants on first."

"Oh ... thank you."

Jessica nodded, listening to him pull on his disguise. He worked slowly. Occasionally he would ask, "How does ...? Why would you ...?"

"Perhaps Unbound can be of assistance?" KT asked. Jessica couldn't be sure, but she thought she detected humor in its voice.

"I am dressed," Orvalus said. "You may open your eyes."

Jessica unclenched her eyes and regarded Orvalus. Keen to get moving, she dropped the pretext and walked up to the large Takki, zipped the fly of his pants, pulled the hoodie out of the waistband, and motioned that he pull the beanie up further on his head.

"I had to dress Poke too, it's like you guys have never worn a two piece before." Jessica shook her head.

"My nephew does not have the same grasp on the world as I do. He ... needs help more than he lets on. It is why we chose Peek to assist him."

Jessica stood back, looking Orvalus in his green eyes. "He's your nephew?" She looked down and shook her head, then back up at Orvalus. "Wait, but you said I was your niece from Atlantis when I was on Bellerophon the first time. He's from Atlantis. I don't know whether to be flattered or sad that you weren't very creative." Jessica laughed, then hugged Orvalus. "Why didn't you tell me?"

"I did not want to confuse you more, you needed to ... focus, and I needed to invent a cover story for your obvious ignorance of our culture quickly." Orvalus smiled.

Jessica stood back, "Okay, I think you look good enough, we're going to be in Jersey City, so I don't think anyone is really going to be looking for aliens." She turned to KT, "You are going to send me home again, right? We can't go all the way from the Ploutonion, I don't know how to get from Turk... Anatolia by myself."

"I will send you back exactly to the spot you arrived from. Do not worry, Unbound," KT reassured.

Jessica pointed to Orvalus, then tapped the back of her neck. "He needs a patch."

Administrator Dux pressed a contact on the control cabinet of the gate. A drawer slid open and in it several dozen vibration patches lay. She took one out and handed it to Orvalus who slapped it onto the back of his neck.

"Let us ... go!" he said.

"When were you off-world last?" Jessica asked him.

"Never!" He responded, then grinned broadly.

"How can you be the keeper of the Terran Gate and never visit Terra?"

"That was Dee's function. I was only needed if something were to happen here on Bellerophon. Dee never went alone, and so my services were never needed."

The portal snapped into life and Administrator Dux ushered them to the gate.

"That's why you were so bored, and why you started this whole adventure with me?" Jessica asked, then smiled.

"Yes, and I would do it again."

The pair stepped through the portal.

Chapter 56: Earth

Jessica landed on the cold concrete floor and started up at the blinding fluorescent light. It blazed down on her like the blue-white sun of Bellerophon; she took a deep breath, all she could smell was mold, lubricant --which she presumed was to keep the fence enclosure for her storage area from rusting-- and dirt. At least she hoped it was dirt. It smelled like home. Quickly, she pulled herself off the floor and out of the trajectory of the portal. Within moments, the hulking form of Orvalus came tumbling through. He smashed into the chain-link fence, bending it in as it absorbed the force of his enormous body. Despite herself, Jessica laughed.

"This is not how I am accustomed to arriving … anywhere," the large alien said as he extracted himself from the fence.

"Nope, not too ceremonious for the Keeper of the Terran Gate, now is it?"

Orvalus stood up and fixed his clothes to the best of his ability then looked around at the cramped space. "As a reminder, we must make haste, your friends are still engaged in … defeating this Eagle back on Gaia. You must be anxious to get back and help them."

"You bet I am," Jessica said, stepping out of the chain-link storage area and motioning Orvalus to follow. "But I can't go back the way I came in there; Eagle was right on top of me. I don't know how I'd get out of there … he's got so much, so much tech."

"We will find a way. There is always another way." Orvalus said, standing behind Jessica as she pushed the call button for the elevator to her apartment.

Jessica raised her left eyebrow, remembering Gabrielle and Administrator Dux both using the same aphorism and wondered if it was a universal sentiment or another side-effect of her creating the multiverse, her multiverse. Regardless, she appreciated his optimism and threw her arms around. Orvalus hugging him tight just as the elevator door dinged open. An old woman stood there, holding an empty laundry basket, clearly embarrassed at having come in at the wrong time.

"Oh, hi Mrs. Ramirez, how are you?" Jessica asked, pulling away from Orvalus, her face flushing red.

"Fine," the old woman said as she stepped out of the elevator, holding her laundry basket between them. Jessica spent no time attempting to explain or even introduce her companion. She grabbed him by the hoodie and pulled him into the car, slamming the call button for her floor and hitting the close button.

"Okay, this might be a bit weird. I don't know how she's gonna react," Jessica said as they rode the elevator up. She counted floors on the display and nodded each time a new floor ticked off.

"Why would you not know? She is your ... best friend."

"Yes, but when I showed up on Terra with a bunch of other aliens, she, well that one Katelyn, almost used a stun gun on me." Jessica didn't look at Orvalus when she explained, her eyes were fixed on the display.

"I understand," Orvalus said. He looked at the number display as well. "Question, what is this 'witch's broomstick?"

Jessica laughed without looking at him. "*The Wizard of Oz*. Dorothy had to go kill The Wicked Witch of the West and bring back her broomstick as proof because The Wizard was a humbug and really had no power."

"I see," Orvalus said. "KT, is not a wizard."

"And I'm not the one with green skin," Jessica said.

Orvalus looked down squinting, then back up at the display. "Yes. I... do not understand."

The car reached her floor and Jessica held her breath as the door opened. Her legs shook as she walked down the hallway to the apartment. Usually coming home was relaxing, this time she didn't know if she could contain her anxiety.

"Are you all right?" Orvalus asked, putting his massive hand on her shoulder.

"Yeah, I just...I'm afraid of either answer, and how she is gonna take an actual extra-dimensional alien in her apartment. No biggie." Jessica reached forward and grabbed the doorknob, forgetting her keys. After two tries turning the knob, she knocked. A knock that she always used to let Katelyn know it was her.

"I swear, girl, you would forget your own head," came Katelyn's voice from behind the door. In a moment it clicked open and Katelyn Finnerty, Katelyn Prime, stood before her. The redhead looked the pair up and down.

"Ah, so this is Orvalus. It's about time you showed up." Katelyn stepped back into the apartment and pivoted to the kitchen, right next to the door. "Can I get you something? We are all out of spaghetti and dumplings."

Jessica stood in the doorway, dumbfounded. Her throat twitched as she desperately tried to speak. Katelyn filled up a glass with water and turned back to the pair. "Are we gonna do this inside, or do you want to talk about all of this in the hallway?"

"H—How ... how ..." Jessica stammered. Orvalus gently pushed her from behind, giving her the extra impetus to walk into the apartment.

"Babe, how long have we known each other?" Katelyn asked, handing Jessica the water, and the returning to the sink to fill up another glass for Orvalus.

"I— this ..." Jessica still could not wrap her brain around what was happening.

Katelyn handed the glass to Orvalus, who took it with a bow. Then she walked into the living room and sat on the couch.

"You talk in your sleep. You always have. You've been going on for the last six months about aliens, KT, your dad, and me. I thought you were having nightmares again like you did when your dad died, but even those weren't as detailed as these were. I talked to your mom, Professor Sterling, even the staff at the restaurant. Everyone knows that you have been out of touch lately. Like you're here but you aren't. We thought maybe the 'bad grade' you got last semester pushed you too far and you were making things up to release the tension." Katelyn patted the couch next to her, and asked the pair to sit down. Orvalus quickly did, taking the blue chair across from the couch, followed by the slowly advancing Jessica. Katelyn laughed.

"Relax babe, it's not that big of a deal." Katelyn looked over at the alien sitting in her living room. "Well, I mean it is. It's a BIG deal." She laughed again. "But it doesn't mean I think you're crazy, or that I love you any less."

Despite herself, and all that she had accomplished in the last six months, hiding this from Katelyn Prime, but being able to share everything with Terran Katelyn bothered her. She felt like she was betraying her best friend. Cheating on her... with her. It made no sense and now that everything was exposed, she burst into tears. The release was exactly what she needed, and she realized just how much it had bothered her. Orvalus stood up to help, and Katelyn waved him off. She pulled a tissue from the box on the table and handed it to Jessica.

"So, you're the 'Unbound' eh? Hopper of dimensions, Ambassador to Terra, blah blah," Katelyn quipped as Jessica blew her nose.

"Yeah, some role model, huh?" she asked.

"Well, you aren't as good as me in physics, but I think you can handle the role." Katelyn winked.

Jessica smiled and punched her in the arm. "By the way, it's Poke who loves spaghetti and dumplings and has the big appetite. Orvalus has never been to Earth. You got your aliens mixed."

Katelyn nodded. "So why are you here? You've been gone again, obviously."

Jessica took a deep breath and started relaying the story, relieved that she didn't have to explain the last six months, only the last six days. Katelyn looked downcast when Jessica got to the part about the agreement with KT and was already prepared with her response when the story finished.

"I can't go with you, babe." Katelyn shook her head.

"Why?" Jessica implored, a fresh round of tears welling in her eyes.

"I kinda like being the only one of me. I think if there were two of us, we'd fight all the time. Besides, I don't like the notion of never being able to come home again. My family is still in Florida, they'd miss me if I was suddenly gone."

Jessica felt guilty at being selfish enough to assume Katelyn would pick up everything and leave her home. This Katelyn wasn't thrust into anything, Jessica had no right to infringe on her desires.

"I don't want to lose you. It would be just like losing Dad again." Jessica said, trying to convince her, but torn with her emotions.

"Babe, you think I'm okay with losing you? Imagine how the other … *me* felt when the other you —this is confusing— died. She lost her best friend and didn't even get to say goodbye. At least I'd get that. Besides," Katelyn pointed to Jessica's room, "I get all of your shit because you can't take this with you." She smiled roguishly.

Jessica laughed, Orvalus leaned back in his chair and shook his head.

"There really is no way you are going to come back? KT is closing Earth off? Forever?" Katelyn asked Jessica.

Orvalus answered for her, "That is correct, Katelyn. Unless something can be found to repair the damage from The Trials. I am truly sorry that we caused this to happen. We did --do not want to damage spacetime."

Katelyn laughed, "I'll bet all the inter-dimensional beings say that. I tell you what, you go get Mom, and convince her that taking her back, into a fight, is a good idea. I'll be sure to say goodbye. She already taught me the dumpling recipe anyway." Katelyn winked.

Chapter 57: Mom's Place

"Ma, it's okay. It's me." With outstretched hands Jessica stood in front of her mother, who recoiled back into the living room and quickly picked up her cane. She brandished it with a speed and severity Jessica had never seen before, as if her mother had been an assassin in some former life, or parallel universe. Jessica stepped back, bumping into Orvalus, who gave way behind her enough to not be rude, but firm enough to let her know he was there. Jessica was acutely aware that she had just walked into her mother's apartment with an alien and that she also bore a glowing patch on her neck and a science fiction communication band strapped to her wrist. She was overwhelmed with the joy of seeing her mother, within a week of leaving her the last time. Maybe meeting Orvalus like this wasn't a good idea on second thought.

"Jess! What the hell is this?! Who--*what* is that?" her mother exclaimed, gripping her cane, ready to swing it. The muscles in her forearms were taut like steel wires.

"Ma! Ma, I can explain. He's with me!" Jessica thumbed over her shoulder to which Orvalus bowed.

"Ma'am, it is a... pleasure to meet the mother of The Unbound."

"Unbound?" Ai Li gasped, her face contorted in fear and suspicion.

"Ma, please, there is something I have to tell you."

Ai Li's hands quivered and tears welled in her eyes, which darted between her daughter and the large, grey-skinned alien standing behind her. "Please tell me you are safe. I don't-- your father-- I—"

Jessica ran to her and wrapped her arms around her mother's smaller frame, who presently collapsed into her arms. "I got you Ma, let me get you to the couch."

Ai Li silently shook her head, dropping her cane.

"Do you require a refreshment? Perhaps some water would help?" Orvalus asked, giving them space but staying within helping distance.

Ai Li nodded to the credenza under the TV on the far wall, "J.D. make it a double."

Orvalus looked around the room, shifting his eyes.

"I am sorry … Jay Dee? Dee is not …" Orvalus looked to Jessica for help.

"Not, Dee silly. Jay Dee, Jack Daniels. It's a drink, whiskey. Over there beneath the monitor." Jessica motioned to the credenza. "The brown bottle. Pour a little in the small glass, then twice as much in another. Bring them both to me." Jessica looked back at her mother and smiled. Ai Li's eyes darted between the pair, but her hands, clutching Jessica's upper arms, no longer bore white knuckles.

"Ma, you shouldn't drink. You know that," Jessica said.

"And you shouldn't terrify your mother like this."

Orvalus came back to the pair, with two glasses expertly filled. "This one is for you… Mrs. Chao," he handed her the half glass, bowing his head slightly and dropping his eyes to the floor. Ai Li perked up a bit, the barest hint of a bemused smile on her lips.

"And for you, Jessica," Orvalus said, speaking in Standard. At the sound, Ai Li downed the drink and shuddered. She placed the empty glass on the floor and looked up at the pair. "Okay, tell me who you are and why you are here," she demanded.

"Are both of your parents so … direct?" Orvalus asked Jessica.

"Both?" Ai Li interrupted.

Jessica sat down. "Ma, this is my good friend, Orvalus, Keeper of the Terran Gate. He is an extraterrestrial from the planet Bellerophon."

Orvalus bowed at the waist, low and slow, in deference to Ai Li.

"Technically, I am an extra-dimensional, since this is not my universe, and Bellerophon is the English translation."

Ai Li sat up, taking it all in.

"Ma, there was this portal in the basement …" For the next twenty minutes Jessica gave her mother the highlights of what had happened in the last six months, ending with her getting pushed into the green portal by Eagle and being diverted by KT into the Hegemony gate system.

"Ay ya," her mother's eyes blinked rapidly, and she stole a sip of Jessica's whiskey that she had so far not touched. "If there are — were two of you, and another … your father … is there another me?" Ai Li looked up into her daughter's eyes. Orvalus stepped back after collecting her glass.

"Yeah Ma, there is another you, she's on Terra. She doesn't know about me yet," Jessica said with a sad hint in her voice.

"Jess, she should know that, that's not very nice of you." Ai Li's left eyebrow arched.

"I know Ma, but I didn't want to," Jessica put her hand on the back of her neck, ostensibly to check on her newly-modified vibration patch, but it was really out of embarrassment.

"Because you thought I'd be jealous?" Ai Li asked, her voice even and deep.

"No, because I didn't want to replace you in my mind. It feels like cheating on you or something. What if I liked her more, or really hated her? It's not something people get shown every day." Jessica explained, quickly.

"Is your father… the same?" Ai Li asked.

"Pretty much. Some things are different, but not a lot."

"I think you owe it to her. Her husband knows. Holding that information is dishonest, whether you are comfortable with it or not."

Ai Li stood up and straightened her shirt. "And I think we need to go see her right away. What have you planned to tell Katelyn? Or will you hide that from her too?"

Jessica felt a pang of guilt, and reluctantly answered, "I already asked her, Ma. She wants to stay."

Ai Li nodded. "Her family. Of course. I couldn't ask her to go either. Are we going back there? Can I say goodbye to her?"

Jessica nodded.

"Okay, let me get a few things. I'm sure the other me has all my stuff there. Although I don't know what versions she has. Hmm, it's best if I bring…" Ai Li's voice trailed off as she went into her bedroom, stepping lightly, without her cane.

Jessica sat back down on the chair, and put her head in her hands.

"Jessica, we should not linger, you still have to return to Gaia," Orvalus said.

Jessica nodded.

"Are you avoiding it? Are you worried that you will not succeed?"

"I don't know. I think I'm missing something and I don't know what it is. A person, an object, something. Eagle just completely had the upper hand there. All we have is Tony and an EMP bomb."

Orvalus allowed himself the seat and looked at Jessica. He thought for a few moments before he spoke. "I will have to come with you then, I will be able to tip the scales in our favor." He said, standing up.

Jessica looked at him, her eyes were puffy and tired. "That's okay, I was gonna ask Dee to come with us. We don't need you risking yourself. It can make a backup, you can't."

"I appreciate your …consideration for my well-being. But I am its muscle, not the other way around."

Jessica wasn't sure, but she thought she heard pride in his voice. "I can't ask you to do that." Jessica shook her head.

"You are not asking. I am volunteering."

Ai Li came back a minute later with a black duffle filled with bric-a-brac. "Okay, let's go," she said, putting her black sneakers on, grabbing her cane, and heading out the door.

"Ma, why is this bag so long, and pointy?" Jessica asked, pointing to the protruding end of the bag.

"Oh," Ai Li said, looking at the bag nonchalantly. "That's my sword, it's balanced for my hand. I can't ask her to share, that's not right."

Chapter 58: Goodbye, Old Friend

Once in the elevator, Orvalus looked at the bag, his solid green eyes tracing over its length. "You are not … concealing the weapon properly, Mrs. Chao. Will you not be noticed?"

"Eh, who's gonna stop an old Chinese woman with a bag? Besides," Ai Li put her cane on top of the bag, overlapping the sword, "I'm no threat," she said, keeping her eyes absentmindedly looking at the readout on the elevator.

Orvalus glanced over to Jessica, who raised her eyes and tilted her head slightly. "Now I see where you get it from," he whispered.

"Her father was the one who had the defiant streak, I could never get him to settle on anything," Ai Li said. "Tell him to do something and he fought it like a little kid. Make it important to him, and he'd do it for so long, even I'd get tired of it. Disciplined was not the first word I'd use to describe him." Ai Li hung her head and took a deep breath, then lifted it back up. "Anyway, gonna be weird to see … him again. This might be hard for me to do."

Jessica reached over and grabbed her mother's hand. "I know, Ma. You don't have to meet if you don't want. I'm sure we can get you another place close by, or back down in D.C. with your family?"

The elevator came to a stop and the doors slowly opened. "No, that will still be her family. I need to make my own way."

Ai Li stepped out into the vestibule of her apartment building, the one she had moved into when her husband died. "Do you think this building has space? It might be easier," Ai Li said, her eyes darted and her lip curled into a frown.

"I will get you in here Ma, I'm sure. Well, if it exists, we didn't go down the street the last time I was there."

Ai Li smiled.

The three headed down the street to Katelyn's apartment in the warm April sunshine. Ai Li asked questions about Jessica's adventures, what Gaia was like, how it felt to be on an alien world. Jessica enjoyed the conversation and was relieved that Ai Li seemed excited to be going. It was a trait both of them possessed; give her a chance to go someplace new and exciting, and she would have a bag packed in an hour. Kevin, Jessica's Earth father, would call it, "desperate to sleep in a strange bed syndrome." But it wasn't the bed, it was the adventure.

Katelyn let them up to the apartment and let Ai Li take whatever she wanted from Jessica's room.

"We need to get back, Jessica," Orvalus said once they had decided on who got what from the room. A second bag was packed full of Jessica's things that Ai Li said were family heirlooms.

"Wait, before you go," Katelyn said, then rushed into her room and back out, green hairband in her hand.

"I want you to have this, I don't know why, but I found it out in the hallway the other day. It smelled like you were burning those candles again. I dunno, it made me think of you." Katelyn shrugged.

Jessica had never seen her at a loss for words before, and she choked up looking at her.

"Goddammit, don't make me cry, babe. Get your shit and get outta here, okay?" Katelyn said when she saw the tears welling in her friend's eyes.

Jessica wrapped her arms around her and pulled tight, "I love you. Take care of yourself. I will get back as soon as I can… if I can. I'll find a way."

"I know," Katelyn whispered in her ear as they embraced.

"Goodbye, Mom, thanks for being there, always," Katelyn said, breaking off her hug and taking Ai Li's hand.

"You're a great woman, I've always considered you part of the family. You'll always be in my heart," Ai Li said.

Orvalus cleared his throat to move the conversation along. "Ladies, we really need to get going. We are not sure if the gates are synced properly to Gaia. Time is… wasting." Orvalus bowed to Katelyn and moved to the door.

Katelyn shook her head and waved them out. She promptly grabbed the glass of wine she had poured for herself and climbed out onto the fire escape, locking her gaze on the Manhattan skyline. Jessica could see her back shuddering; she knew she was crying. The three left, closing the door quietly behind them.

Chapter 59: The Last Time

"Okay, Ma, this is going to be a little weird," Jessica said as they approached the chain-link storage area where the portal had opened six months ago, and in which she had returned in the last two hours. "It's gonna feel like you have too much static on you, and you will get a bit dizzy. When we arrive, I'll give you a vibration patch like mine. It will sync you up to the vibrations on Bellerophon. Then we will have to do it for Terra once we get there." Jessica rolled her eyes and shook her head. "It's crazy, I know. Three planets and as many dimensions in the same day." Her thoughts drifted to her friends on yet another dimension that she was desperate to get back to, and in the middle of a fight she still had no idea of how to win.

"I will go first," Orvalus said, then stepped in front of the women. "I am sure that KT--" as he spoke, Jessica's comm band lit up, and Administrator Dux's voice cracked over the connection.

"Gatekeeper, can you hear me? Unbound? Are you ready to return?"

How did she get the signal?

Jessica's eyebrows furrowed over the thought that *this* might be the last time she would see her homeworld; the musty basement of her apartment building. She still couldn't forget the point that KT would never really stop watching Earth and took solace in the fact that someday she might get back home, despite all the assurances to the contrary.

Orvalus spoke, "We hear you, Administrator, we are ... ready to return. Please activate the portal at your convenience."

"Portal? I thought there was a gate here somewhere. Don't you travel by gates?" Ai Li asked.

"They do, gate to gate is the best way, but you can open portals that aren't gate dependent. It's hard though, harder than the technology for the gate system itself."

"This is what Eagle wants? To be able to open a portal wherever he wants?" Ai Li asked.

"Something like that. He doesn't have a network, and it's probably more 'hacker' credit for him if he can pop them open at will."

Ai Li shook her head.

Their hair stood on end as the lights in the room dimmed. A glowing, gunmetal-blue spot grew on the wall. Jessica cleared the boxes as far away from it as possible just in time for the portal to open.

"You stuck your head in that? Are you crazy?" Ai Li said.

"Well, actually I couldn't see it, it was just a space." Jessica shrugged.

"I've failed you," Ai Li replied, a smirk growing on her lips.

"I am prepared to step through," Orvalus said, taking hold of Jessica's duffel bag. "Mrs. Chao, you should follow me, and Jessica can bring up the rear. In case you need … encouragement."

Ai Li shook her head and raised her eyebrow. A look Jessica inherited in spades.

"Ready to receive," Administrator Dux said.

Without hesitation, Orvalus stepped through the portal and vanished. Jessica realized at that moment that KT trusted her more than she probably deserved, knowing that all Jessica had to do was refuse to enter the portal and it would be as if she never left six months earlier. She also knew that all her friends and family on Gaia would be facing Eagle alone. A problem that she was responsible for. Resigned to her fate, Jessica moved her mother forward.

"Okay, Ma. You go next. Don't worry, you'll be fine. Orvalus will be on the other side of the portal as well as Administrator Dux and KT. I'll be right behind you."

Ai Li looked around the basement, and clutched her duffel tighter. Her lip quivered and tears flooded her eyes.

"I…can't… your father is here… I can't leave him."

Jessica leaned forward and hugged her tightly.

"Ma, some of Dad's ashes are in my duffel, he's... well he's already there." Jessica felt guilty at sneaking part of Kevin through the portal before the rest of the family, but she knew this would help her mother move along.

Ai Li laughed through a sniffle. "I've got the rest here too," she said.

"With a sword," Jessica said. They both laughed at the absurdity of the situation. Jessica wondered if her father was now the first person to posthumously travel through multiple dimensions. A quiet fear crept into the recesses of her mind, *What if I've split his soul?*

"Ladies, I am here, we are awaiting your arrival," Orvalus's voice crackled over the comm band.

"Right, sorry, just saying goodbye," Jessica said, letting her mother go. "I'm right behind you," she said, pointing her mother to the glowing field in front of her.

Ai Li held her breath, and slowly stepped in, when enough of her body cleared the event horizon, she disappeared.

Jessica looked around the basement, taking in as much of it as possible. She looked down at the plastic cups and makeshift poker she created when she first entered the portal. The urge to stay was overpowering, but she forced it down like an errant thought.

"Holy hell, this is something. I'm here sweetie, come through," her mother's voice crackled over the comm band. The truth of the situation suddenly became both real and surreal, and in the deepest part of her. Her mother was in another dimension, she wasn't dreaming this. Her last familial connection to Earth was severed, and Jessica jumped with excitement.

Taking one last look around the room, she took a deep breath, not to steel herself, but to remember the smell of her homeworld as best she could. She had no idea if she'd ever be back, and this time it felt real.

"Let's do this," she said, and stepped into the light.

Chapter 60: Pit Stop

Jessica stepped out of the gate and into the familiar confines of the Library. Dee was there, facing the portal, and her mother stood across the room chatting pleasantly with Administrator Dux, who laughed softly. Jessica's mind raced as she tried to figure out how her mother could so easily get the administrator to be relaxed enough to laugh when Jessica could barely get her to crack a smile on several occasions. Maybe it was the severity of her situation every time she had met the tall Takki, or the possibility that she was always under too much pressure to relax enough herself and couldn't be as personable as she would have liked. After a moment, Jessica shook off all those thoughts, and remembered that Ai Li was just better at talking to people than she was.

Orvalus worked the controls of the portal system as KT's shifting form appeared on the large monitor.

"Orvalus has informed me that he will be returning to Gaia with you, having volunteered to assist you in your dealings with Eagle," Dee said.

Jessica nodded. "I need some extra help. I thought about asking you, but he made a better case. I'm glad KT allowed it, but I think it's in all of our best interests. I know he's got other things to do, I'm just 'borrowing' him."

Dee stood back briefly, as if it were offended at the suggestion that it was not capable of providing support. Its whiskers flashed blue momentarily, then returned to a blue and white pattern.

"I would not be able to help you in a physical altercation, as you know. Unless you were in danger. Knowing that you could potentially be in danger would compel me to act first," Dee explained.

Jessica studied him for a moment. "But, doesn't you knowing that I will be in danger compel you to come to my aid now? Before we even leave?"

Dee froze, its gold-irised eyes flashed blue, along with its whiskers. "I… I see… I cannot…"

"Gotcha." Jessica said, then smiled.

"D417a is under orders to not assist you in your mission on Gaia." KT explained, its voice coming from everywhere and nowhere in the library. "I cannot have it run the risk of getting stuck on yet another planet and having more technology leak out of our control. More lives could be lost. Whereas Gatekeeper Orvalus is—"

"Expendable," Jessica interrupted.

"Something like that," Orvalus said, lifting Jessica's duffel bag and bringing it to the quietly pulsing gate.

"How am I going to get back without ending up in the same place I started? Eagle had me like a sitting duck. There was nothing I could do." Jessica asked, running her hand along the control cabinet. "Can you put me somewhere to give me an advantage? Like the other side of a wall or something?"

"The portal opened on Gaia is a fixed point. We do not know the geology of the location well enough to place you with pinpoint accuracy," Dee said, finally able to overcome its struggle with the Three Laws and function again. "You could end up in the floor, or a wall, or a hundred feet in the air. We could not allow it."

"In the air…?" Jessica mused aloud. "Hey, Ma, how would you like to go flying?" she asked Ai Li, a devilish smile grew on her face.

"Flying? I don't understand," her mother responded, breaking off her conversation with Administrator Dux.

"We do not have wings, Jessica. Poke had them when he left earlier. He has not … provided them to you?" Orvalus said.

"No, he didn't. I think they disintegrated, but you could always make new ones, right?"

"Icarus …?" Dee asked, referring to the Greek legend, which in reality was a human irresponsibly using gifted alien technology.

"Was an idiot I know. We don't need to fly up to the sun here, just enough to drop down on the building from the top. We could, literally, get the drop on him. He'd have no idea we were coming that way." Jessica said, her eyebrows raised and she sucked on her lower lip.

"This could work…" Orvalus rubbed his chin and gazed over to the shifting image of KT. Its quiescent visage shifted back and forth from green to amber. "This is more of our technology you will be bringing to another world. I cannot allow it," it finally said.

Thinking quickly, Jessica blurted, "We don't all need them, we just give one to the big guy here. He can hold us till we hit the roof. I know how they work; we won't be able to fly with all the weight, but we can definitely glide down." Jessica smiled and nodded. "If we can't do that, we are going to get picked off one by one by Eagle and we will still get nowhere. We won't be able to stop him or control anything."

KT shifted again for another few moments then spoke, "And what of your mother? She does not need to go to Gaia with you and she can remain here with us, where it is safe."

Ai Li frowned at the suggestion.

"One more person could put us over the edge. It could be all that we need to make the difference. Look, I know this isn't what you want, but a lot of the time a perfectly laid plan doesn't work at all. It's better to have as many options as you can." Jessica said.

Ai Li smiled and grabbed her duffle, stashed the cane in it, and pulled the sword out, strapping it across her back.

"This is insane," Dee said, its gold-irised eyes switching to blue. "I cannot allow you to do this. You are speaking as if you are some kind of strike force. You are assaulting a nanite-enhanced supervillain with only the three of you, a sword, a pair of wings—"

Jessica interrupted, "—and seven other people who are waiting for me to do something. If this goes to plan, it could be the best distraction we could possibly have. All you need to do is drop us a hundred and fifty feet or so above the spot where the gate originated on their side. We were in the basement three floors down, and the hospital was four up. That would give us a thirty-foot drop to the old roof, give or take. He flattened half the building, so it will be much lower. We drop in, climb down and take him out."

"And the nanites?" Dee asked.

"The EMP Tony, uh, my... brother, was carrying, we need to get it away from him, get him to a safe spot, and then detonate it." Jessica's eyebrows stitched together, unsure if she was making sense to herself, let alone anyone else.

"I will drop you on the roof," Orvalus said. "Then I will... distract him, while you find him and secure the EMP." He stepped over to one of the smaller cabinets and opened a drawer to pull out a silver block, like a shiny card deck. It unfolded to a set of silver wings, with green lights flashing on the edges. "Dee, when we are through, please get as much telemetry of the area as possible for our ... eventual return. You will need to contact us from your side."

Dee's eyes flashed blue. Administrator Dux held out a small box and handed it to Ai Li, "Please keep these, they are extra vibration patches. This box is EMP shielded." She then nodded and wished them luck.

Orvalus practically hopped to the gate and lifted himself off the ground with the resplendent wings, the reflected lights dancing throughout the library.

"Ladies... if you would," Orvalus said, turning to the women and holding out both of his arms. Ai Li quickly zipped the box into her duffle, jumped into one of Orvalus's arms and adjusted her sword, "Let's go kick some ass!" she practically squealed.

Jessica stepped into the embrace and turned to her mother, realizing there was so much she didn't know about her. "Who the hell are you?"

Orvalus tipped himself back, and when more than half of their collected mass crossed the event horizon, they vanished.

Part Three:

The World Set Free

Chapter 61: Not Exactly as Planned

"SHIT!" Jessica screamed as her stomach jumped in her throat. Desperately, she clung onto Orvalus's torso as he pumped his wings to no avail. They were too heavy to fight against the gravity of Gaia. That was never part of the plan, of course, drifting down to the roof was the plan, and it was supposed to be smooth enough that they wouldn't need the wings except to slow down. There was no roof, no place to hide or spring from on their opponent, only piles of rubble.

Eagle saw them as soon as they appeared out of the portal, and his nanite tentacles reached out for them instantly. Jessica kicked frantically to keep them from grasping her feet, as Ai Li climbed up Orvalus as far as she could.

"I CANNOT SEE!" he roared as he tried his best to look around the panicking women.

"Orvalus! Turn! Turn in any direction! We're falling toward him!" Jessica screamed holding her feet just beyond the reach of the nanite pseudopod.

Orvalus craned his head attempting to use his body to redirect the falling trio. With a thud, the three slammed into the detritus of the broken hospital.

"MA! MA! Are you okay?" Jessica flipped over Orvalus, who lay prone, his wings twisted underneath him. She saw her mother several feet below on the hill of debris, sprawled out and motionless. "MA! Move, please!" Jessica pleaded with her mother. Jessica flipped back and rolled over onto Orvalus again when she heard Eagle laughing. Slow and almost quiet, then gaining in volume.

Orvalus coughed and whispered to Jessica. "Stay nearby, do not let him know your mother is here with us."

Jessica nodded and balled her fist, attempting to push herself up on it.

"Now that, that was impressive," Eagle said, his pseudopods carrying him over the debris to the pair. "I had no idea you would come out of the sky at me like that. And on wings no less!" A tentacle reached forward and grabbed Orvalus's wings, lifting him straight off the ground.

"Another alien, splendid. I'll kill you just like the other one, I can't have you contaminating this biosphere now can I?" Eagle snarled.

"You ... lie ..." Orvalus said, struggling to pry Eagles tentacles off his throat. "Poke is not dead."

"And how would you know this, alien?" Eagle asked, pulling Orvalus's face right up to his.

"Because ... he is behind you."

Eagle's face dissolved from staring at Orvalus, and resolved on the back side of the seething mass of tentacles that was its body. Its glowing green eyes scanned the area. Nothing moved.

"Ah, now you are the liar, alien. I see nothing behind me. Did you think I'd be so easily distracted by the 'look over there' trick?" Eagle's face dissolved and appeared in front of Orvalus again.

"No, I did not. But it was enough time."

Jessica reached up and shoved a long piece of rusty rebar into the tentacles holding Orvalus off the ground. She jumped, rotating the bar counterclockwise, and loosened the nanites just enough for Orvalus to break free. He then disappeared completely; Jessica turned and ran across the rubble, jumping from pile to pile. Eagle's head bounced to the side, taking a blow from the unseen Orvalus.

"Invisibility! I didn't know they could do that! Again, you hide the truth," Eagle said. He shot tentacles in every direction attempting to hit the flying Takki without seeing him, the tentacles shot through the air hitting nothing.

"You know I can still see you right? Have you forgotten that the nanites allow me to see in infra-red?" Eagle mocked as he took more stabs at the sky, he took another swipe into the air and made no connection. Waves of vibration rippled off him as his frustration grew. "I'm tired of wasting my time on you, alien. Besides, your master is easier prey." Eagle redirected his gaze to the ground, throwing chunks of debris through the air, searching for the Unbound. After moments of increasingly frantic searching, he found Jessica, as she jumped from one pile to another. He grabbed her around the waist, then lifted her straight into the air.

"Now, where were we the last time?" Eagle said, a staccato combination of his voice—and those of the people he held inside his body—vibrated from the mass of nanites. "Ah yes, blah blah, keep away or I'll kill her." Tentacles wrapped around her torso, and then her feet, slowly Eagle pulled in opposite directions. "Or should I just rip you apart and get this over with? I can mimic you anyway" he said in Gaian Jessica's voice, then proceeded to pull harder.

"I think that would be… unwise," Orvalus said, sailing through the air and hitting the center of the nanites mass. Eagle shifted forward and Jessica screamed from the pain.

"Do you think this is something you should do? You can see this is the painful way," Eagle mocked.

"How about we don't do this at all?" Katelyn said as she crested a pile of rubble, running full-speed at Eagle. When she got close enough, she tore her comm band off and threw it at the mass. In a flash another tentacle reached out and grabbed her, flinging her into another pile.

"Katelyn!" Poke yelled from the other side of the fray. He held his comm band with his right hand, sliding controls on the display. "Yeah, I know! Hurry!" Poke yelled in Standard. Peek flashed in his temple.

"Jessica! Hang on!" Jason yelled, running alongside Meera. The two carried another piece of rebar, and when the pair were close enough, they plunged the bar into Eagle's mass, driving it as deep as they could.

"FOOLS!" Eagle howled. "I can absorb all of you, you won't be able to stop me. Anything you throw at me becomes me!"

Gerard tore out from the basement level, Amanda's electric baton in hand. He swung at the base of the mass, hitting the nanites and sending electric blue sparks into the air. "You can't deal with all of us at once!" he yelled.

The mass of nanites that was Eagle swung out in all directions, every time it dealt with someone, another person was there, swinging and hacking with anything they could find. The spot from Katelyn's comm band, entangled in the mass of nanites, glowed bright blue and ebbed and flowed like ripples on a bioluminescent lake. Jessica pulled her arms free from the mass and swung at her captor with a vigor unrivaled.

"HA HA! MORE! MORE!" Eagle yelled, as his mass slowly increased. The more it did, the larger the glow from the comm band grew in response.

"Getting more! Keep him busy!" The synthetic voice of Amanda screamed over the rest of the bands. "Don't give him a second!"

"Drop my daughter!" The fiery voice of Ai Li pealed through the confusion. She ran at the base of the mass, swinging her sword at   any part of Eagle that got close. With an eerily calm affect, she swung, one after another. As she did, the black and green mass of Eagle's nanites slowly reduced in size, and the blue nanites slowly being hacked by Amanda and Poke increased.

"ENOUGH!" The polyphonic voice of Eagle roared, and in an instant, he drew all the tentacles back into himself, forming a sphere around Jessica, who disappeared inside it.

Chapter 62: The Sphere

"HEY! HEY! DAMMIT LET ME OUT!" Jessica screamed from inside the nanite ball. Although imprisoned, she was provided a resting place of sorts, a floating chair that swung around as the ball rolled about her.

"Why don't you just absorb me you bastard? I thought that was what you are good at?" Jessica kicked all the inner side of the sphere, which moved out of the way with each thrust.

"No," Eagle's polyphonic voice replied. "I need you; I want to make sure you remain untouched. You are the only connection to Earth, and those aliens give you special privileges to go back. I need you on my side and without any physical changes."

"You just said you were going to kill me anyway because you can mimic me. Who is lying now?" Jessica hissed.

"I was not lying; I was simply motivating your friends to show all their cards. You're the key to The Hegemony. You can't die Jessica, you're my ace in the hole."

"Yeah, like that's gonna happen. They cut me off, I can't go back to Earth anyway. Dude, you are so screwed up. What the hell is it with you? Two whole planets aren't enough?" Jessica spat.

"An interesting point of view from a woman who calls herself 'Unbound.'"

Jessica waited before speaking as she tried to assess the situation and looked for his weakness. "And how do you think you are going to get me to 'play ball?'" she asked, then gestured broadly inside the sphere.

"I want to show you everything I can give you, and to the world. If you'd only listen."

"Bullshit, you aren't interested in making a deal, you are just trying to get away with something and feeling out your options. You can't convince me of that, I know your kind. You're a bulldozer, you'll do whatever it takes and do whatever is expeditious. And if you can use me to get around The Hegemony, you'll keep me around until you are done."

The sphere rocked, hard.

"What's going on? Are they kicking your ass?" Jessica asked.

"Your friends are fools if they think they can stop me. They don't realize how powerful I have become. I can create anything that I want. Do whatever I want. Be whatever I want to be."

"Maybe they don't see what you want as viable. They see you take and give nothing back. I don't trust you, why should they? You'll lose and you know it. That's why you need me. You know in the end that a totalitarian regime will always fail. You need me for respectability," she hissed.

Jessica looked around the sphere, glowing green and black surrounded her. She wondered which nanites held her friends and if they could ever be brought back. Her sister Jessica, the Chargers, Richard and Sally must be there somewhere. As she scanned, a section of blue rolled past her face, and her comm band lit up. Looking at the display as quickly as possible, she caught an image of the sphere in the middle of the cornfield. The sun streamed down on it through clouds of smoke. People were everywhere around it, brandishing sticks, farm implements, even horses with riders on top. The image blinked out as soon as the spot rolled past her line of sight.

Jessica.

"So, what are you going to do once you get to Terra? Convert everyone or just take revenge?"

Keep him talking.

"I intend to show them how they have been invaded by aliens from multiple dimensions. They had no idea you were there. Once I show them, they will panic and see you as an enemy. Then all I have to do is let them continue to act like the children they are. I'll show them how I can bring order and keep them safe. Society will be on the edge of collapse; they will beg me to lead them."

Jessica saw the spot swim by again, and her comm band lit up. She caught a glimpse of Amanda and Poke standing on top of a wrecked truck nearby, their line-of-sight was perfect.

"Jessica..." whispered over the band. The voice was soft and broken.

"Richard?" Jessica let slip accidentally.

"Yes, I have Richard," Eagle answered. "Your friends are still here; I can't prove to the world I am no monster if I killed them."

"Where's my sister?" she asked.

He doesn't know about the band, or he's just too arrogant.

"She's here. She doesn't want to talk," Eagle responded.

"How do I know this?" Jessica questioned, "You could be lying to me again."

"I am not lying to you." The sphere rocked, throwing Jessica right into the glowing spot as it passed, she slipped out and took a breath of the acrid, scorching air.

"Jessica, get us out, darlin'. Your sister isn't here." Jessica heard, this time in Sally's voice.

"Nanites...hacking..." in Richard's voice.

"I want to see them!" Jessica said, falling back out of the spot and into the floating chair. "If you're as powerful and benevolent as you claim, it should be no problem for you."

"Fine, I will do so to prove to you that I am no monster," Eagle responded, using only his voice this time.

The sphere expanded, and two figures quickly took shape as it was hit yet again. The glowing spot grew.

"Jessica?" Richard asked as he finished forming, looking exactly the same as he had before he was absorbed. Jessica peered into his glowing green eyes.

"Richard, are you okay? Are you with me?" Jessica asked.

"I'm fine, don't worry. Eagle has set me free." Richard's right eye briefly flashed blue.

"We're good, darlin'. I like it here. Eagle takes care of us." The fully formed Sally added, blue filaments snaked through her body in perfect counterpoint to the green.

"I'm so happy to see you!" Jessica forced a smile trying to play along. "I am sure you are happy where you are, and I don't want to take that away from you. I think you are perfect together. No one can stop you this time. Well. Almost no one." Jessica pointed to the rest of the sphere.

"Oh, I think it will be fine darlin', Richard knows he's all mine. And now, that we're one…" Sally's voice drifted off in mid-sentence, the spot rotated by again and Jessica's comm band flashed. Poke and Amanda lay on the ground, with dozens of the farmers surrounding them. Gerard was holding a hoe and running full speed at the spot in the side of the sphere. Tony was running behind him, darting from debris pile to debris pile.

In an instant a pseudopod launched out of the sphere and grabbed Gerard around the throat and tossed him a dozen feet into the air, throwing him up like a rag doll.

"Ha ha, not so fast old man. I am much quicker than you will ever be." Jessica heard Eagle growl. Her heart sank, seeing Gerard tossed from one pseudopod to the other, his face quickly turning purple as each catch wrapped a tentacle around his throat before tossing him.

"Stop it! You'll kill him!" Jessica screamed from inside the sphere.

"And? I just need you undamaged. These puny things on the other hand…" Eagle said, then dropped Gerard ten feet before catching him around the throat. He dangled Gerard right in front of the spot, tantalizingly close to Jessica's position.

Jessica's mind flashed back to the recurring nightmare she had had about her Earth father, Kevin. In it he fell, desperately grabbing for Jessica's outstretched hand, each time he missed and fell to his cancer-filled death. She could never catch him, and now she knew why. She was too afraid in the dream, too afraid to sacrifice herself and reach down into the void with both hands to pull him up.

I needed to let go.

Eagle lifted Gerard higher than he had been, and then dropped him again. Jessica launched herself out of the seat Eagle had made for her, and flew through the spot. She focused as hard as she could on his torso and opened her arms wide as soon as they cleared the opening. Once she connected, she willed her arms to close and hold on as tightly as possible. As they wrapped around Gerard's torso, she could feel Eagle's pseudopods snake around her feet then crawl up her legs. Pulling her muscles as tight as possible, Jessica held on as the spot closed around her torso, her ribs compressing against the nanites. From the corner of her vision, she saw Tony leap out from behind a pile of bricks; in his hands he held the EMP. She knew she couldn't stop him. He was too fast. She couldn't even scream before it detonated.

Chapter 63: The EMP

Jessica's ears rang, although she couldn't figure out why. Her arms were still wrapped around Gerard's waist, and she looked at his face. His throat was bright pink and blood trickled out from several lacerations along the neckline. Resting her head against his chest, she heard him breathing softly, with only the slightest rasp in his lungs. Pushing his foot with hers, she relaxed when he moved it back upright, slowly.

"You should be okay. Please be okay," she whispered.

Jessica looked around her quickly as fried nanites fell from the sky and piled up around her. The smell of ozone filled the air. Shaking her head, she tried to clear it. The blast rattled her senses, and left her feeling queasy, as if her patch was gone. Shooting upright, her hand flew to the back of her neck. The vibration patch usually left a warm spot but it was cool to the touch. She felt nothing at all, just the material of it, like gauze taped onto her skin.

"The patches! TONY!"

Jessica scanned around desperate to find anyone. She flipped her comm band to her face, it was dead. "TONY!" She yelled, slowly getting to her feet.

"Here! He's here!" Meera yelled, as she ran to a spot a dozen feet in front of Jessica. Jessica pulled herself toward her brother, wobbling legs dragging her forward over piles of fried nanites like pebbles on a black sand beach.

"Tony, why did you do that? I already said it was a bad idea!" She croaked out.

Meera was holding Tony in her arms; she clutched him against her chest.

"Had to save you… only way to stop him… he was too…" Tony

responded, each word becoming more strained than the next.

"His pacemaker, the EMP shut it down. We can stabilize him, but he needs to get to the hospital. The one in the city I mean. We need to get him to The Trunk." Meera stood and attempted to pull the arms of her exosuit down to give her the long legs she needed to traverse the wastes. But nothing moved.

Amanda rushed up to them, signing frantically. Jessica squinted as she tried to follow as quickly as possible.

"The caravan... those horses are here." Jessica nodded emphatically. "Right! Where are they?"

"Here," the tall form of Razlo, the leader of the caravan, said. The other three riders and their horses were behind him, all with downcast expressions.

"Sir, I'm sorry... I couldn't get Sally out," Jessica said, then swallowed hard, she did her best to look him in the eyes.

"I know you did the best you could. This is why we attempt to not take sides." He responded, then signaled the other riders who got on their horses.

"If you don't mind my asking, why did you?" Jessica asked.

"Eagle was a threat to the stability of the area; we couldn't let him succeed. He wasn't held up in a building like the Chargers. We couldn't ignore it."

Jessica nodded solemnly, and Meera lifted Tony up so Razlo could take him. "We should also take his father. It will be faster if his sisters remain," he said, nodding his head behind Jessica.

She spun around and stood face to face with her older mirror image who held up Gerard, his eyes drifted but he smiled weakly. Unbound steeled herself against whatever retribution her twin had decided to dole out, clenching her jaw and holding her breath. The Gaian walked past her, helping Gerard to the horse, then kissed Tony gently on the forehead. Razlo reached down and pulled Gerard up, who took Tony into his arms.

"Look for others who need help, I will take them." Razlo nodded to the sisters, then spurred his horse. The three rode east.

Left with her sister, Jessica could only feel an absolute sense of guilt. Worse than anything she'd felt before. The Gaian walked up to her, tears in her eyes, lips trembling. Unbound closed her eyes and mouthed, "I'm sorry."

She expected a slap across the face, or worse, a blade in the stomach, or a boot to the head. If her own temper was any guide, Jessica expected, and deserved, a painful response.

Gaian Jessica wrapped her arms around her tightly, pulling her in against her body. Unbound started as she felt the weight from her sister drop, and she instinctively looped her arms under her arms, keeping her twin from falling to the ground.

"It's okay baby, we're here," came Ai Li's voice from behind.

"Ma?" The Gaian said, barely squeaking out the words. "Ma? Is that—you?"

Ai Li extended her arms and took a step forward, careful not to rush Gaian Jessica. "What's the difference?" she said, then smiled.

Gaian Jessica got to her feet and ran toward her, laughing and smiling at the same time. She flung herself into Ai Li's arms.

"Babe, she knows that's *your* mom, right? Not hers?" Katelyn asked, taking a step up from behind. The Unbound didn't turn to look at her, and held out her hand; Katelyn immediately took it.

"It doesn't matter. Mom's right. She always is."

"Peek!" Jessica exclaimed, turning around to Katelyn, who smiled and put her arm on her shoulder.

"It's okay, the storage device is EMP shielded, it's still chattering away. Poke though…" —she pointed to the ruined truck he and

Amanda were standing on— "He's blind, again. We think the relay is fired." Amanda waved to them as she and Meera were heading toward Poke, who was sitting with Jason.

"What about the Chargers? And Eagle?" Katelyn asked.

The pair looked back at the piles of burned nanites, like so much black snow.

"I don't know. I guess they aren't shielded. I can't believe all of them are fried though. But I have no idea how many there need to be for them to have consciousness," Jessica explained. Katelyn bent down to poke the piles with a stick. She pushed through the layers and scraped the top of a buried car, its rusted frame still intact.

"I saw Richard and Sally, they were… alive, then they fell apart right in front of me." Jessica said.

"Why didn't he… absorb you or whatever?" Katelyn asked.

"Said he needed me to get to Earth, wanted to show everyone how benevolent he is or some shit. He wanted me to be unspoiled. But I know he needed me to get around The Hegemony."

"Eww, that has some serious creep vibes. I'm glad he's dead," Katelyn said.

"I hope so. I'm tired of dealing with that dude."

The two best friends surveyed the blasted landscape around them. The force from the EMP had flattened much of the corn, and the farmers were already in the fields lifting as many of the stalks back upright as possible. Gaian Jessica had broken off from Ai Li and was already directing other settlers to clean up the hospital.

"This is going to take them so long to fix. How am I supposed to feel good about fixing a problem I started, when it has so much collateral damage?" Jessica asked.

"I don't know, babe, but did you notice everyone is working together? Medmads, Wayfarers, and whatever your sister's people call themselves." Katelyn laughed.

"I guess. I just have this feeling that something isn't finished."

Jessica turned back to see Amanda sitting on the ground, watching the caravan ride off into the distance, Poke and Meera chatting behind her. Jessica sat down next to her and put her arm around the Wayfarer's shoulder. Amanda tugged at her afro, twirling the hair into knots.

"Not going to ask if you are okay." Jessica said to her after giving her a hug. "I know what you are going through. I lost my father too."

Amanda pulled her right hand away from her hair, and fingerspelled to Jessica, "Not my, Dad. I know this is dangerous."

Jessica nodded silently. She could see Amanda's back shaking as she started sobbing. Katelyn came over, putting her arms around the two of them. "It's not going to be okay anytime soon. That's bullshit. We all know this hurts. That's our advantage, we know what it feels like. We can get through it."

Amanda nodded, snorting hard to keep her nose from running. Jessica reached up and wiped the snot from her face with her hand. Amanda scrunched her face and shook her head.

"Gross," she signed. Then laughed softly.

Katelyn continued, helping Amanda unknot her hair. "This one died on me on another planet. Heh, then I almost killed her another time. It's something we all have to deal with eventually, and it's much easier doing it with friends."

Amanda nodded, and signed, "Friends."

Orvalus came over and smiled, his green eyes reflecting the sunlight. Ai Li turned and waved to him, then came over to the pair.

Katelyn looked up at him, "Okay, so can you explain to me where you went, how Orvalus got here, and how you convinced mom?"

Chapter 64: Aftermath

"That will take... a bit of time to explain," Orvalus said.

Jessica looked at him, but wasn't really sure what she was looking at. Grey skin, green eyes, but the image was swimming, like she was under water. His voice got distant, like she was listening through cotton.

Patches

"Gotta get— patches." Jessica said, dropping to her knees and clenching her stomach. Katelyn likewise dropped.

Ai Li raised her hand to her head, then looked around. "The duffel. Dux gave me extra patches, they are in there." She gestured over to Amanda and Meera then pointed to the hospital.

"We will find them soon," Orvalus consoled, following the women with his eyes.

"EMP, useless—" Jessica croaked out.

"These patches were shielded. They are kept in a special box," he explained.

Jessica nodded, "Them first," then gestured over to the others.

"We will treat them as fast as we can. In the order we come to," Orvalus explained.

"No, not me..." Jessica pleaded.

"Sometimes," —Orvalus knelt down to Jessica, and reached out to stabilize her— "you have to accept help when it is given you."

Jessica couldn't find the strength to argue with the Takki, and laid down on the rubble.

"Why aren't we sick?" Ai Li asked, running over with the duffel Meera and Amanda recovered.

"I do not know. Possibly we have not been away from our home dimension long enough." Orvalus looked around the landscape, taking in the surroundings. "This is a desolate place. Earth and Terra appeared much more… hospitable."

"So was Gaia once," Meera said. "We're trying to fix it, but it will take us time."

Orvalus reached into the bag and pulled out a metal box, six inches on a side. He opened it and inside where vibration patches, resembling a stack of party coasters. He took the first one and carefully lifted Jessica's head. He pulled the existing one off, tossed it on the ground, then pushed the new one onto her neck.

Jessica's vision swam. She grabbed her stomach and wretched.

"Give it a moment," Orvalus said.

She blinked quickly to get her bearings, then took a slow breath. "Thanks, I feel better. These need to be modified. They don't work perfectly here."

Orvalus showed Meera how to apply the patch onto Katelyn, and then instructed her to apply them to everyone who needed it.

"When did Dee say they will contact us to get you back?" Jessica asked.

"It did not. I am… not sure when that will happen. It is probably best that we stay nearby the hospital to be ready to return."

Jessica stood up and straightened out her clothes; coughing and stretching, she tried to get herself looking presentable. Gaian Jessica and the farmers were busy with the task of cleaning up the rubble pile that was the rest of the hospital.

"We need to check on Tony, I have to be sure he is okay." Jessica looked over to her sister. "I promised her I'd take care of Tony, one way or another."

Amanda looked up at the sky, then signed to Jessica, "The Trunk ends in Reston. It took us all day to get there last time, but once you get on it, the transport will have him there in minutes."

Jessica's eyebrows knotted together. "Why can't they just use nanites to fix it? I don't understand why we couldn't fix him right here."

"These are just industrial and field-kit nanites. Basic programming for simple functions and they are expendable. Think of it like triage," Amanda signed.

"You're taking him to the city? DC?" Ai Li asked.

I forgot mom knows ASL too.

Amanda smiled. "Yes, do you want to see it?" she asked.

Ai Li looked at the sky and wiped the sweat from her forehead. Her cheeks were flushed from the heat.

"It has air-conditioning," Amanda signed.

Ai Li picked up her sword and slung it back into the scabbard onto her back. "Sure, I'd love to check it out."

Katelyn's jaw swung open. "Holy shi—"

"She's pretty bad-ass, and I had no idea until today. I thought she was an old lady doing tai-chi," Jessica said, then pretended to close Katelyn's mouth for her. "You're gonna lose water if you gape around like that," she teased.

Amanda explained, "The city has a quarantine. We can take you into the hospital on the Potomac, but you won't be able to get through the city wall without two weeks in temporary housing."

Having lived through the worst pandemic in a century, Jessica shuddered at the thought of quarantines and hospitals.

"Don't your nanites screen out bugs?" Jessica asked.

Meera answered, "They do, and they are really good at it. But it can't find a novel virus. There won't be a sequence to match it against, and if we didn't quarantine, something could slip in and it would be bad before we knew what happened. SARS was devastating in 2046; we were barely keeping people alive."

Jessica jumped on the statement, "That's when you made the Medmads, wasn't it? You figured you'd keep it out of the city by dealing with it outside."

Meera nodded. "Yep. We got good at setting up field hospitals and quarantine tents. We just rolled out the first nanites, and the caravans started telling everyone about what we were doing."

"The Wayfarers," Amanda said from her band, "were created to start outquisitioning any other settlements to make sure we could keep an eye on stuff like that."

"So, it's self-preservation, not altruism," Jessica said, a hint of disappointment in her voice.

"No act is completely selfless." Ai Li said as she started walking west.

"Mrs. Chao," Amanda signed after tapping Ai Li on the shoulder and pointing away from the sun, "It's east of here."

Jessica stood and looked back and forth between her mother and her sister.

Which one do I go with?

Orvalus broke the silence. "Jessica … we have to be here for Dee to retrieve us. That is part of the agreement we had with KT and the administrator."

Jessica's legs shook as the realization hit her. She might have to leave her mother, her real mother, behind to tend to her adoptive brother. She had no idea if KT would keep her promise and allow her to come back. She didn't want to let her mother out of her sight.

"Orvalus— I," she stammered.

"I'll be fine, sweetie," Ai Li said, coming up to hold her hand. "Give me some credit huh? I spent all this time raising you, taking care of your father when he was sick, and now spending that time away from you. I trusted you to go out into the world on your own, you have to trust me."

"Ma, I trust you, I know you can handle yourself it's just— "

"I'm old? I don't need a babysitter."

Katelyn erupted into laughter. "Babe, you'd better let her do what she wants, she's armed."

Ai Li turned to Amanda, pointed to her sword, and signed, "Is this, okay? Will I have to give it up?"

Amanda tapped the electric baton that she had strapped to her right arm. "All weapons are checked in when we get to The Trunk. They will give it back," she signed. "We should go though; it's a long walk and we don't have horses or school buses anymore."

The little girl Jessica had spoken to when they had first arrived at the hospital ran up to Ai Li, a heavy pack on her back.

"Ms. Ai Li, Jessica wants you to have this. It's water and food for the trip."

Ai Li smiled, then looked across to the hospital where Gaian Jessica was still directing the clean-up. Meera stood next to her, treating the cut hand of a farmer. The Gaian smiled and waved, then continued working.

"It's gonna be fine, sweetie." Ai Li repeated to Unbound. "Besides, your father, well you know, is there. I'm not going to be alone."

Jessica smiled and hugged her mother. "Get going, you have a lot to catch up with I suppose."

Ai Li kissed her on the cheek. "Be good, I'll see you soon."

Amanda smiled and waved, and the pair walked off to the east, toward the city. Jessica held them in her gaze as long as she could, waving back when Ai Li occasionally turned around to wave.

The hair on the back of Jessica's neck stood up, and she could smell cinnamon. In front of the hospital, a blue portal popped open and the regal form of Administrator Dux stepped through.

"Unbound?" She called. "It's time."

Chapter 65: The Administrator

Fighting off the feeling that everyone she knew should know each other, Jessica made introductions. Poke, still blind from the EMP, bowed, and Peek spoke from its storage device. Katelyn presented her elbow, and held it there, smiling jovially. After a moment the administrator grabbed it with both of her hands and shook, her regal countenance betrayed by slightly squinted eyes.

Administrator Dux addressed Jessica, "Dee and I have been watching you throughout your ordeal with this Eagle fellow. It's amazing how thoroughly he managed to take over machines from another civilization." Dux kicked a pile of charred nanites with her iridescent purple boots, then looked up to Jessica. "I hope this has not spread this time. KT is probably tired of making rules for you."

Jessica looked around at the destruction that was the hospital and at all the damage dealt to the farming community. "No ma'am, I think most of this is here." *I hope.* "Although this is my fault. Again."

Dux quickly responded, "You may have been the catalyst, but you are not at fault for this. There may be a broader reason you are brought into all of this and we don't understand it yet. Even KT cannot figure that out, no one has the power to see into the future." The administrator turned around slowly, surveying the landscape. "This is not all random, even though it is chaotic."

Jessica looked at her feet again, unsure of how to feel. "So, what do we do now?"

Administrator Dux tapped the communicator in her ear, and shook her head when it was unresponsive. Then she pulled her table computer from her pocket, it was similarly inactive. She frowned.

"None of that should work," Jessica explained.

"How do you bear being disconnected like this?" Dux asked.

Jessica shrugged her shoulders. "I dunno, I kinda like it."

Orvalus gestured to the portal floating in front of the hospital. "We need to go. We should not… keep KT waiting."

"Quite right, Gatekeeper," Dux said, then turned and stepped to the portal. "I can let you say goodbye to this place for five minutes, but I expect the four of you to come back, Jessica last, as part of the arrangement."

"Okay," Jessica started, "Wait, what about Katelyn and Jason?"

Dux stopped and lifted her head up, studying the event horizon around the portal.

"Why do you *accumulate* so many others?" Dux dropped her head again.

"Because she's a good friend," Katelyn said, stepping up between Dux and Jessica; the purple light of the portal caught in her eyes. Poke shuffled toward them, guided by Orvalus.

Administrator Dux turned back to them, the right corner of her mouth curling up in a smile. "I knew that part of your personality would always save you. You're lucky to have them. But the deal was for you alone, not the Gaians, Terrans, or Earthlings."

"Administrator, I can't leave them here," Jessica started, "They don't belong here anymore than I do, and they aren't choosing to stay." Her eyes darted to Katelyn, silently asking if she was on the right track and could speak honestly for her friend. Katelyn slowly blinked her eyes in agreement.

"What would you have us do, Unbound?" Dux asked.

"They come with me," Jessica demanded.

Dux responded, "Impossible. There has already been too much contamination, we aren't going to allow more off-worlders into our gate system, to say nothing of allowing them access to the Library."

"Then I'm not going. You can tell KT the deal is off and that I won't be its errand girl."

Dux turned and walked back toward Jessica, looking down at her from the tip of her aquiline nose. "KT has already fulfilled its part of the bargain. Your mother has been allowed to come here. You have to live up to your responsibility."

"With all due respect," Jessica said, holding back her anger well enough to surprise herself, "I am living up to my responsibility, and it comes to them first." Jessica stepped back into the group. "This is my family, all of them. I'll not abandon them." Poke stood as upright as he could at her statement, chin held high.

"You are already leaving your family here. The Hegemony is not an inter-dimensional taxi service."

Katelyn laughed hard, releasing the tension. "Wow, okay you two need to chill. Listen Dux, you can drop the tough girl facade. Jessica isn't going with you unless she is sure we are back where we want to be. If you think that she is here for some special reason, then disagreeing with her on the most important parts of her life has to be the stupidest thing you can do."

Dux stepped back; her breath became labored. "We can't send them back to Terra when they left. We have no idea when they left the dimension, and would have to use the last known configuration. That was five years ago in their time."

Jessica's eyes narrowed, "Can't you calculate the difference from their bodies? You have a point of origin; you can just figure the rate of change by scanning them… or something."

"That information is more sensitive than just a scan can provide. The vibration patches, by design, change the signature. The only way to accurately tell would be to take a patch off a Terran, which would kill them at this point, or similarly scan something from Terra."

Jessica dropped her head in thought.

"Administrator?" Dee asked from the portal, its voice loud and clear. "I am sorry to interrupt your conversation, but KT wants everyone back now. You have also gone too long without a patch. Your life is in danger and I will be forced to retrieve you if you do not hurry."

Dux addressed Jessica, "You must make the decision, Unbound. We cannot send them home, and if you stay here, KT will maroon you all on this planet. You will lock them here forever because you continue to be obstinate. You have five minutes to decide. Choose wisely." The administrator turned and stepped through the portal.

Chapter 66: Diaspora

"Well, isn't that nice of her," Katelyn spat, cocking her hip.

"She's probably under a lot of pressure, you know a whole city to run and all. I'd hate to have KT as a boss," Jessica said.

"I want to stay with Katelyn, wherever she is," Poke said, and reached out to take Katelyn's hand. She, uncharacteristically, blushed and took his.

"What about you, my friend?" Jessica asked, touching Peek's storage device, safety strapped to Poke's arm.

"Stay with Poke. Already discussed." Its child-like voice spoke out of the device's onboard speaker.

The three turned to Jason, who was busy consuming a protein pack that Meera had produced from her backpack. Amanda was standing in front of him, curling her fingers and gesturing toward her mouth, giving the sign for "food." Jason smiled, and then focused his attention closely on Amanda's hand, he nodded emphatically.

"Well, that was easier than I thought. Except…" Jessica said, then turned to Orvalus.

"It is… okay, Jessica. I can stay here," he said. "I always wanted to get away from Bellerophon. Now I have an entire planet to explore."

"I can't let you do that," she said. "I'm not going to be responsible for marooning you here. It's not your home."

"Are you planning on staying here on Gaia?" He asked.

Jessica looked over the fields and at her sister and her people rebuilding. If there was any place she would be needed, it would be here. If there was anywhere she would be able to get away and lead a life less ordinary, it would be here. Her mother was here now. Her family as she knew it was here. Why would she need to go back?

She caught the eye of her sister as she crossed into the cornfield, carrying a large aluminum jug full of water. They smiled at each other. She had everyone she wanted. She wasn't alone. Then she noticed her mother's eyes reflected in her sister's. Her Terran mother and father would be alone now. Terran Katelyn's family would never know what happened to her. Professor Sterling and everyone at Echo Mountain; a dozen lives would be shattered without their loved ones. She had to go back. If anything, then to just let them know.

Jessica took a slow breath and held back the panic that was slowly creeping its way into her body. "I can't. I can't let everyone down. Your families need to know. We have to find a way back to Terra, even if it is five years in the past. I could leave a message at least. Explain what happened, or what will happen. At least they will know. Then I can come back. It will work. It has to work. God, I can't stand this. There has to be another way."

She jammed her hands into the pockets of her pants. Both were filled with grime, charred nanites, and bits of shattered brick. The left one also held a USB drive, in the other was Gabrielle's bracelet. She pulled both of them out, and her mind raced.

"We have another portal. The one Eagle shoved me in." She spun around to look at the wreckage of the hospital, and tried to see the MRI machine buried under the rubble. "We can fix that one. Turn it back on. We know how to use the time-displacement, and we have this." She held up Gabrielle's bracelet.

"That is not the Silver Stone, Jessica. We cannot use it to circumvent the targeting subroutine of the gate system." Orvalus reminded her.

"Right, it's just an ornament; a knickknack. But I'm going to play a hunch here—" Jessica gestured over to Meera who was walking back from the hospital, "—can you scan this please, and tell me if you see anything unusual about it?"

Meera stepped up and took the bracelet, her eyes narrowed as she turned it over in her hands. "It looks like a bracelet to me, this stone on it is a piece of metal. What are you asking me to look at? I mean, I can look at this all day and tell you the same thing that you can see—"

Jessica cut her off, "Scan it with a microscope, not just your eyes."

"Ohh right, yeah sure." Meera held up her comm band and turned it over. "My band is dead. I forgot."

"Let Peek try," Poke said, pointing to the storage device strapped to his arm. Which, in reality, was nothing more than a beefed-up smartphone.

Meera handed the bracelet to Poke, making sure to place it firmly in his hand. Poke moved it to the camera on the storage device, and Peek's light turned on. It flashed for a moment, then went dark. "Copyright 2027. Afghanistan. 16972321049165205." Poke said, translating for Peek.

Jessica beamed. "I knew it."

"The command code number?" Orvalus asked.

"Yep, just like on the Silver Stone to Earth. I'll bet we can use that to open a portal to Terra, without needing the Hegemony gate system. I mean, we can't click it into the control cabinet, but did we really need that anyway? We can send everyone back to Bellerophon who wants to go, and then we can use Eagle's gate to get everyone else back to Terra." Jessica hopped on the balls of her feet.

"Jessica, this is a… piece of jewelry. How can it possibly control an inter dimensional gate system?" Orvalus protested.

"Hacking it, of course," Amanda signed.

Jessica laughed and translated, "Hacking it."

Orvalus asked, "Does that not make us just as bad as Eagle? Was he not a… hacker too?"

Jessica explained, "There are many flavors of hackers, my friend: Black Hats, White Hats, and Grey Hats. Eagle was a black hat. The bad guys. White hats, the good guys, stop the black hats…. grey hats do good, but bend the rules."

"I knew I was rubbing off on you!" Katelyn whooped.

"Where's the EMP?" Jessica asked, looking around.

Amanda pointed to the hunk of twisted metal on the ground which bore absolutely no resemblance to the bomb it had been before. Jessica ran over to it and picked it up then spun it around in her hands. "There you are…" she said, putting her hand on the vibration patch.

"That no longer works, Jessica," Orvalus said.

"That's exactly what I am counting on." Jessica tore the vibration patch off. The device felt soft and pliable in her hands, almost unreal. It was disintegrating rapidly. "Not much time."

The portal popped back open, and Administrator Dux stepped out.

"Have you made your decision, Unbound?" she asked.

"Yes, I have. I will go back to Bellerophon and complete my part of the bargain. The rest…will stay here."

Chapter 67: Bellerophon

"Okay, everyone who is going to Bellerophon, follow me," Jessica said, addressing the crowd. She pointed to Poke and Orvalus specifically.

"Librarian, are you unwell?" Dux asked Poke.

"I'm fine Administrator, the EMP pulse damaged my connection to Peek. When we return to Bellerophon we can fix the connection. Don't worry, Peek is fine." The display on Peek's storage device flashed the "thumbs up" emoji.

"Hey, come back soon, huh?" Katelyn said, taking Poke's other arm.

"As soon as they allow me, my dear," Poke said, looking at her, but not able to focus.

Dux looked at the pair, but made no recognition of their connection. Jessica smiled and stood next to her, and waved to the rest of the people gathered. She worried she may never return to Gaia, or Terra for that matter, but there was no time to second guess, and she had to have faith in the arrangement.

Dux thumbed the tablet computer in her pocket nervously and took a labored breath, she turned and stepped back through the portal, leaving it open. Jessica stepped in behind her; the smell of cinnamon was overpowering.

As soon as Jessica exited the portal, her head swam. KT's shifting form was already on the main monitor of the library. Dee was standing nearby, wearing the 'android' head it had when she first met it; cold, with harsh lines, it was lifeless and sterile. Administrator Dux laid all her devices on the gate console, and they immediately began to recharge. Orvalus excused himself and walked toward the alcoves, pulling his hoodie off as he went.

"That was exceptionally well done, Unbound. It made no logical sense, and the potential for failure was staggering, nevertheless you achieved the objective," KT said.

Jessica raised her left eyebrow and chose her words carefully.

"So, this means I held up my end of the agreement? I brought everyone back—" she pointed to Poke whom Dee had rushed over to assist. "—in one piece anyway. Does this count?"

"Count?" Dee jumped in, while it tilted Poke's head to get a better look at his eyes. "Every time you go to a new dimension, someone ends up getting hurt, Unbound. Why is this a pattern for you? Do you not understand that even though we are a superior species, we are still not immortal. We can die and never come back, and our medical science, although years ahead of yours, is not perfect?"

Jessica kept the eyebrow arched and stuck out her hip, crossing her arms. Dee was wearing its android head, and that meant it would be less empathetic than with its other, more human, head. "Okay, Dad, I go wild in other dimensions. I destroy androids, contaminate cultures, lick doorknobs, and run with scissors. I'm a mad woman. I even bring EMP bombs." She held up the spent device, and it had disintegrated so much it squished in her hand like warm butter.

Dee stopped and looked at her. "This is what you call sass, is it not?"

"Yeah, and this is me taking it easy." Jessica put the EMP on the top of the control cabinet, right on the spot they last used the Silver Stone. "Scan this before it disappears."

Dee turned back to Poke and led him into the main room of the library to one of the alcoves. It reached down and put one of the teaching helmets on Poke's head and placed the EMP in another alcove.

"The Teacher will fix your nerve connections. It should not be long." Dee said, gently locking the helmet in place. Poke nodded silently. Dee continued, "Forgive me, Unbound. Sometimes it is difficult to speak when someone is hurt. My obedience to the Three Laws makes it nearly impossible to focus on anything else."

Jessica remembered Dee throwing all caution to the wind when it saved a Terran child from being hit by a truck on Halloween.

"It's okay Dee, no offense taken. I know you'd protect me just as strictly."

"Indeed, I would, Unbound," Dee said.

Jessica looked around the library as everyone reintegrated themselves in their home dimension. "You with us, Peek?" She asked into the air.

Peek was silent and dark on Poke's arm.

Jessica frowned. "I don't understand. Why can't it connect and recharge?"

KT answered for it, "We expressly forbade that, Unbound. If Peek were to reconnect to the network, the information it contains would contaminate our entire culture, plunging it into chaos. At the very least, it would embolden the separatists. It shall remain powered down until you leave Bellerophon."

Jessica held her speech, she knew this was the plan. Silently, she cursed herself for condemning a friend to a reduced existence. "But… the portals, every time we go through Peek gets drained, Poke goes blind, and we have to wait until he recharges. I'm not walking into some strange place with them both out of commission. How do we deal with that?"

KT's face switched to the more angular amber visage. "Yes, Unbound, I am aware of that. You have brought the solution with you, and you carry them in your body."

Reflexively, Jessica put her hands on her chest and patted, as if she were looking for a lost set of keys. She stopped and tilted her head. "The nanites from Gaia. They use body fat and cholesterol to run. They could use that energy to… charge a battery. Your nanites didn't know how to do that. They ran on the network to process everything, they were inert. I had to teach Poke how to pee. So, when

Peek opened the code, it found a way to incorporate that bit of data."
Jessica smiled, and satisfied with herself decided not to belabor her
explanation.

"Exactly, Friend Jessica," Poke said. "The teacher has already
analyzed the code and added it to the nanites codebase here on
Bellerophon. We should be able to get him up and running within
moments upon arrival. At least fast enough to get my eyes working."

"We are heading back right away?" Jessica asked.

"As soon as we are done here," Dee said.

For an instant, Jessica's stomach flipped and she felt a shock of
elation thinking that Dee and Orvalus would be coming with them.
"We...?" she asked.

KT answered for them, "D417a and the Keeper of the Terran
Gate will remain here. We don't need them at the moment. It will
be much more difficult for you to move around with an entire
entourage."

"That makes sense," Jessica said. *Except that I'm taking the Gaians
with me.*

Jessica ran up to Orvalus and hugged him. "I'm not doing this
again, you know I will see you again, soon."

"I do not doubt this. I will... await your return." Orvalus stepped
back after their embrace and bowed, then handed Jessica a black bag,
about the same size as the one that contained the EMP, but far less
heavy. "Do not open this until you get settled on Terra," he said.

Jessica took the bag and returned the gesture, then turned to KT
and Dux, where she bowed to them.

"Safe journey, Unbound," Dux said, putting her hand over her
heart and bowing.

KT switched to her green image, "I expect updates when you
have found anything at all. I would like to update our database of

information so I can come up with an appropriate response. Peek should know the last world we lost contact with during The Trials, it may be the least feral one, start there."

Jessica squinted at 'feral.' *Not the politest term.*

"Are we ready, boys?"

"I am ready, Friend Jessica. Let's do this!" Poke said, then stepped up to the portal. It flashed open with the unmistakable smell of lavender.

"This is when I left, correct? Not weeks afterward?" Jessica asked, still not trusting them fully. She looked at the control cabinet; the EMP was gone.

"Yes, Unbound, this is one day after you left, according to the residual time signature from the EMP. You will arrive exactly at the location you left." KT answered.

"Great!" Poke said, and jumped through the portal.

"Wait no! That was in the landfill!" Jessica reached out to stop Poke, but he had already crossed the event horizon. "Why would you send him there?"

KT's face switched to amber. "Because that is the last reliable data we have that is close to you. We could not send you to Anatolia."

"Why not Echo Mountain?!"

"We do not have the address."

Jessica shook her head and dove through the portal, waving goodbye as she did.

Chapter 68: Back Where They Started

Jessica closed her eyes and took a breath as her vibration patch adjusted to the new dimension. The smell of lavender was overpowering and she clutched her stomach as she wretched.

As the room faded into view, she could see Poke standing over the control panel for the gate, which she had last seen as they were thrown in by Eagle and Jason.

One more, she though, prompting her to remember that Katelyn was coming through the gate behind her.

"Wait, no. It's just the two of us here," Jessica said aloud, forcing her mind to catch up with reality.

"Three," chirped Peek's voice from the storage device.

Jessica laughed and rattled her head, trying to get the marbles to fall back into the right holes. "Wait, you can see! Peek can talk!"

Poke nodded as he looked through the screens. "The nanites work great, it only took a few seconds before we reconnected. But I am hungry."

"You're always hungry," Jessica teased. "We'll get some food as soon as we get out of here. What are we looking at?"

Poke took off the storage device and put it on the control panel, a data line emerged from it and snaked its way beneath the keyboard.

"The device was left on. Someone must have used it then left, leaving no one to turn it off," Poke answered.

Jessica turned back to the gate, studying it for a moment.

"Can Peek find out…"

"The last location? Yes, it is looking for it now, the targeting information is encrypted."

The display on the control panel flashed between screens, slowly at first, then faster and faster.

"Encryption easy. Data is missing," Peek said from its device.

"Missing? How can that happen. It was left on?" Jessica asked. The LEDs in Poke's temple flashed quickly.

Poke explained, "Ah, yeah. Peek says the data was encrypted, it broke it, and found the database is empty. The last location called from here, was here. Whoever went through it last had it call back here when it was done. Then we arrived after it reset."

Jessica's eyebrows knitted. "How long between those events?"

"About five minutes," Poke answered.

"We just missed them!" Jessica scanned the room. "Okay I just want to verify, this is the same place we were, and it's relatively the same time, right? I jumped in and out of the library half a dozen times before I realized what was going on."

"Yes, Friend Jessica," Poke said, "this is the same location we all left from a week ago. It's the same dimension."

"Peek, can you find anything in there that can give us a clue as to where they went? And who? I mean, I know it's the Eastern Syndicate, but who? Look in an obscure place."

Peek chirped and the screen on the control panel flashed, switching through image after image until it was all a blur. Jessica turned away, overwhelmed with the stimulation.

"Got it," Poke said eventually, and the screen displayed a list of numbers and names.

"Our database. My bad," Peek said meekly.

"Damn. It was Eagle." Jessica said, turning again to the gate behind her. The rudimentary frame was dark and silent. "He must have survived and got through Gaia, then took our database he hacked out of the nanites. How? How the hell did he do that, we were only gone a few minutes."

"Time," Peek said.

"Shit, that's right, the whole reason why they were there was to find how to control the time of the gate." Jessica's mind ran through the possibilities. "That bastard probably intentionally jumped back to here to screw with us."

"They have the same information we do. The same addresses," Poke said.

Jessica said with a sigh, "So, somehow Eagle wasn't destroyed, got out and slipped past the Gaians, jumped back here, and then went to who knows where?"

"We need to contact your sister, Friend Jessica," Poke said.

"Peek, do you think you can open the gate here to communicate with Gaia?" Jessica asked.

"Gate primitive. Easy," Peek said from the storage device. The gate jumped to life, filling the frame with green light. The smell of chocholate filled the room. The display panel changed and a video of Eagle appeared. His face glowed green along the edges of his tattoo, and his eyes pulsed in sickly green light. When he spoke, it was the polyphonic voice, replete with hints of the Chargers, and Richard's and Sally's voices.

"You have found me, just as I planned. I knew you would come back here. You're so predictable it's shameful. If only you'd decided to join me, I could have made this so easy for you. We could rule the multiverse together. But you chose a different path.

"Obviously I was not destroyed on Gaia as you had hoped. Your pathetic plan was futile, as I anticipated. I have the database that your little emulated friend so easily gave to me, and I know all about the separatists and the lost colonies. I will unleash a great power across the multiverse, and the Eastern Syndicate... I... will rule over them all. With the other gates, I will be victorious."

The screen went blank, then returned to the Gaia's gate address.

"The other gates?!" The three said in unison.

"Hello? Umm, hi?" a young male voice crackled through the speaker on the control panel. Jessica ran over to it and spoke toward the screen.

"Hi! Who is this?"

"Ummm… I don't know… mommy said I'm not supposed to talk to strangers."

"Sweetie, this is Jess—ica's sister. Are there any adults around?" Jessica asked, and immediately felt angry that a child was keeping an eye on an interdimensional portal. No wonder Eagle could get out so easily.

"Oh hi! Umm hang on…" there was a muffled sound of moving furniture, the child giggled, and then Gerard came on the line.

"Hey there, sorry, I was cleaning out the technician's station. We are going to use that for an observation room in case anyone decides to open the gate."

"Dad, there was a kid watching it," Jessica said.

"I was right there, Jessica. He ran to it as soon as it turned on."

Jessica let it go quickly, there was no reason fighting it. "How's Tony?"

"He's fine. They fixed him up, good as new, even upgraded the pacemaker and shielded it. Just in case. He should be out of the hospital in a few days. They wanted to keep him there until he got some rest. He loves it, all the tech. It's like a carnival."

Jessica smiled, and that knot she was holding in her stomach since Tony nearly died trying to save her loosened.

"Dad, did Eagle turn on the gate? Did you see anything happen?"

"Eagle? We wiped him out with the EMP. We're still sweeping up fried nanites."

"Unfortunately, he survived somehow. He activated the gate and jumped back here to Terra. Then he took off again. We don't know where he is."

Can he rebuild from a handful of nanites? Some of them must have survived somewhere. Some kind of Faraday cage…A car?

"That's…" Gerard waited a few seconds before continuing. "That's unfortunate. All that effort…"

"I know, Dad. Since we don't know where he is or how he's getting around, we can't leave the gate unattended."

"Jessica and I were talking about that. She's okay with us keeping the gate, and asked the Wayfarers to watch it. They are sending some folks back with Amanda. But they are only allowed to stay at the hospital. We never worried about security inside the building before."

Jessica nodded her head in agreement. "How's Mom?"

"She's... something else," Gerard said. Jessica knew he was smiling when he said it.

"Yeah, I think so." Jessica smiled. "Dad, we need to get back to Echo Mountain and let everyone know what's up. I'll give you a call from there. I don't trust anyone coming through this gate, who knows what the Syndicate built into it." In the back of her mind Jessica instantly regretted calling from here at all.

"Hey, when are you gonna let me see my boyfriend?" Katelyn yelled.

"Ha! Never!" Jessica teased.

"I am right here, my dear. I hope to see you soon." Poke said, his face darkening with a blush.

"Okay, talk soon! Ummm... Landfill out." Jessica shook her head, not liking the name she had assigned to the location. She pressed a contact on the panel and the screen went dark.

"Peek, can you find a way to keep people from using this gate?"
"Only way, call back over and over," the emulant said.

"Keep calling itself to tie up the line? Okay, that sounds good. Do it."

The portal flashed open; the purple light filled the frame.

Jessica nodded and headed for the door.

"Wait, Friend Jessica. What if they are here still? Remember last time?"

With her finger poised on the release for the door, Jessica paused.

"Yeah, that's a good idea. Peek, can you call Professor Sterling and let him know we are back please?"

Peek chirped, and then ringing came from the speakers. In a moment the line picked up.

"Hello?" Was the curt answer from Gabrielle.

Jessica responded, "Hey, we're back. Can you give us a lift from the landfill? You might want to bring some extra folks with you. We're downstairs and not sure who's still here."

"You stole my EMP, ran out the door, and then disappeared for a week. No communication and no attempt to tell us where you were. Nothing."

Jessica cringed, over-exaggerating the expression to Poke.

"Um, sorry. It got pretty intense." Jessica threw up her hands in exasperation.

"… where were you?"

"Another dimension."

Chapter 69: Gaian on Terra

"You mean you pulled the 'Damsel in Distress' again on the same dudes?" Jessica asked, standing in front of Gabrielle.

"Yes, Jessica. Those aren't the smartest of people. The professor is talking to them now. He is convincing them that the EPA has given us access to the offices here to study the leachate and methane wells. My 'boyfriend' is the new inspector and I am leaving a note for him."

Jessica raised an eyebrow, as that countered what she knew of landfills and how they are kept safe. "Those dudes probably already know the state inspector. Why would they believe him?" Jessica asked, signaling Poke to follow them out the door to the tiny office aboveground.

"A little money in the right hands buys a lot of influence," Gabrielle said. She wrinkled her nose as she looked around the gate room. "This is a very crude build; I am surprised it didn't scatter your atoms across the multiverse."

Pantomiming patting her body and looking for holes, Jessica smiled. "Nope, still in one piece. For now."

Gabrielle nodded, "Let's get out of here before people look too closely at our friend." She tossed Poke a black beanie, and he quickly pulled it over his head. Jessica picked up her bag and took one last look at the gate locked in repetitive callbacks, then left.

The three walked down the hall to the stairs behind the refrigerator. "How do we keep people from getting in and using the gate?" Jessica asked.

"We will keep some of the students here to study this gate, maybe the Syndicate did something we haven't thought of. At the very least we can keep them from using it, and can dismantle it if we need to."

Poke climbed the stairs first, and pushed the refrigerator away from the wall, letting them out into the office. The smell of formaldehyde and garbage overwhelmed them, and Jessica suppressed another retch. "Why do I get the feeling this will be punishment for something?" she said, waving the air in front of her nose.

Gabrielle said nothing and headed for the door quickly. Stepping out into the spring air, she pointed to the bent fence that Jessica and Poke had snuck under to get into the facility a week before. "Go back under. Wait for us to pick you up."

Jessica nodded and gestured to Poke.

Minutes later one of the professor's black Econoline vans pulled into the parking lot and several grad students jumped out, including the guitar player. They scrambled into the double wide trailer waving hello to the two technicians who were loading their pick-up truck with their gear.

"How does Professor Sterling do that?" Jessica asked, her fingers threaded through the chain-link fence.

"Is this how money motivates people?" Poke asked.

"Yes, but, it's more than that for these kids, it's about knowledge and exploration."

"Isn't that what Eagle said?" Poke asked.

Jessica nodded and frowned.

The black Model X pulled up on the road behind them and the gull-wing doors opened, letting them in. On the way back upstate, Jessica and Poke relayed the story of the last week to the professor. No one looked at the road as the crossover drove itself to the farmhouse.

"This database must be huge. Peek, do you understand that you need to encrypt this kind of data before you go off world next?" Professor Sterling asked the emulant. "We can't have you unknowingly give away more information, or the location of Echo Mountain."

"Yes, Professor," Peek said from the storage device. The display screen flashed blue then displayed the thumbs up yellow emoji.

When they arrived, Jessica immediately took the elevator down to the gate room to call Gerard and let him know they had arrived safely, and she wanted to get Katelyn back with her as soon as possible. She felt weird having Poke and Peek along, but not the fourth member of her group, like it was a three-wheeled cart that didn't quite move properly.

As she headed to the gate room, she quickly glanced at an entire hallway she had previously not seen before, Ellwood was walking down toward her. She ran up and hugged him.

"What is this place?" She asked, gesturing over to the hallway with her chin.

"Ah, this is the dormitory. We can't have all the grad students stay in the house upstairs, there isn't enough room. I was just checking on your rooms. The professor texted me to let me know you were back."

Jessica shook her head and accepted that there was a lot more going on here than she had realized. She needed to stop thinking that this was the same Professor Sterling she had known back on Earth. The Terran version had a lot of money. Too much. And she decided right there that the less she knew, the better.

She turned into the gate room with Ellwood on her heels, to find another student she didn't know sitting at the controls and Gabrielle already plugging the address to Gaia into the other panel. Jessica's eyes narrowed. She didn't remember giving it to her, nor could she figure out how the teacher's assistant had beaten her to the room.

Within moments the gate flashed to life, filling the room with green light and the overpowering smell of chocolate. Jessica grabbed a headset that was connected to the speakers in the gate room and spoke.

"Hi, this is Echo Mountain, come in... Gaia. Are you receiving?" She shook her head, glad to not call it something vague like "landfill." After a moment, she repeated the call.

"Hey there, Sis!" Tony's voice chimed in over the speakers. "How are you?"

"Little Bear? What are you doing out of the hospital?" Jessica asked.

"That was a week ago. We've been waiting for you to call us. I was just about to ask Jessica if we could, we were getting worried," Tony replied.

"The time difference. We haven't calculated the variables. We were gone a few hours," Jessica said aloud.

"We needed to make the connection from here to derive the difference. We can sync them next time," Gabrielle said.

"Sorry, Tony. It's hard to make a person to person call across dimensions," Jessica explained.

"A what to what?" Tony asked.

"Never mind. How's Katelyn?"

"Okay, enough chatter. Can we come over? I miss my boyfriend," Katelyn's voice crackled over the connection.

"Yes, but we should make sure that we aren't using this a lot. I'm sure KT will be watching somehow, and you are all supposed to stay there."

The gate flashed briefly, then returned to its quiet state. Everyone looked at the controls and then back at the portal. Its smooth surface undulated peacefully.

"Waiting on you, Kate?" Jessica asked.

"She sent me over to test it out first," said Tony from behind her, his bear-skin hood pulled tight over his head. Everyone at the control panels jumped from the sudden appearance.

"Dammit, Tony! You can't keep doing that to us!" Jessica said, then started laughing despite herself.

"Sorry, Sis," Tony laughed.

"Feeling better?"

"I am, the Medmads did a good job. Where is my room?" He asked, already out in the hallway.

"Ummm, Dad is there, he will let you know."

"Cool, the other dad, this is gonna be…" Tony's voice trailed off as he disappeared down the hallway.

Jessica turned and laughed, just as Katelyn stepped through the gate. It snapped closed behind her. The smell of chocolate slowly dissipated.

"Hello, my dear." Poke said, stepping into the room and taking Katelyn into his arms.

Shaking her head, Gabrielle took off her headset and threw it on the console. Pulling out her smartphone, she opened an app, and thumbed the screen quickly, always swiping right.

Jessica rolled her eyes and entered the hallway.

Chapter 70: The End

Days later, Jessica Unbound sat at her desk in her room at Echo Mountain. The calm hum of the air conditioners was the only noise in her sound-proof space. She looked around at the artifacts and decorations that she and Katelyn had collected from their apartment in Jersey City. They all sat on a wooden desk, that was haphazardly decorated with vibration patches. She smiled, reminiscing.

Still, Jessica felt sad that she would never see Katelyn Prime again and knew that KT would never allow the gate to be opened. Although she knew that they could fix the problem with spacetime if given enough resources and time to work on it. KT was defending an entire civilization now that the separatists were breaking off the Hegemony, and was justified in its caution. Jessica didn't agree.

There was also her worry about Eagle and what he planned to do with this "Great Power," whatever that was and if he would return to Gaia.

She missed being on that world despite the searing heat. Further, she missed her friends, especially her counterpart. They had work to do, restoring an entire world from the hellscape of climate change was difficult.

Jessica stood up and walked over to the wardrobe next to her bed. Its old oaken panels were worn, but strong. She opened it up and took out the black jumpsuit that Orvalus had given her. It hung on the far-left hook, right next to the black uniform her Terran counterpart had worn to her old job before she died.

I still can't shake black.

She laughed knowing that she had the opportunity to pick any color she wanted, and even have it change on a whim thanks to the Hegemony's technology. But she went with black anyway, unchanging. She took off her NYU hoodie and PSU sweatpants and climbed into the jumpsuit, pulling the zipper closed and taking her green hair out from under the collar. It was tighter than she wanted it to be, but the jumpsuits had to stay sleek in preparation for gating to worlds without any prior knowledge of the conditions. They needed to be ready for anything; The Eastern Syndicate, Eagle, Separatists, or Lost Colonists. They had to be able to make contact and deal with any situation. Jessica pulled the comm band on her wrist and clicked it into place. Her blue icon flashed onto the screen along with two others. She smiled as one moved closer to her location, faster than any icon she had ever seen move.

Breathing deeply, she looked at the pictures on her desk, one of her as a child with her deceased father Kevin and her mother. They were smiling and sitting on the grass. She couldn't have been more than two years old and had no recollection of the photo. They were so young, all of them. The grass was bright green, and the dappled sunlight that shone through the trees gave the pink and white azaleas an iridescent glow. Next to the photo Gabrielle's Silver Stone bracelet, and Katelyn Prime's hairband. Next to those, a small hologram of Orvalus stood on a glowing pedestal, the glowing image bowed occasionally. Laughing quietly, she remembered the first time she met him all those months ago when she stupidly stuck her head into a portal that mysteriously showed up in her basement. If she had known that day would turn into all of this, she might have thought better about what was really important to her: her friends and family. The warmth of her family, now augmented by three; her friends from multiple worlds; and a mission to save three universes from danger, even if none of them were her home was what mattered to her the most. Anxiety be damned. She was content, and full of purpose. Her mind and her body completely relaxed. She looked at the picture of her parents again and smiled.

"I love you, Dad."

There was a knock at her door, and she straightened up, wiping a tear from her eye. "Little Bear, do you have to hide all the time?" Jessica asked, smiling and not bothering to look for him in the room.

"Yep," came Tony's voice from inside the wardrobe. "It wouldn't be me if I didn't."

Jessica rubbed the back of her neck, feeling the vibration patch shimmering under her touch. She couldn't see it, but she knew it was glowing a faint green, powering itself from her body heat and fat, and keeping her molecules stable in this alternate universe. Katelyn's voice chimed in over her comm band.

"Babe, it's time, Peek wants to get started, you know how it gets when there is somewhere new to go."

Jessica smiled, hearing the door to her wardrobe click closed, Tony had already left, headed toward the gate room.

"I'm on my way, Kate. Thanks. Thanks for everything," Jessica said.

"Yeah, I love you too. Now come on! Ellwood has some of mom's dumplings ready before we head out."

Jessica opened the door to the hallway and stepped though; grad students came rushing by and they pinned themselves to the walls smiling and making room for her to pass.

Jessica Unbound took one last look around her new room, and did her best to memorize it. She didn't know when she'd be back, and the thought electrified her.

She closed the door softly and, with a quiet click, it locked.

A moment later she opened it again, leaving it ajar.

"Just in case."

THANK YOU FOR READING!

A year of work went into this novel, throughout many changes in my personal and professional life. I am excited to have finally given life to Jessica and her new adventures, and I hope you enjoyed reading it as much as I enjoyed writing it!

The Jessica Unbound series has many connections to my other works, and a good deal of the characters have been featured in other stories. Essentially, I have created a metaverse within a metaverse, and it is as complicated to keep straight as it sounds.

Please leave a review on my Amazon page:
S.G. Kubrak

Follow me on Twitter: @sgkubrak
Visit my author page: www.sgkubrak.com
Support me on Patreon: www.patreon.com/sgkubrak
Visit me on Royal Road:
www.royalroad.com/the-adventures-of-void-cat-and-shadow

ABOUT THE AUTHOR

S.G. Kubrak grew up in Jersey City, just across the Hudson from New York City, where he spent his youth running barefoot on concrete and unsuccessfully avoiding trouble. Ever the wanderer, S.G. has traveled the world in search of new experiences but has always lived within a few hours' drive of home.

S.G. currently lives with his wife, daughter, and two rescue cats in suburban Virginia, but his heart is always in his native New Jersey.

This is his first sequel in the *Jessica Unbound* series.
His acclaimed short-story collection, *Dreams of a Freezing Ocean: Volume 1*, is available on Amazon. He is currently writing the sequel to that book, *Dreams of a Freezing Ocean: Volume 2,*
He is also writing his web serial *The Adventures of Void Cat and Shadow*, available on his Pateron page and on Royal Road.